THE
BEAUTIFUL WEST
&
THE
BELOVED OF GOD

ESSENTIAL PROSE SERIES 105

Canada Council for the Arts **Conseil des Arts du Canada**

ONTARIO ARTS COUNCIL
CONSEIL DES ARTS DE L'ONTARIO

an Ontario government agency
un organisme du gouvernement de l'Ontario

Guernica Editions Inc. acknowledges the support of the Canada Council for the Arts and the Ontario Arts Council. The Ontario Arts Council is an agency of the Government of Ontario.

We acknowledge the financial support of the Government of Canada through the Canada Book Fund (CBF) for our publishing activities.

THE
BEAUTIFUL WEST
&
THE
BELOVED OF GOD

MICHAEL SPRINGATE

GUERNICA

TORONTO • BUFFALO • LANCASTER (U.K.)

2014

Michael Mirolla, general editor
Lindsay Brown, editor
David Moratto, book designer
Guernica Editions Inc.
1569 Heritage Way, Oakville, ON L6M 2Z7
2250 Military Road, Tonawanda, N.Y. 14150-6000 U.S.A.

Distributors:
University of Toronto Press Distribution,
5201 Dufferin Street, Toronto (ON), Canada M3H 5T8
Gazelle Book Services, White Cross Mills, High Town, Lancaster LA1 4XS U.K.

First edition.
Printed in Canada.

Legal Deposit — Third Quarter
Library of Congress Catalog Card Number: 2014934785
Library and Archives Canada Cataloguing in Publication

Springate, Michael, 1952-, author
The Beautiful West & the Beloved of God / Michael Springate.

(Essential prose series ; 105)
Issued in print and electronic formats.
ISBN 978-1-55071-858-4 (pbk.).--ISBN 978-1-55071-859-1 (epub).--
ISBN 978-1-55071-860-7 (mobi)

I. Title. II. Title: The Beautiful West & the Beloved of God.
III. Series: Essential prose series ; 105

PS8587.P74B42 2014   C813'.54   C2014-900217-3   C2014-900218-1

For Carolyn Combs and Alan Heffez

To Nikola
with thanks!

Michael
July 2014

Chapter One

Montreal, March, 2008

─══ 1 ══─

"The light wasn't on," Sharon said, throwing her thin arms about her mother's neck.

"You're cold. Do you want a bath?"

The child nodded, then leaned forward to rise on her toes as her mother quickly rolled the wet tights down her legs. She helped at the end by kicking vigorously, first hopping on one foot, then the other.

"I stayed outside because I thought nobody was home. Because the light wasn't on."

Roused from the growing darkness in which she had been sitting, Elena scooped up the wet tights from the hallway and placed them in the laundry hamper. She ran water in the bath and placed a fresh towel beside it. She returned to the kitchen and broke four eggs into a small mixing bowl before shredding cheese on top and whisking. She sliced bread for the toaster and put the kettle on for tea. There wasn't any milk. She would have liked to give a glass of milk but at least there was cheese. She grated more cheese.

"Are you almost done?" she yelled down the hall.

"Do I have to wash my hair?"

"No."

"Can I wear your robe?" Sharon swirled the water this way and that, following with her eyes a fleeing bar of soap.

"Why don't you put on your pajamas?"

"I don't know where they are!"

"Your bedroom."

"Your robe is on the hook."

"If you want."

Sharon emerged in a terrycloth robe many sizes too big, carrying the towel and shaking her lowered head. Her mother grabbed the towel to dry the dripping hair and then tied it tightly with two effective twists. She moved to the counter to butter the toast and serve the scrambled eggs. Sharon ate eagerly.

"How was your day?" the child asked when almost finished, capturing her mother's usual inflection.

"I'm supposed to ask that."

"But you didn't!" the child squealed.

"Homework?"

"A little."

"Go get it." Elena continued to sit, loose hands around a warm cup, looking out the window and noticing that it really did seem to be getting dark later.

Sharon returned with an illustrated book, a blank piece of paper, and a thick pencil gripped with determination. Elena stood to wash the dishes and tidy the kitchen. She found her own small piece of paper, the back of a receipt, to make a quick list of food needed for the rest of the week. She entered her bedroom to separate and bundle clothes for the Laundromat. In the bathroom she went down on her knees to wash the still wet floor.

Sharon looked thoughtfully at the illustrations in her book. She turned the pages slowly. Finally she made a few abrupt marks on the piece of paper, printed her name boldly at the top and dropped her pencil, which rolled unnoticed under the table.

Fifteen minutes later Elena was reading to a restless child squirming this way and that between mismatched sheets. After the second chapter she lost patience. "That's it, that's all for tonight."

She rose to flick off the light and then sat back on the bed, briefly noting how the hallway light spilled onto the bedroom floor. She reclined to share her child's pillow. Then, softly, as much to herself as to Sharon, Elena recited the nightly prayer.

> *Jesus tender shepherd hear me*
> *Bless thy little lambs tonight,*
> *In the darkness be thou near me*
> *Keep me safe till morning light.*

Sharon tucked herself against her mother's steady breathing and settled. Her eyes fluttered and shut.

Elena's eyes also closed. She imagined the yellow canola fields receding on either side of the highway, mile after mile, during the two and a half hour cruise from Brandon to Winnipeg. While she had studied the fields, her father had paid careful attention to the plates of the passing cars.

"Two from Minnesota," he had said.

"Oh yeah, interesting."

"Only four cars passed us and two from Minnesota."

It was the sort of conversation he could sustain for hours, if not weeks and months, maybe years, a litany of small comments about changing details in a barely comprehensible world.

"Two isn't many," she had ventured.

"No, but two of four is high. Half of the cars that passed us are from Minnesota. That's unusual."

"Why don't you ask why there aren't more cars from around here passing us? That's what you should be asking. There's no reason to believe a lot of people are up from Minnesota. Two cars, probably each with one person in it, not exactly a major historical trend."

"You're a treat," he had replied. "A real treat." Then his voice had slid into that familiar mutter: "I want this to work for you and the child."

"Yeah, well, I want that, too."

He turned to look in the rearview mirror to see his grandchild. "You'll take good care of your mother, won't you, because as far as I can see she's going to know no one else there." A Manitoba car passed them. "Now it's three to two. Odds are like that, keep changing all the time. I really hope this works out."

"I'll be fine."

"I want you to do well."

"What do you mean by that? What do you mean by 'do well'?"

He shook his head in a kind of impatient frustration. "Well, you'll have to figure that out because I never did. I wanted to, but I didn't."

"You always talk as if your life is over."

"I don't."

"Do you mean make money?"

"Don't insult me. It's not about money."

How would you know, have you ever had any? The question

she hadn't asked. But she couldn't help smiling, considering it. She should have asked. It would have been funny.

"It's not faith either." He had restarted the conversation in another direction. "At least not the faith you learn early and agree to for all time." And then he had looked at her as if there was something particular in that insight.

"I'm hoping, in Montreal, that I won't have to put up with conversations like this."

"I re-mortgaged the house so that you could study and get ahead. I put money in your account. I'm paying for the tickets."

"Do you want me to thank you again?"

"No. I just want you to study hard and do well. I know how capable you are. Don't forget that. I know you in a way that no one else does. The bible"—he said as if discovering the point of the discourse—"says seek and you shall find, knock and the door shall open, ask and it shall be given to you. So you do that. Have confidence. Know that even though I'm not on the front lines, I'll be there for you, whatever happens."

"Front lines?"

"You know what I mean, I'm ready to help."

"Front lines?"

"What's your problem?"

"Why does an ex-Hutterite like you use military terms?"

"That's the point, Elena, I was never good at it. Never felt I was in the right place. Anyway, all I'm trying to say is that I'm here for the both of you. Is that so difficult to understand?"

Elena, softening, wished she had acknowledged her trust in him, or at least her trust in his intentions. She could have done that.

"I guess you'll figure it all out in your own good time," he had concluded.

They're at the Winnipeg bus station and he's holding two tickets in his hand. "I have them here. Right here. You know they both cost the same. A seat is a seat, the lady said, a seat is a seat. Christ, I know that, I said to her. I wasn't asking if a seat was something else. I never thought a seat was something else. I was asking for a reduced fare for a seven-year-old child. How are you supposed to travel with kids if they cost the same as an adult?"

Elena silently gives the bus driver standing outside two suitcases and then climbs on board, keeping one hand steadily pushing on the small of Sharon's back. The bus pulls out.

The father she had left now sits on the seat beside her, gazing out the window, still counting cars.

A moment of blinding panic: Where's Sharon? Didn't she get on? Wasn't she in front of her as they both climbed the stairs? In that very second Elena's body jerked into a sitting position in one strong contraction. She saw the dark bedroom, the light reflecting off the floor, the sleeping child.

It's alright. Yes, yes, alright. She had fallen asleep.

She gently placed her hand on Sharon's shoulder, reassuring herself of its fragile reality. She leaned forward to kiss the smooth forehead and to feel the lightness of the child's steady breath upon her face. She rose, moved quietly to the hallway, looked behind her into the shadows and left the door ajar.

She wanted to call her dad. Should she? Just pick up the phone and see how he's doing? It's 11:15 p.m. in Montreal, an hour earlier in Brandon, he might be up, watching the news on television, harvesting yet more details for the daily grist of futile conversation. She wants to tell him ... well, what exactly? What, really, can she reveal about herself to him who knows her so well but never gets her right? Perhaps she should tell him that it's difficult to achieve goals that aren't defined. What would he say to that?

No, she had nothing to tell him.

She fried an onion, cut in some garlic. The smells pleased her. The sound of sizzling in a quiet world pleased her. Refreshed by her short nap she opened the window and let the cold air chill her face. She closed the window but not all the way. She liked the sharpness of the fresh air mixing with the scent of frying onions and garlic. She opened a can of chickpeas, emptied it into the pan and stirred. She sat and ate.

Finished, she left the kitchen, moved the two piles of sorted dirty clothes off her bed, undressed, put on a large white T-shirt and rolled down her bedcovers but didn't get in. She unplugged the radio and carried it with her into the kitchen. She measured out rolled oats and put them in a pot with water to soak, placed brown sugar on the table ready for the morning. Still no milk. She plugged in the radio and turned it on oh so lightly. She looked about, trying to remember anything forgotten, then sat and folded her arms on the hard table. She stared out the window as large wet snowflakes, lit by the streetlight, tumbled in the night sky.

Her father, she thought, knew his own beliefs confused yet remained confident that other beliefs, still undefined, would be clear. Why did he believe that? It was wrong, wasn't it?

She lowered her head onto her arms, her eyes still open.

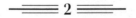

2

IN FRONT OF Mahfouz and on his left were the steaming pans: fried eggplant, diced chicken mixed with vegetables, fresh falafel, fried cauliflower and two kinds of rice; one white and plain, the other yellow with raisins, nuts and onion. To his right were the cold pans: vine leaves, tomatoes, raw onion, pickled turnip, tubule, feta cheese, olives and sliced lettuce. Behind his back two spits rotated in the heat of glowing electrical coils. There was a surplus of moist lamb on one and a thin column of dried-out chicken on the other.

He gazed through the window to the street, his head tilted in such a way that, should one order, he was ready to serve.

Elena asked for a vegetarian platter.

He served her generous portions from the warmest part of the steaming platters and ensured that the three sauces were not indiscriminately mixed as they most certainly would have been across the street.

She paid, sat alone, and began to read as she ate, starting at a page near the end of a thick book. Such a thick book. What could it be? Really, not that many pages to go. Would she stay to finish the whole thing? That's what he'd do. But people leave abruptly all the time. There's no way of knowing. And think, her coat is over her shoulders, she must be chilled.

"I thought you would like this," he said, bringing a coffee to her table.

"Are you going to charge me for it?"

"I wasn't going to charge you. I thought you might like something hot."

"I'd love a cup of tea."

He took the coffee away and re-emerged with a new cup and a small metallic teapot.

She looked up. What did he want? Surely he wanted something?

He moved away from the table and stood very still, his gaze elsewhere. Maybe he didn't want anything. She turned the page and continued reading.

He retreated noiselessly behind the counter.

The evening continued. A steady stream of people passed on the street, a few entered. Mahfouz served. Elena drank tea. He refilled the pot. She continued reading. She looked at him looking out the window, watched as his lips moved silently in time with the song crackling on the inferior speakers.

In her book, set during the Second World War, the main character, an Italian woman named Ida, part Jewish, has been raped by a German soldier and had a child whom she fiercely protects. What is that supposed to mean, Elena wondered. She closed the book, replaced the tome in her over-shoulder bag and stood to leave, paying Mahfouz no heed.

He was hurt. Did she really think the presence of the teapot a small miracle? Did she not know that human agency was involved in her comfort?

But no, at the door she allowed her eyes to seek his. She smiled and gently nodded good-bye. Mahfouz found her beautiful. Not beautiful in looks, not exactly, but she entered quietly, ate with restraint, read with concentration, didn't take what was first offered but asked for what she wanted, and then discovered his eyes at the end for a personal thank you. What a wonderful woman. Some people are a delight. They make the world glow.

He began to sing while cleaning. He placed the bills from the cash register into the commercial deposit bag, left the cash register drawer conspicuously open, activated the alarm, closed the lights, locked the door.

Standing on the sidewalk he stared back through the window into the shadows of his workplace. The spits were motionless, the coils behind them a dull black, the pans at the counter cold and empty, and yet he was happy with this space and the role he played within it. *I stand there*, he thought. *That's who I am, the one who, standing, oversees. And it's not wrong is it, or demeaning, to serve others to earn a living?*

He walked briskly to the bank to drop the night deposit bag down a metallic throat which clanged as it closed. Finally free of obligation he didn't want to disappear down the stairs and under the streets to ride the Metro home. He decided to walk to the next station. But as he reflected upon his life from the changing perspective of the larger city, the image of himself as he who oversees began to fail. Didn't he have more ability then an endless servitude to the appetite of others? But how could he become something more if he wasted all his time, day after day, repeating the same actions? And why had he spent all that time and effort getting a business degree if this was the extent of it—an annual lease, old kitchen equipment and a few matching tables and chairs? If he had known he was going to work forever for his father it would have made more sense to take a course in second-hand refrigerators and how to keep them running.

He descended into the station, a stern look on his closed face, and stood on the platform still and subdued. The train arrived, the doors opened. He entered and gripped a pole, eyes lowered to the floor. He looked up. In front of him sat the young woman to whom he had served tea.

He turned away.

Why the hell had he done that? Why had he turned away? He had had a chance to smile and make a comment or ask a question and he had missed it. What a fool! The surprise had confused him. Yes, it had. How, now, could he turn around and pretend he hadn't done what he'd just done?

The train ground to a rapid halt before fully entering the next station.

"*Quelqu'un a sauté devant l'maudite train*," calmly proposed a young man with a baseball cap and earmuffs. "*Maintenant on va être retardés de vingt minutes pendant qu'ils ramassent les morceaux.*"

The possibility was widely considered, but no one immediately endorsed the premature opinion. The Metro did grind to a halt for other reasons. After the briefest pause the train restarted, moving forward and pulling smoothly into its accustomed place.

Mahfouz turned as several people, including Elena, exited onto the platform. It wasn't his stop but he, too, left the car. When they reached the escalators she stepped up and moved to the right to let others pass. He stopped one step behind her. People filed by on their left, eager to get to the street.

It surprised him, the tight knot in his stomach, and now the tightness gripping his throat.

At the top of the escalator they funnelled towards an exit, she leading, he following. She turned to glance at him and then faced forward. In her eyes it was clear, he was sure of it, there was no one in front of her to recognize. He didn't exist. She hesitated, turned again to look at him. He must speak. He must speak now.

"I served you in the restaurant."

She nodded. "I thought so."

"You live near this stop?" he asked so easily one would think that he did, too.

"Yes."

Keep talking. He must keep talking. "Had you ever come in before, to the restaurant? I don't remember ever seeing you."

"No, but I liked it."

"We're known for being cheap."

"Don't knock it. The food was good."

She was smiling and they were walking side by side. Now he dared not say anything else, any word or question might reverse his great good fortune.

"I go this way," she indicated a turn.

"I would normally go that way," he pointed down a street he's never seen before, "but I can walk this way, too."

"If you want."

They continued in silence.

"That's my building."

"It's very nice," he said, lying. "Do you have time for a cup of coffee, or tea? I know you prefer tea." He hoped beyond hope that some unlikely seam in the fabric of probability would open.

"I don't live alone," she said.

"I didn't mean ... I mean, of course you live with somebody. I'm sorry ... I wasn't thinking." He didn't know how to continue.

His confusion encouraged her. "I live with my daughter."

"Your daughter?"

"Yeah. She's seven."

"Why don't you bring your daughter to the restaurant? Why don't you? I would love to meet her."

"I liked the restaurant."

"As my guest."

"Alright."

"Tomorrow, come tomorrow."

"I can't tomorrow. Maybe next week."

"It would be nice to see you and your daughter."

"We'll come at the end of next week," she said before climbing the three concrete steps and pushing against the heavy outer door.

He waved to her receding back, floated back towards the subway, past St. Cunegonde Church with its twin cupolas — two firm breasts with crosses as nipples —then again descended beneath the streets at Georges Vanier Station, this time to sit contentedly while crossing the city and anticipating his future.

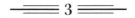

3

ELENA ALMOST MANAGED to forget her easy words to Mahfouz and when, on Friday evening of the following week, she flopped onto her bed to decide whether she would go as promised, she resented the obligation. Could he really expect her to show up? Did he think she owed him something for a free ... what, hot water and a tea bag? Besides, if she never went, what of it? She had no responsibilities whatever towards the shy, skinny, waiter who had imposed himself upon her.

But she didn't want to make dinner — the vegetables in the freezer were unappetizing frozen clumps wrapped in plastic — and he had said that if they went she wouldn't have to pay. Why not get out, eat well, and save money as well?

She dressed Sharon with a sense of occasion, finding red knee socks that matched a blue smock patterned with small crimson flowers. She fussed carefully over the dark, thin hair, pulling it neatly off the forehead and weaving it into a perfectly balanced French braid before fastening the loose ends with butterfly barrettes. Then she sealed her good work by centring the open and trusting face between two palms and gently kissing both eyelids.

As for herself, she pulled back her unbrushed hair into a tight ponytail and left the apartment in faded jeans and a green nylon winter coat which, opened, exposed a flannel shirt washed and rewashed from a royal purple into an inadvertently most elegant mauve.

4

MAHFOUZ, ALL PLACES at once, catered to the Friday night crowd grown tired of burgers and pizza who still want change from a ten dollar bill. He filled the plates, worked the cash, bussed the tables. Even though there was frost at the bottom edge of the large front window, perspiration stains visibly spread beneath his arms.

"You came!"

"This is Sharon."

The child. He looked down at her. "My name is Mahfouz."

"Do you remember my name?"

"You never told me."

"Elena. Do you want me to spell it?"

"Elena. I got it." His heart quickly filled with the importance of the event, an importance evident in the obvious care she had taken dressing the child. Such a well-dressed child, such a selfless and dedicated mother. "She's beautiful."

Elena couldn't help but smile. "You seem busy. Is this a good time?"

"Yes."

"But there's nowhere to sit, I mean, I don't see anywhere to sit."

"By the time you're ready there'll be a place. It's a miracle on busy nights but you'll see, it works."

Elena took charge by letting him be responsible. "Do you want to order for us ... just, you know, put things you think we'll like on the plate? We're vegetarians."

He turned to Sharon. "Is there anything special you want?"

She shyly pointed to the yellow rice with raisins.

He immediately put two stuffed vine leaves on the plate and covered them with rice, steaming green vegetables, oily eggplant, perfectly fried falafel, pickled turnip and tomato slices. He began on the second plate, working to build a contrast of nourishing colours and ended by carefully spraying sauces on each.

Two men entered. They were laughing in an open, good-hearted way. One had his arm draped over the other's shoulder. Mahfouz launched on the offensive, haranguing in Arabic, but his father, happy to see so many customers rather than being stung by the accusation there weren't enough hands to serve them, simply ignored the complaint.

"Look," said Mahfouz hurriedly to Elena, "there's a small table clearing over there. You sit down and I'll bring these to you." He picked up the over-flowing plates and began to walk around the counter.

"What are you doing?" asked his father. "First you complain you have too much to do and now you act like a waiter?"

"She's my friend. I told her to go ahead and save a table."

His father looked over, noted the attractive young woman with a child, shrugged, then propelled himself and his friend through the swinging door into the kitchen. He knew he should help his son, but first he needed something to assuage his hunger.

Mahfouz placed the plates in front of Sharon and Elena with a broad smile on his face. "Eat," he insisted. "Eat!"

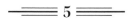

5

THE BUS COUGHED its way through the night while Sharon sat on her knees facing the window, her head bobbing rhythmically,

"Why are you doing that?"

"I'm not doing anything," she replied, her head still bobbing.

"Don't."

She stopped. Everything moved back into focus. Boring.

"Do you have to go to the bathroom?"

"No. I liked it there. I liked being behind the counter. People talked to me. Mahfouz is nice. Do you like him?"

"I don't know him. You talked to him more than I did."

"You could have sat behind the counter, too."

"Don't be silly."

"I got the soft drinks from the fridge if someone wanted one. If you were behind the counter he'd let you get the drinks, too."

"Right," said Elena, "and maybe if I behave I can work there as a waitress one day."

"That'd be good," said Sharon.

"We're getting off at the next stop. I want to get milk."

Elena moved quickly beneath the buzzing, flickering, fluorescent tubes casting a greenish light in the all-night convenience store. Sharon followed her closely. Then they were on the street.

The wet snow, again falling, covered the sidewalk with a thin layer of slush. Elena slipped and fell on her back. Winded, unable to get up quickly, she lay on the cement gasping for breath.

"Are you okay, Mommy?"

"I will be."

"Why don't you stand up?"

But even when breathing more easily Elena preferred to lie there, feeling the refreshing moisture of the melting flakes on her face.

"Mommy, you have to get up."

Yes, I should get up, she thought, discomforted by the broad wetness seeping through the back of her nylon coat.

She rolled to her side and saw the horizontal length of the wet sidewalk. There were so many beautiful colours reflected upon it. Strange, how differently the world presented itself from here. She placed her palms flat on the rough surface of the concrete and pushed against its cold hardness to help her shift to her knees. She hesitantly stood, attempted to brush the slush off her coat, then leaned forward and gingerly picked up her bag.

"Why did you lie there?"

"I was catching my breath."

"Are you hurt?"

"No."

They entered their building. The light in the foyer was very dim because someone, once again, had stolen two of the three light bulbs.

"I want you going straight to bed when we get in."

"Can I sleep in your bed?"

"No."

"Why not? Don't you like it?"

"Yes, sometimes. Not all the time. Not tonight."

In the apartment Elena turned to Sharon. "I invited Mahfouz to our place. I shouldn't have done that but we didn't really talk in the restaurant and I wanted to get you to bed. Since I don't have a baby-sitter I said he could come over."

"You invited him here?"

"I don't know if he'll really come."

"You like him."

"I don't know him."

"Where will he sleep?"

"My god, he's not going to sleep here. If he comes it's just for a tea or something. Then he'll go home. Really, I don't know why I invited him. Now I'll have to stay up and figure out how to get rid of him. But he lives near here so it shouldn't be too hard. Why did I do such a stupid thing?"

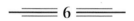

6

"THAT'S GOOD." MAHFOUZ took another small sip of tea. "It's very good."

"I used fresh mint."

A pause. "Do you go to school? I mean the book you had, it looked pretty thick."

"That wasn't for school, but yeah, I go to university."

"You like it?"

"I don't know to be honest. Sometimes I feel too bored to go. Then at night I start to worry, stay up late, drink tea, make imaginary plans about how I'll study. The next day, I'm exhausted."

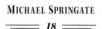

"You miss a lot of classes?"

"Like now, here we are drinking tea and it's after midnight."

"Tomorrow's Saturday."

"I'm talking about a pattern."

"Are you failing?"

"No, of course not."

"Were you married?"

"You're asking because of Sharon?"

"You don't have to talk about it."

"I don't mind talking about it."

"You don't have to."

"I wanted the baby."

"You didn't want to marry?"

"When I told him I was pregnant he said it was impossible and that the baby wasn't his. He said I must be lying. So I guess marriage was really never a part of it."

"He said that! Why?"

"I don't know."

"We don't have to talk about it."

"You were nice to her tonight. She liked being behind the counter."

"I liked it, too. She was helpful."

"Would you like something besides tea?"

"What?"

"Something stronger."

"Muslims don't drink alcohol."

"I'd forgotten that."

"Good Muslims won't touch it."

"So, not all Muslims?"

He smiled in spite of himself. She was, indeed, a subtle and quick woman. "It's hard to be good all the time."

She got a small bottle of vodka with two shot glasses and set them on the table. "What does it mean to you, being a Muslim?"

"What does it mean to you, being a Christian?"

"I'm not a Christian. My parents are, were, whatever ... especially my father. My mother didn't think much about it. It's his religion, not mine."

"But still, it's who you are, it's how you think."

"I don't know, is religion genetic? Don't I have a choice?"

"It's in the air you breathe, in the alcohol you drink."

"You say that as if you don't think very highly of us."

"See, you said 'us'. You can't help it. You're Christian, even if you don't believe." He poured himself a shot. "And even if I drink this, I'm still a Muslim. It's odd, but true." He tasted the cold vodka and enjoyed it in measured sips.

Elena went to the washroom, hesitated as she returned past her bedroom, momentarily confused by the form in her bed. She sat on the edge of the mattress and shifted the hair from the sleeping face. When did she get up and crawl in? Was she awakened by Mahfouz's arrival? Such a young face. Seven and a half years, so, counting the pregnancy, more than eight years without — what would the word be — intimacy? Not exactly. Whatever it was that got her pregnant it wasn't intimacy. Eight years without it, whatever it's called. And now this strange man, everything about him unusual, in her kitchen late at night. She didn't know him. Maybe she didn't even like him, but everything she was doing was telling him to stay. She recognized that. But as to why she was doing it, she didn't know.

Footsteps came towards her.

He stopped at the doorway and leaned against it. He was accustomed to think of sex as something primarily visual.

It happened on screens, restrained in the cinemas and completely without shame or limits on the computer. Standing like that, peering into a dark room, he saw almost nothing. It wasn't sexual arousal he felt, but a desire to share the darkness. He listened to the soft cadences of her breathing.

"I was just checking on Sharon. Let's go to the other room." Together they re-emerged into the light of the kitchen. But now, both sensed it, some scent of a desired possibility was disappearing, becoming less definite, more vague.

"Just hold me," she said, as flat as that.

He held her.

"Follow me."

They entered Sharon's room. Elena's hand rose as if to turn on the light but then fell away. They held each other's hands in the dark, simply. They moved closer and, perhaps without knowing, began to sway.

Mahfouz moved closer still, believing he was transforming into wax, molten and slow moving, covering with warmth the places of least resistance on the person in front of him. He poured himself into the moment, unconscious of everything except his proximity to this remarkable person who, made up equally of heaven and earth, understood so much.

They were on the bed. Everything was new for him. She opened the condom she had purchased at the store and put it on him.

Elena, too, floated away from the world with its ceaseless burdens, content to let her body guide him, hoping that the waves washing over her would remain gentle, for he was that, gentle. She was surprised, then, when only minutes later her body arched to drive his home. She held tightly onto his slight shoulders as he shuddered uncontrollably.

Mahfouz withdrew, stunned and unsure what to do. Without chancing a word he walked to the washroom to dispose of the condom. When he returned he heard the muffled sobs. He stood in the doorway, paralyzed.

What had he done? What was he to do?

Elena rose. She stifled her sounds as she passed him, entered her bedroom and crawled in with Sharon. She circled her arms around all that she wanted to protect in this life and cried, wishing herself asleep.

Mahfouz dressed quickly, imagining he was supposed to run, imagining he was supposed to console her, knowing he was filled with confusion and anxiety because of something he couldn't understand. What had he done wrong?

He sat indecisively on the bed in Sharon's room. He heard Elena still crying. He didn't want to run, but neither did he want to intrude upon her.

7

MORNING. SHARON SLEPT on her mother's arm. Mahfouz slept on the child's bed. Elena, awakened, wondered what last night meant.

Why did it always seem that she would never know herself, not really, not at that fundamental level that seemed to express itself in spite of her? What had she really wanted? What had she really expected? And why, after, had she turned into a fountain of tears? But now it was day. Surely he had left. She could forgive herself the mistake. She could forget the mistake. It wouldn't happen again.

She entered the bathroom, began the shower, scrubbed with soap beneath the cleansing flow of steaming hot water.

Hearing the running shower Mahfouz roused from an unsatisfactory slumber. Elena, he realized, was up. He wanted to do something simple and obvious, one suitable in its plainness for the strangeness of the occasion. He went into the kitchen.

Sharon, hearing two familiar and comforting sounds, the water of the shower and noises from the kitchen, wondered how both could be happening at the same time. She got up, put on the protective robe of her mother and wandered out.

The morning light fell steadily on the kitchen and the objects within it. Sharon stared seriously at Mahfouz. "Were you here all night?"

"Yes. I slept in your room."

"Are you going to make breakfast?"

"I was thinking of coffee, but I suppose breakfast is a good idea."

"What will you make?"

"I don't know. I haven't really thought about it."

The child paused, then queried: "Do you have any money?"

"A bit," he answered. "Why?"

"Sometimes on Saturdays my grandfather would make a special breakfast, fruit and yogurt and French toast. I liked that. We would go together to the store to buy the stuff."

"Would you like that?"

"Yes."

"Would your mother?"

"I think so."

"Okay. Get dressed and we'll go to the store."

"Should I ask her first, if I can go?"

"Of course. You must ask her."

Chapter Two

— 1 —

Elena's exams came and went and she managed to miss them all. She felt good about that, relieved that her future no longer relied on that particular form of hypocrisy she associated with classroom success. It wasn't that school was too easy, though it often was, but that the questions asked never started at the right place.

She found a job on Sherbrooke Street, in Montreal's Westmount area, selling expensive clothing in a tiny store where the majority of clients entered in clusters of unripened adolescence. In spite of uncertain hours, poor pay, and strains on caring for Sharon, she felt herself moving in the right direction: a new city, a new relationship, a full-time job.

The walk-in business came in predictable waves with long, slow, troughs during which she refolded clothes, rearranged shelves, dusted, mopped the floor, or sat patiently on her stool at the cash. She listened to the music of the on-line radio station selected by the owner, a stream of songs miraculously arranged to be immediately recognizable and totally indistinct.

Elena knew nothing about fashion but accurately visualized how people would look in the clothes they admired. She addressed the concerns of her young clients in a straightforward, guileless manner. Her advice on fit, cut, and fabric was sensible and simple. People liked to buy from her.

She learned that the older ladies who strayed in, those over twenty-five, were likely seeking a bit of social interaction. To them she was naturally amusing and deferential.

She wasn't permitted to read while at work but did so anyway, holding the book open on the counter with a heavy stapler on one side and a paperweight meant for the bills on the other. She was reading while at the same time turning a pair of patterned tights inside out, carefully avoiding snagging her nails on the thin material, when the owner suddenly appeared at the front door.

"How's it going?"

"It's quiet now but there were people at lunch. They liked the new colours."

"Did they buy?"

"Yes."

"Are you reading?"

Elena's response was surprisingly uncensored. "Read? Me? You gotta be kiddin'. I don't like it, hurts the brain." The nasal voice, high and slightly aggressive, didn't belong to Elena, but to the puppet instantaneously brought to life by her hand in the stocking. The words out of her mouth, Elena was appalled by her own boldness, yet pushed forward. The puppet confided: "If you don't tell no soul nowhere, especially not the owner, this ditzy broad behind me was reading but, you know how it is, she dusted, she mopped, she squared all the piles. I mean, she has to do something for her mind. You don't want a brain dead cashier."

"No," the owner said, moved to a tired smile. "I don't want a brain dead cashier." She gazed around cursorily, confirming that the store was in good shape. "I suppose you can read, if everything else is done and there aren't any clients."

"Thank you," Elena said, beginning to peel the stocking off her hand.

"Don't kill your little friend. She's amusing."

"Yeah, that's it. Keep me alive! Keep me alive!" cried the puppet, even more animate now that it had been given the right to live. But the reason for its short life had passed and Elena, herself beginning to laugh, cautiously plied the little creature from her arm.

"Can you work until closing?" asked the owner.

"That's the shift."

"I'll come back about eight and work with you for that last hour. We'll cash out together."

"You don't have to come before closing if you don't want."

"I like to put in a few hours."

"That would be nice."

"What are you doing after work?"

"I need to pick up my daughter at a friend's place."

"Is it far?"

"Not really. St. Laurent Boulevard.

"I can drive you."

"That'd be great, it really would."

"If my husband comes, tell him I'll be back at eight. Tell him that I came in for a bit and then had to leave. Okay? And if he asks where I am you don't know because I didn't mention it. If he gives you a hard time, have your little friend talk to him. That'll really drive him crazy." The owner exited, a nagging sliver of her personal life embedded in the capable hand of another.

Elena regained her stool and gazed out the large plate glass window. Overcast since morning, the high grey sky had been rapidly overtaken by sombre masses of darker clouds racing in at low altitude. The rain started, hitting the glass and smearing the surface. Elena slid off her stool and moseyed to the front.

Waiting at the light at the corner of Claremont and Sherbrooke, not more than twenty yards from her, a young girl, younger even than Sharon, stood wearing a red raincoat. Elena thought the child would always remember that coat. How could one not remember something so brilliantly, exuberantly, red? What a colour! The girl held the hand of an older male who must be her father. The traffic light turned and the pair began to cross.

A car, travelling east, accelerated to make the yellow light. The driver couldn't possibly stop in time. Elena turned her face away and, when there was no sickening thud, turned back to see what had happened.

The car, having swerved to barely miss the couple, now fishtailed dangerously on the wet street in front of her. It decelerated, eventually coming under control and continuing more soberly. A fresh downpour fell in a series of pulsing, vertical sheets.

Elena peered through the rain to the receding girl, still hand in hand with her father, an ever-fainter smudge of once brilliant red. She had expected them to be hit and couldn't quite explain how they weren't. Feeling a wave of acute nausea, she went back to the stool and sat in silence. She was shaken, upset, angry and relieved all at the same time. She turned off the ridiculous music. God, that was close.

The owners' husband entered from behind her, having parked in the alley. "Whoa! Is it raining or is it raining?" He looked at Elena, "Isn't Rachel here? She said she'd be here."

"She just left. Just just."

"She's not here?"

"She was for a bit, but then said she had to go."

"Do you know where she went?"

"I'm sorry."

"It's not your fault, I just wish ..." He walked to the front of the store and looked out at the street which seemed to him common and uneventful. He turned and considered the low table on which were piled several short columns of sweaters, all the same colour but of various trims and sizes. "Is this the new colour?"

"Yes."

"I don't know, what do you think? I mean, there's purple and then there's ... what do they call this colour?

"Aubergine. It looks good on some people."

"You tell them that, that they look good?"

"If they do, of course."

"You look good, fabulous, just like an eggplant! Is that what you say? They have a right, don't you think, to know that aubergine means eggplant?"

"You think that would help sales?"

"Maybe. Never know. Actually, it's not a bad colour. It beats fuchsia."

"Nothing wrong with fuchsia, especially as an accessory. Your wife wears it."

"Smart girl. You are a smart girl."

"No, I'm not."

"Smart people are modest. I tell my kids that. Where're you from?"

"Manitoba."

"Winterpeg? You're from Winterpeg?"

"No, Brandon."

"I know Brandon."

"You've been there?" She couldn't help the happy lift of her voice.

"No, but I've seen it on the map. It's on the map, isn't it?"

"Of course, it's the second largest city in Manitoba."

"Right. I'm sorry. I didn't mean to imply it was small and insignificant ... well, just how many people are in Manitoba's second largest city?"

Elena didn't answer, which didn't stop him from rambling on. "I was in Winterpeg once. I remember seeing this big map, it was on a wall somewhere, maybe at the airport, and it showed how the city was at the very centre of everything. It was roughly the same number of miles to Moscow as it was to, I don't know, some other famous place. And it was the same distance to New York as to Vancouver, or somewhere. Anyhow, it struck me that if you really are equidistant from all the important places, doesn't that just prove, logically, that one is as far as possible from anywhere important? So I ask myself, why would a city pay for a big map in a public place to prove conclusively that it's in the very middle of nowhere?"

"That's not how we see it. We see it as a hub. Being at the centre of a hub. And it's Winnipeg, not Winterpeg."

"Really? Winnipeg? I should have known that." He was teasing her.

"The reason we live in Manitoba is that's where we were allowed to settle. We were accepted there."

This interested the owner's husband. "We. Who is this we?"

"The Hutterites. I'm not a Hutterite, my father was. He was *Schmiedeleut*. All my cousins live on the colony but I never have."

MICHAEL SPRINGATE
30

He considered for a moment and then continued: "I'm looking at you sympathetically, is that right? Doesn't one sympathize with that kind of news? You don't watch television? You ride buggies and don't drive cars? You wear thick shoes and black hats? Sort of like our Hasidim, sufficiently backward that outsiders can almost be fooled into believing there's some special purity to it."

"You're probably thinking of Amish, not Hutterite. Anyhow, no, it's not backwards. Just because they own things in common and wear similar clothing doesn't mean they're backwards. You'd be surprised. Besides, I don't live like that. I live like everybody else. I just said I didn't grow up on the colony. My dad left when he was young."

"How old was he?"

"Eighteen, nineteen. Maybe not that young, but before he was baptized."

"Would you prefer he'd stayed? I mean, you wouldn't be working minimum wage selling *schmattas* for someone else if you were in the colony, would you?"

"No, but I wouldn't have been born either. My dad met my mother on the outside."

"On the outside, I love that, like a prison escape."

"It's not a prison if you can leave when you want."

"So we assume your dad did the right thing?"

"I'm glad I exist."

"When my wife comes back, ask her why she has a cell phone if it's never on."

"I can't ask her that."

He rephrased his frustration: "Okay, mention to her simply that it's been empirically proven that cell phones work much better when turned on."

Elena wanted to help him. "She told me she was coming

back at the end of the day to work the last hour and help me close-up."

"Why are you working here?" he asked. "A bright kid like you, why aren't you in school?"

"Students need to work, too." Not exactly a lie.

He opened the back door, looked up at the unsubsiding rain and left with his shoulders hunched. Elena refolded the clothes on the low table, wondered if she'd remember anything about this job a year from now. Surely she'd remember something, but what? Would she remember the conversation she just had with the owner's husband? Not a chance. Strange man. Nice. Heart on his sleeve.

I can't see into the future, she thought, *but I have a sense of what I'll remember. But knowing what I'll remember is also seeing into the future. How does that work?*

She gazed out the window and tried to recall the almost accident. She could explain the experience in words — if there were anyone who wanted to hear — but the nausea, that visceral dread she had felt so immediately and sharply, where had it come from and where had it gone? And without it, in the present, the memory was ... well, lifeless. Without the immediacy of that dread, the memory seemed trivial.

2

"MAHFOUZ, I WANT you to go to Cairo."

Mahfouz looked up, surprised. His father had never said that to him before.

"Cairo?"

"You can stay with my brother Ibrahim."

Mahfouz bent to pick up two boxes of tomatoes. He

carried them into the small room used for cool storage just off the kitchen.

"Why do you want to send me to Cairo?" he asked, re-appearing.

"Am I sending you?"

"Isn't that what you just said?"

"I gave up telling you what to do years ago. I'm saying I want you to go because there's an opportunity for you there." Samih finished sorting through a bag of onions emptied onto the table. "Put the hard ones in storage, Mahfouz, and we'll use the soft ones now. I also want to tell you that you should be careful of your commitments to the woman you're see-ing. I'm not saying don't see her, I'm just saying be careful."

"It's none of your concern."

"None of my concern?"

Samih decided to take the two remaining unopened bags of onions into the cooler himself, one over his left shoulder and the other gripped in his right hand. Mahfouz looked around estimating the amount of work left to do before he could leave for the day. In any case, he had to return later for the night shift.

"Sit with me," Samih said when he returned, taking a stool.

"I'm not a boy," Mahfouz said without moving. Maybe half an hour, he thought.

"I know, and as a man you want a wife. I just want you to choose a good one." Samih paused. "Not the first cute girl that sleeps with you."

"Did you have to add that?" replied Mahfouz, moving to pick up two more boxes.

"You know what I mean."

"She's not the first."

"There's a woman in Cairo my brother wants you to meet. He says she's young and beautiful."

"To your brother, I'm sure she is."

In spite of himself Samih laughed, but then added: "Think of it as having a choice. You meet another woman, you have a choice. Is it wrong to think like that?"

Mahfouz shifted from Arabic into English: "I'm not going."

Samih remained in Arabic. "Are you worried what to tell your girlfriend? Is that it? You don't have to lie. Tell her you've been invited by your uncle for a visit and then see what happens. Why not open the door just a little?"

Mahfouz returned to Arabic. "It would be a betrayal."

"No, simply a moment to reflect, a little bit of time away. You're rushing into things here. Why don't you at least meet this woman?"

"We'll have nothing in common."

"That's not true. When I first came here I wanted to turn my back on everything that had anything to do with that cursed country. I wanted to forget where we came from. I don't feel that anymore."

"No?"

"No."

Mahfouz returned to English. "You're crazy."

"I'm crazy?" replied the astonished father, also in English.

Their intimate lives flowed in Arabic, their public lives mostly in French. English, however, was regularly called upon when there was need for a blunt tool. Mahfouz continued in it: "Why won't you meet Elena properly? Why won't you sit and talk to her? Or have her over for dinner? Why don't you actually listen to what I'm telling you? You can't hear me, can you?"

"She already has a child," Samih replied forcefully, remaining in Arabic.

"So?"

"What do you mean, so?"

Mahfouz slipped back into Arabic, trying to remain calm. "Sharon is one of the best reasons to be with Elena. You'd think that, too, if you actually knew her."

"I like children as much as you do. Don't try to make me look bad."

"You're making yourself look bad. She's a wonderful person with a wonderful daughter. Give her a chance."

"Will you go if I agree to meet her?"

"Yes."

"Alright, I'll meet her."

"Okay, then I'll go." Mahfouz was satisfied with the success of his difficult negotiation. His parents would meet Elena properly. Talk to her. One has to start somewhere.

"That's not why I want you to go to Cairo."

Mahfouz suddenly felt angry. "Why don't you just tell me?"

"My brother sees a business opportunity. He exports, we import."

Mahfouz considered this. "He wants us to buy something from him?"

"He sees an opportunity."

"He wants our money."

"It's my brother you're talking about."

"What opportunity?"

"Fragrances. He thinks we should import fragrances into Canada. He'd help with suppliers. I told him I was too old to start something new but that you were young, educated and smart. Maybe I exaggerated. Anyway, we agreed that you should go and look around, see what he's talking about. It was only later he mentioned that one of his friends has a daughter you could meet."

Mahfouz began to understand. His father didn't want to refuse outright, but neither did he want to agree. Mahfouz would go to Cairo to make the decision, which would also get him away from Elena.

"My brother is smart," Samih said. "My parents always thought he was the gifted one of the family. But you're smart, too, and have a business degree. I'm hoping that means something."

Mahfouz felt a growing pride. His father, at long last, was giving him some real responsibility.

"You don't have a passport, do you? You'll need to get one. Since you're Arab it might take longer than normal. You should apply soon. I admit she's pretty."

"Who?" asked Mahfouz, momentarily confused.

"Your girlfriend. I admit she's pretty."

"I like her very much."

"What do you know about her family?"

"Almost nothing."

"Almost nothing?"

"It's her I like, not her family."

"So, you'll apply for a passport and you'll go?"

"Yes."

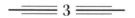

3

MAHFOUZ STROLLED TOWARDS work that evening imagining a life of new professional challenges: product launches, customs agents, currency fluctuations. Life, he concluded, was full of unexpected twists and turns. Yesterday he was a lonely nobody slicing chicken and lamb and tomorrow he'd represent his family in an international business venture while being desired by two beautiful women, both with claims on his future.

In a rare moment of nagging doubt he wondered why he always had difficulty clinging to the real. But Elena was real. Her eyes were real, her hands, her smile, the smell of her, the taste of her. There was nothing as real as the taste of Elena's salty sweat. She was smart, courageous, generous, and she had this — Mahfouz struggled to find words to fit the vague generality of his thoughts. An aura. That was it. But the sweat of that woman in Cairo, what might it taste like? If she ate meat, and she would, would that change the taste?

It's true he knew nothing about Elena's family. In fact, he knew very little about her, too. Sometimes she talked a lot; other times remained silent for long periods. But he knew her touch and through that he was convinced he knew her. Why imagine another woman? His father found Elena pretty? Good! Let him suffer the frustrations of all old men.

An ageing musician stood beside the open door of the Café Royale, blowing what he thought was an Andean tune into a large set of panpipes. Feeling worldly and comfortable, Mahfouz dropped a few quarters into the upturned hand and entered. He ordered a double espresso at the counter — his pre-work ritual — and proceeded with it to a vacant table by the window. He stirred the slick of foam into the thick liquid, enjoyed the hot initial sip.

Fragrances? He knew nothing about them except that one pays a lot of money for a pretty bottle. Admittedly, people did like pretty bottles. As a young boy he had bought a small bottle for his mother, mostly because he had been attracted to the graceful curves of the deep blue glass. He had thought it expensive, but smiled as he realized how cheap it must have been. It wasn't even perfume: it had been called Toilet Water. His mother, having had all her teeth pulled, had hid her mouth during two long weeks in which her gums hardened and dentures were prepared. When she spoke she veiled the lower half of her face with the palm of her hand. He remembered seeing the tears in her eyes over the edge of her fingers. He had known, even then, that it hadn't been the physical pain that made her cry, but the humiliation, the vulnerability of being toothless. So he had bought the fragrance both as a cure for her humiliation and as an expression of his loyalty. He had to remember that. It would help in the marketing.

Of course his parents must have discussed his uncle's proposition, but that didn't mean they had agreed. Maybe his mother had argued with his father. Maybe she had thought he shouldn't go. Or maybe she had suggested it? And what about Sharon? Didn't he have an obligation to her? He saw again her open face, basked again in her unreserved affection. It'd be wrong to abandon a child who needed and wanted him in her life.

It was Saturday. After Elena's shift she'd bring Sharon and they'd eat dinner. Sharon would help behind the counter and, when tired, would either draw at the table in the kitchen or fall asleep on the bench behind it. They'd all return to Elena's apartment together. In the morning he'd serve her coffee in bed and Elena would roll over to sit up and not hide her naked breasts. He'd go with Sharon to buy the ingredients for breakfast, maybe choosing a ripe mango to slice into the yogurt, or finding seasonal berries to spread on the toast.

He looked out the window and smiled at the silhouetted forms flowing in currents along the sidewalk, phantoms in the long shadows. What could they possibly know of the intensity of his happiness? And for that matter, what could he know of their feelings, or anything about them beyond momentary flickerings of perception and judgment?

Bolstered by caffeine, unperturbed by unanswerable questions, he arose content with his expectations.

SITTING AT THE table in the kitchen of Mahfouz's restaurant, Elena closed her eyes to assimilate the last chapter. She opened them to observe a drawing emerge from Sharon's fistful of crayons. She wondered what the bundles of vigorous red marks now colliding all over the page could possibly represent. "What are they, those red lines?"

The question delighted Sharon. "People."

"People? What are they doing, other than bumping into each other?"

"They're going into that building. I first drew its roof in yellow, like in the picture, but I couldn't see it so I drawed it again in blue."

"I drew, not drawed. I drew, past tense of to draw." Elena looked at the faded poster on the opposite wall. "Do you mean that mosque? Is that what you're drawing?"

"The what?"

"Are you drawing the building in that poster, the mosque?"

"What's a mosque?"

"Like a church, but for Muslims."

"What's a Muslim?"

"Mahfouz is a Muslim."

"Oh." Sharon looked up, unsure of what to do with a definition like that. "Oh," she repeated, accepting it. "Do you like my picture? I like it. I want to bring it home and put it on the wall in my bedroom. Is that okay?"

"Yes, of course, I think it's beautiful."

Sharon was pleased with the word beautiful.

"There are no people in the picture on the poster," said Elena.

"I added them."

"Do you want to draw a picture of me? I can sit still as I read."

"You don't have to sit still, I know what you look like. Do you want me to draw a picture of you and granddad together?"

"That would be interesting. But what about you? Can you draw all of us?"

"Okay. I'll draw all of us."

"I wish you could draw your grandmother, too."

"I remember the picture of her."

"In the living room?" Elena saw in her mind's eye the photograph of a thin woman in a wheelchair taken during that terrifying, final year of suffering, drug treatment, hospitalization and death.

"I could draw her, too."

"That would be all of us."

Elena also remembered her mother vigorous and in good health, reading Dr. Seuss to her when she was the same age as Sharon is now. No, younger, she must have been even younger. Her mother would miss a word and she, the eager child, would supply it. In the beginning only the rhyming words had been dropped, but later her mother blanked on whole sentences, and still later, complete pages, all of which she as a child enthusiastically supplied. She recalls the physical gestures used to help her remember: holding a fishbowl in the air, shaking hands with two things, catching the things in a net as they flew kites in the halls ... an improvised but repeatable choreography which always left her mother laughing. How long had it been before she could recite the entire book? And how much longer before she realized she had been taught to do so in a simple and effective way?

Her mother had enjoyed some good years. Is that as much as one can wish?

In the long period of mourning following her death, Elena had read each of the books her mother had left behind — not only the children's books — all of them, of whatever length: *Fox* by Margaret Sweatman was balanced on one arm of the living room chair while the *Egyptian Book of the Dead* claimed the other; the collected stories of Mavis Gallant splayed on her pillow while Carol Shields' *Republic of Love* lay open on the kitchen counter: books too adult by far but each more interesting for that. Some were read twice, and then again. And although each left its trace upon Elena's absorbent mind, the cumulative effect was not to define her mother more clearly, but to simply enrich the enigma she remained.

Sharon stood up to show her the completed drawing. In the foreground, along the bottom of the page, stood a small figure with two perky pigtails. One of her stick arms, much longer than the other, reached right across the page to entwine with the hand of a thin person sitting in a chair bracketed by large, emphatic wheels. Higher on the page were three looming figures: Elena's father, identifiable by his beard and big ears; herself, for what other woman could it possibly be; and then, quite unexpectedly, another male.

"Who's that?"

"Don't you recognize him?"

"No."

"Mahfouz!"

Elena wanted to exclaim that he wasn't family, that he wasn't even close to family. How, in fact, could Sharon have thought to draw him on the same page as her mother and grandparents? But then she'd have to explain why they were waiting in the kitchen until he was ready to leave, and why he regularly slept over.

5

"DID YOU KNOW that you sing at work?"

"No."

"I can see your lips moving. Not always. Sometimes."

"Maybe sometimes I sing in my head," Mahfouz responded lazily. "At work I hear the same songs over and over, it's hard not to know them by heart." He paused. "Do my lips really move?"

"Yeah."

"I must look stupid."

"Sing now."

"No, I can't."

"Yes you can. Pretend I'm not here."

"When I clean, after the place is closed, then sometimes I sing out loud. That's the only time."

"You sing when you clean?"

"It's the best time."

"Well, you can scrub the pans in the kitchen if that would make it easier."

"You want me to get up, go to the kitchen and scrub your pans and sing?"

"I'll still hear you from here."

"Do you want me to put my clothes on or wash your dishes naked?"

"I promise not to laugh."

"That's generous."

"It'll be a struggle." And she exploded with laughter. They rolled from their backs to their sides, smiling at each other through the darkness. "Imagine if we were blind, really blind."

His hand reached for her shoulder, smoothed the length of her arm, closed on her wrist. He twisted it gently towards his mouth and softly bit.

"Don't bite. Sing."

"No."

"All right, then don't sing."

"You are ... silly."

"Why is it silly?"

"You wouldn't understand a word of the song."

"It's music, you don't have to know the words."

"That's true."

She saw his outline. It was dark in the house and dark outside and yet there was a strange light in the room making him dimly visible. Could that light really be from the window? The pane is black—no, not really, a midnight blue. Some unexpected light through an almost black window illuminated him. "Sometimes, when I'm alone and you're not here, I lie in bed and listen to the radio. Some nights I sleep the whole night with it on."

"Why?"

"I can't explain. I just feel ... I like the talking and the music. It's as if they're, you know, as if they're talking and singing for me."

"They don't know you exist."

"Well, they don't know I exist but they know somebody's listening and they're talking to that somebody."

"It's a job for them. They do it as a job."

"I'd like that job. I wish I had it. Who chooses the music in your restaurant?"

"My father."

"Your dad?"

"Yeah."

"Would you choose the same music?"

"No. I've gotten used to it but I don't like it. He likes old music, especially the recordings from the cafés in Cairo. He loves that stuff. He can spend hours listening to it. He can tell you the names of all the singers, male and female. He talks about the styles and how they changed and why, the effect of the different wars. He even has a collection of 45's, those little records with only one song to a side with a big hole in the middle. He's very proud of those."

"You like your dad?"

"Of course."

"Not everyone likes their dad."

"Not all the time, most of the time."

"Does he sing at home?"

"Sometimes he sings."

"Do you ever sing with him?"

"I have done."

"Sing for me."

Why should he refuse? Her voice was entreating, the room dark, he knew the words.

"Sing one verse," she urged.

So he began, but so softly that the words were barely more than clicks of a wet tongue on teeth. He finished the stanza and waited during her silence.

"That wasn't the whole song," she finally said.

He started again, this time giving clearer shape to each sound, pulling at vowels to ensure that each was distinct from the next. Again, he stopped. Again, he started, his voice sliding more confidently into the rhythms he knew so well. By the fifth and final verse he sang with the assurance that each and every person in a distant and long forgotten café leaned forward to hear his nuanced and heartfelt interpretation.

After he finished Elena straddled him in one quick movement, the inside of her thighs resting on the top of his hips, her palms firmly flat against his torso. "That was amazing."

"What do you think the song was about?"

"I don't know. I don't care."

"Elena!" he said, her name an exclamation of wonder.

"What?" she replied, hanging forward and kissing him lightly on the lips, allowing her breasts to softly brush his chest. "What?" But she knew he had nothing to say, that the act of singing in the dark had moved him as much as her and that in some unexpected way it was her presence that had permitted it.

She gently slid off him to one side, one leg remaining over his. She wanted this feeling of closeness to last. She wanted to protect the moment from harm. She didn't move.

Mahfouz shifted his weight and let his hand fall lightly onto the small of her back. There was a complete stillness before his fingers began to make small circles on the smooth skin. The delicacy of his touch pleased her.

The small of one's back, she thought, can be an intimate place.

Now his full palm glided up the long back muscles. She inhaled deeply into her lungs, expanding her torso. Mahfouz, amazed by the living volume beside him, the solidity of her bones, the living flex of her muscles, the way her breath sometimes deepened sometimes quickened, wanted to ask what she really thought of him. He wanted her to list words that would help him to see himself.

He considered saying "I love you", but he'd never said that to a woman before and besides, the sentiment was large and clumsy. When might be the right moment to say it? Not now, that's for sure, but maybe when the words came without thinking. Or perhaps one should say them only after long deliberation? No, of course not, love can't be thought the sum of a list of calculations. The words should only be said in a moment of true spontaneity. He was convinced of that. And therefore now was not the right time.

"I love you," he said, in spite of himself.

And, in spite of herself, Elena believed him. She began to wonder if she really might love him in return.

Chapter Three

—— 1 ——

Mahfouz stood in front of the security gates at the Pierre Trudeau International airport. The uncle's business proposal — on this he and his father had eventually agreed — most likely reflected pressing personal needs which he was not comfortable to disclose, so Mahfouz carried five thousand dollars secure in a money belt. It was the amount his father had thought reasonable for a brother who'd never before requested financial assistance.

But Mahfouz wasn't thinking about that. He had spent the previous night laughing and drinking at a noisy outdoor terrace. Elena had been there, attractive and witty. His friends had all liked her. So why leave now? What fool would choose to visit an uncle in the unrelenting heat of a Cairene summer while letting his lover wander alone during Montreal's long summer nights? It would be smarter to simply wire money to the uncle and give up the pretence of a business proposal; or at the very least postpone the visit until November, when the only swaying limbs in the night air would be those on the naked trees.

"Don't forget me," he said, embracing first Sharon and then Elena. Elena called him a fool and kissed him again softly, lingering on the lips.

"You're coming back on my birthday," Sharon reminded him.

"How can I forget when you keep telling me? What would you like?"

She answered immediately. "Sand from the desert. I can keep it in a jar in my room."

He thought that doable, and offered to bring her some of the very sand in which the ancient Pharaohs were buried. Would she like that? Sharon nodded, impressed by his access to special things. With a final, hesitant, self-conscious smile, passport and boarding pass in hand, he disappeared behind the opaque security screen.

Elena felt a moment of guilty relief. She imagined herself having more time, getting more accomplished. But then again, she had just enjoyed a special day, sweet and sad, as a day of parting should be.

Both Elena and Sharon were dog tired, but Elena refused to spend the equivalent of four hours' work to go home by taxi—for that was how she now calculated all her expenses: by the time it took to pay for it. They walked until they found their stop for the express bus. Once on it, Sharon put her head on her mother's shoulder and fell asleep. She roused slightly, but never entirely wakened, as they held hands and walked the short distance home from the last stop. Elena started to hum. She remembered the words so she sang them softly.

There's a land that is fairer than day,
And by faith we can see it afar;
For the Father waits over the way
To prepare us a dwelling place there.
In the sweet by and by,
We shall meet on that beautiful shore;
In the sweet by and by,
We shall meet on that beautiful shore.

They entered the familiar darkness of the lobby and climbed the worn stairs. Sharon dissolved into her bed and Elena sat on hers.

Where was Mahfouz now? Would he be high above Nova Scotia, or would he be farther north, over Labrador or Newfoundland? It was interesting how flights arched over the globe. Could he be even further away, over the ocean? Amazing — in the two hours it took them to get home he was already so far away, hurtling through the dark. But it wasn't dark, not really. In a plane one soars above the clouds to join sparkling stars infinite in number and a polished moon. He may be flying above a darkened world, but through an incomparable illumination.

She turned off the bedside lamp, slid between her sheets and rolled onto her back. She stared into the unmoving shadows of her bedroom, envying him his night flight.

2

IN THE CROWDED fuselage six miles above ground, rendered silly by lack of sleep and two inane movies watched back-to-back, Mahfouz reached for the newspaper that the man dozing beside him had stuffed between their seats.

Among the articles was one profiling the fighter pilots at the Creech air force base in Nevada, northwest of Las Vegas, who guided the unmanned bombers in their around-the-clock sorties over eastern Afghanistan. The drone aircraft, called "The Reaper," one generation evolved from 'The Predator', was reported to carry the same explosive load as an F-16 fighter. The article noted that the air force was rapidly shifting its budget to buy many more of these remote-controlled devices.

Mahfouz twisted sideways to shove the newspaper back where he found it, but then, reconsidering, meticulously tore out the disturbing article and folded it into a small square which disappeared into his breast pocket. Then he replaced the refolded newspaper. He had no idea why he saved the article except that it spoke to him of all that seemed wrong in the world. Not that anyone cared what he thought. He tried to close his eyes and find a comfortable place for his head.

Just then the cabin lights turned on and the coffee service slowly began down the long aisle. People stirred. The old couple beside him awoke and smiled in all directions.

Mahfouz remembered another article, one which praised the skills of a Canadian sharpshooter. The marksman, with the aid of a telescopic lens, had shot an Afghani at almost two and a half thousand metres, far enough away to be certified as the world's most distant sniper kill. Mahfouz had been surprised to learn that anyone actually kept track of such things, and then had felt outrage that the sniper had been honoured with an award for bravery. Did no one ever wonder about those little dots of men falling dead within a profound silence, killed at great distances by foreigners who rewarded each other for bravery? Did the west really have the right to demand no resistance? And when they encountered it, did they really think it was all the fault of assorted madmen and Persian mullahs?

Mahfouz hated the bitterness of his thoughts. What did the Qur'an say? "Whoever sees something reprehensible, let him change it with his own hand, and if he is unable, with his tongue, and if he is unable to do that, with his heart."

But it was hard to hold the heart steady.

He shouldn't have watched the films, stupid and forgettable as they were, nor have read the newspapers, which only infuriated him. He should have slept and dreamt of Elena. If she had simultaneously dreamt of him, could they have reached out to each other?

Mahfouz raised the plastic blind on the airplane window. The red sun, attached to the horizon's edge, enflamed the sky. Before him and below, not too far away, was the city of his birth. He was mesmerized by the clustered, rose-tinted stumps on both sides of a thin red ribbon, the glass surfaces of the high-rises reflecting the fires of dawn. He suddenly recognized the pyramids and noted that the city had grown to almost engulf them, as if they were a phenomenon of the suburbs. As the plane banked for its final approach Mahfouz leaned forward, fatigued and disoriented, and began to recite, ever so softly, the *salatu-l-fajr*, regretting as he did so that he hadn't washed himself first. He was surprised to remember the words, and found himself oddly moved by them.

The plane landed as the sun lifted. The city, sprawling and undulating, gave up its crimson highlights to emerge resonant with umbers and ochres, accented in green.

3

IBRAHIM PUT MAHFOUZ'S bag into the trunk and they
headed towards the city centre. He shifted quickly through
the gears and guided the small car aggressively. "Your father tells me that you're hard working and intelligent, speak
three languages, have a university education and run a successful business. He's very proud of you."

Mahfouz had never heard himself described quite like
this before and his heart tightened. "My father has always
been supportive. If not for him I wouldn't have had the op-
portunities I've had."

"Yes, I'm sure that's true. Your father works hard, I've
always thought that."

"My parents send their warmest greetings."

"How are they?"

"Well. Both are well."

"I'm glad. It's too bad that we don't see each other more
often."

"That can always change, uncle."

"You're right," Ibrahim said, smiling. "I'm sure it will."

"My father wanted me to tell you to visit soon."

"Perhaps I will, perhaps I will."

There, thought Mahfouz, the formalities were over.
He was surprised by the quiet authority with which Ibrahim
managed himself. He expected a more broken, even tragic
figure, but it's clear his uncle had no experience playing that
role and little desire to begin. He'd be a daunting partner in
any negotiations, if that was, in fact, the intent.

"As for three languages, uncle, everyone in the immigrant community in Montreal speaks at least three. It's a
minimum. And to be honest, our business is small. It only

survives because we work long hours without proper pay."

There, he had said it, and it didn't hurt anyone for the truth to be known.

Ibrahim smiled good-naturedly, understanding the boy's swift positioning of his brother's business. "Listen, we'll have time to discuss the proposal later. Right now I'm happy just to have you as my guest. I want to be your guide and take you wherever you want to go. Nor do we have to stay in Cairo. It can get hot here. We could go up the Nile to the Valley of the Kings, even visit the High Aswan Dam. Did you know that you have a great grandfather from Luxor?"

"No, I didn't."

"On our mother's side."

"How long would that take, Luxor?"

"How many days do you want it to take? Or we could go north to Alexandria. It's nice there now. We have some say over these matters." Looking at Mahfouz slumped with fatigue in the passenger seat he added: "You don't have to decide right now. Believe me, you don't have to do anything today."

"This morning, flying in," Mahfouz replied, the slowness of his voice betraying his altered state, "I saw the sun rise over Cairo. It's something I shall never forget. It shocked me, somehow, seeing the city like that from up high. And I prayed. Can you imagine? I said the dawn prayers. I can't remember the last time I did that. I was moved and I thought, sitting there ... well, I thought ... prayer is better than sleep."

Ibrahim nodded, said nothing.

"I'm not religious," added Mahfouz.

"Are you political?"

"No. I spout off with friends sometimes, in conversation, but I'm not active."

"You don't talk politics with your father?"

"Rarely. I think he's paranoid. He thinks I'm naïve. We don't understand each other."

"There are reasons for his paranoia."

"Perhaps, but I don't know them."

Ibrahim remained silent.

"When I was a student," Mahfouz said, stifling a yawn, "I avoided the so-called controversial classes."

"Why?"

"I wanted my education to be useful. I didn't want to hear people say the same thing over and over as if I must be hard of hearing."

"I'll try not to repeat myself," Ibrahim said, enjoying his own humour.

"But don't you find most political conversation useless? One sees the obvious, one hears the public lies about the obvious, and then one sees that those who tell the truth are punished and those who lie are rewarded."

"You're disillusioned. Nothing wrong with that. It's a sign of intelligence."

"I don't deny that politically I'm disillusioned. But personally, I'm happy."

"Are you?"

"Yes I am. I have a girlfriend who I like very much."

"My brother said nothing of that."

"She's not Egyptian, nor even Muslim, so he has his doubts about her."

"It shouldn't be important whether she's Muslim."

"She has a child." Mahfouz saw no reason not to get this, too, out of the way.

"She has a child from another man?"

"Yes. I like the child. Very much. Her name is Sharon."

"She was married before, the woman?"

"No. She had the child when she was very young. A teenager. When I'm with them the world makes sense. I make sense. I don't know why it happens, but it does."

"You're a disillusioned romantic."

"I don't deny it." Mahfouz finally yawned fully, his eyes heavy.

"Romanticism is suitable for the young."

"But not a sign of intelligence?"

Ibrahim smiled but said nothing. Mahfouz closed his eyes and gave into the soothing rhythm of the engine. Of course his uncle, like his father, would assume that Elena was a passing affair to be briefly enjoyed. Had his uncle ever been in love? Well, surely everyone had been in love at some point. Maybe his uncle remained unmarried because he had loved too desperately.

"Have you ever been in love?" Mahfouz thought he was asking. But he heard no answer to what was only an incomprehensible muttering. Safe in Ibrahim's presence, his body collapsed in the passenger seat, Mahfouz had fallen asleep.

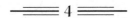

4

HE AWOKE SWEATING in the same clothes he'd worn on the flight. He couldn't remember getting from the car into Ibrahim's apartment, but obviously he had. He must have fallen asleep again as soon as he touched the bed.

It hadn't been a peaceful sleep. He'd been disturbed by dreams; something about moving furniture up and down stairs. Yes, with his father, as they used to do before the restaurant. He hadn't dreamt about that in a long time.

The tiny room had blank grey walls, the old plaster

patterned with long thin cracks. A shuttered window looked over a tin roof that covered the alley below. Although the room was in shadow, it was extremely bright outside. There was no dresser, no table, no chair. His watch lay on the suitcase on the floor in front of him. He must have taken it off and put it there habitually, as he usually placed it on his side table back home. He looked at it. Mid-morning in Montreal — add six hours — late afternoon here.

He stood, took off all his clothes and changed into fresh underwear, socks and shirt, and the same pair of now heavily wrinkled black pants. He stuffed his dirty clothes into the plastic bag he had brought for that purpose. He fastened his watch, straightened the sheets that were wrinkled but not soiled, went to the door and opened it.

"I've been waiting for you." His uncle's voice came from the kitchen. Mahfouz followed the sound to discover his uncle standing at a counter in a small kitchen, squeezing lemon on diced onions. "This is for later, although I know you must be hungry. Right now we can go to a restaurant that's close, known for its *koshari*. Would you like that?"

"I'd like to shower first."

"Of course. I put a towel for you in the washroom."

The bathroom had been freshly painted a deep green, which nicely offset the more recent porcelain fixtures. Mahfouz removed his clothes, refolded them, and placed his watch back on top. He studied his face in the mirror. No need to shave, not yet.

A coiled hose was attached to the faucet. He turned on the water and cautiously directed it away. After a disturbing pause water began to trickle out. Mahfouz stepped into the tub and held the hose over his head. After several minutes his hair was wet. He smiled, then laughed. Is this all the water pressure there was?

Chapter Four

=== 1 ===

Rachel looked around and sat. "This place isn't pretentious, is it?"

"Will Josh be okay here?"

"If the food's good. Where's Sharon, I thought she was going to be with us?"

"She's in the kitchen, she'll come out soon. She likes it here. They spoil her."

Rachel noticed the book Elena was putting away. "Did Josh lend you that?"

"No. Why?"

"He often lends books to people he likes." She changed the subject: "How's Sharon adapting to Montreal?"

"It hasn't been easy. It takes time to adjust to a new school. It'll be easier next year."

"I imagine."

"But I'm glad we're here. It's more interesting to live in a place where no one knows you or really cares what you do. It's liberating."

"Not lonely?"

"No. I didn't really have friends — not after I had the baby — you know what I mean? Just before we left we bumped into Sharon's dad and I said to him, isn't she beautiful? And he said she wasn't his. He said that right in front of her. I was so angry I said to him there's no way she's anyone else's, like no way, unless you think I'm capable of a virgin birth. I shouldn't have added that. He told me he knew I wasn't any virgin, but he also knew he couldn't be her dad."

"Why couldn't he be her dad?"

"He says he didn't cum inside."

"I'm sorry I asked that."

"It's okay."

"How old were you?"

"Sixteen."

"How old was he?"

"Same."

"Another Hutterite?"

"No. He was normal. I mean, not normal. Hutterites are normal, but a friend from school. I liked him at the time. Besides, I'm not a Hutterite. That was my father."

"Is that Mahfouz's father behind the counter?" asked Rachel, twisting slightly.

"Yeah. Can you see the resemblance?"

"No, not really."

"Me neither, thank God."

Rachel laughed. "You're being unfair. I think his father quite handsome."

At that moment Josh walked through the door. He smiled when he spotted them. "So this is the place."

"How was your day?" asked Rachel.

"The rise and fall of the mighty Canadian dollar is taking up my time. I don't know how we can keep the film industry alive if it stays above par."

"Josh is a lawyer who works with a production company. Did he tell you that?"

"I don't think I did," said Josh, turning to Elena. "I'm a Robin Hood in reverse. I help the local poor give to the foreign rich."

"How do you do that?"

"I make sure that as much Canadian taxpayers' money as possible goes to rich American producers. That, effectively, is my job. For some reason the government has convinced itself such generosity makes Canadian culture possible."

"Josh is not a great fan of government hand-outs," said Rachel.

"That's not true, I support them. I'm just amazed that they almost always go to the well off. I think it peculiar."

"It's cafeteria style, we have to go up to order," Elena said.

They all stood and moved towards the front of the restaurant.

"This is Rachel, the owner of the store where I work, and her husband, Josh," Elena said to Samih. "And this," she added, turning to Rachel and Josh, "is Mahfouz's dad."

"Call me Samih."

"Good to meet you," said Josh. They looked each other in the eye as they almost, but didn't quite, shake hands over the counter. "Tell me, which of your dishes do you recommend?"

"They are all good."

"Of course."

"If you eat meat, try the lamb kebob. We marinate it in my own recipe. Our regulars swear by it."

"I'll have that."

"I will, too," Rachel said.

"My son says nice things about both of you." Samih wasn't sure if that was true, but he was confident saying it wouldn't hurt.

"Oh," exclaimed Rachel, "that's nice. You know, if you have a free moment during the evening, why don't you join us?"

"Usually I'm too busy at this time of night, but if I can, I'll come over."

When Josh got to the cash, Samih refused to ring anything in.

"Are you sure?"

"You're my guests."

"That's kind," said Josh. "Thank you."

The three of them wound their way back to their seats with loaded trays.

Sharon appeared from the kitchen with several drawings that she was eager to show. The adults put down their plates and she put down her pile of papers, flattening the top one with both palms. "Do you like it?"

"Very nice," Josh offered. "What are the red marks? People?"

"How did you know that? My mother didn't know that."

"Really? I think your mother pretty smart."

"Do you?"

Josh laughed at the earnestness of the child's surprise. "Yes," he said, "yes, I do. Tell me, that upside down bowl-like thing, what's that?"

"It's the one in the kitchen."

"They have an upside down bowl in the kitchen?"

"A picture of one."

"A poster of the Dome of the Rock," Elena explained. "The mosque."

"We went there. We've seen that on Temple Mount." Rachel tried to compare the drawing to her memories of the actual building.

"It's not a mosque, it's a shrine," corrected Josh. "Mohammed's foot left an imprint on the rock just as he began his Night Flight, or so they say. That's why it's called the Dome of the Rock. It's not a mosque."

"Ah," Elena said.

"It was a busy location. It's close to where Abraham was going to sacrifice Isaac, or Ishmael, if you prefer the Qur'an."

Rachel turned to Elena. "I've never understood that story. Why would a father agree to sacrifice his own child?"

"Not to mention that on the same spot, or almost, Solomon built his temple. A lot of people would like to see that Dome come down and a new temple go up."

"Do we need that conversation now?" Rachel asked.

"What's a sacrifice?" asked Sharon.

"It's when you kill something, or have it killed, for no real reason," Elena said.

"That's not quite right," Josh muttered.

"Nice colours," Rachel said to no one in particular, eyeing the drawing.

There was a sharp sound of shattering. Everyone looked up. A woman had dropped her glass of water near the cash. Mahfouz's father quickly appeared from around the counter with a small broom and brushed the shards into a dustpan. He reappeared with a mop and, in a few quick passes shaped by the rapid twisting of his wrists, cleared the water. The line at the counter again moved.

"Notice that Sarah wasn't asked her opinion," said Rachel to Elena. "Abraham just assumed the right to kill her child without talking to her. What gave him that right? I think that's the question to ask, not whether Abraham was faithful to god, but why he thought he could do what he wanted with the woman's child."

"I've never thought about it that way," Elena replied.

"I thought it was about Abraham's trust in the wisdom and mercy of God," suggested Josh, "even if God should ask the sacrifice of a child. Or am I being too conventional?"

"That's dreadful enough, a god who asks for such things," Rachel said. "But that's not what I'm talking about. I'm asking, quite simply, why the man has the right to kill the child without asking the mother's permission — not that she'd give it."

"Well, Abraham didn't actually kill his son, did he? A sacrificial goat was provided. It's only in Christianity that God actually sacrifices his child. Why that's considered by some as moral progress is, I confess, a bit beyond me."

"You're avoiding my question. You think it's not important that the woman be asked because God gave Abraham the right. But who was that God other than a voice in a man's head?"

"Ouch," said Josh.

"Abraham not only claims the right to kill Isaac, he asserts that all the children of all the generations are his as well, to the very end of time. They are like sheep in his flocks, his to kill or not. And all the lands his children live on, they, too, are his. Children and property, his. And by what right? By the voice in his head which he calls divine. So the story is really about men establishing the rules of patriarchy, pure and simple."

"Ouch, ouch," repeated Josh, amusing himself.

"Do you want to know the real kicker? It's that Abraham pretends he's not claiming anything, but rather he's obeying. Obeying! He makes outrageous claims and then says he's only being faithful! Make no mistake, when they talk about faithful Abraham they actually mean conniving Abraham, cunning Abraham, who somehow ends up owning all the property for all time, children included."

"Perhaps you're right, my outraged wife, but I don't want to argue with you."

"If you did want to argue with me what would you say?"

"Times change. Now, when parents divorce, everyone thinks the mother is right and all the father can do is send the cheques on time."

"That's not arguing with me. It's suggesting that historical progress is possible, which I'm happy to consider."

"They don't all send cheques," Elena said. "I know a father who can't even admit he has a child."

"She means my dad," added Sharon simply, with a shy smile on her face.

Josh turned to the soft-spoken daughter. "If he actually knew you he'd be sorry. He doesn't know what he's missing."

"You're nice," whispered the child.

Mahfouz's father, meanwhile, had turned towards Sharon and by the tilt of his head and the wriggling of one bushy eyebrow posed a silent question. "Can I help at the counter, mommy?" asked Sharon as she squirted out of her seat. "Samih needs me."

"Aren't you hungry?"

"No, I ate in the kitchen." She scurried to the vacant stool by the cooler and climbed onto it as if mounting a lookout. She gazed about, smiling broadly, ready to bring the drinks she knew Samih would request.

"She's comfortable here," Rachel said.

They began to eat in silence, the restaurant noisy with others. Elena was suddenly unsure how to continue the conversation. "Thank you for hiring me," she said, turning to Rachel.

"You're a treasure."

"I like the lamb here," Josh said. "It's good. The guy wasn't lying."

The music on the sound system changed and Elena heard the soft words Mahfouz had sung to her in the darkness. For a moment she was lost in a different set of associations. She smelled his scent, bore the weight of his slight body. She saw the restaurant as she first remembered it, almost empty, and looked over to the counter as if he'd be there. Her daughter waved at her, alert and happy. Elena couldn't help but smile.

"That's better," Josh said. "You looked sad there for a moment."

"I was thinking about Mahfouz."

"When did he leave?" Rachel asked.

"Last week."

"And you miss him already?"

"I guess I do."

"Do you ever wonder if Jesus really existed?" Josh asked Elena.

"Are you saying he didn't?" Elena cautiously replied, allowing Josh his *non sequitur.*

"No, I'm quite sure he did. The historian Josephus wrote about him. But I doubt very much he was as you imagine."

"How do you know what I imagine?"

"Josh likes to provoke people, Elena," Rachel said with obvious irritation. "But that doesn't mean we have to go along with it."

"Given your background, wouldn't you think it strange that Jesus, if he lived now, might be called an insurgent?"

"I take offense at that," said Rachel, "I really do."

"Why?" asked Josh. "After all, he said he came to bring

the sword, his disciples were armed in the Garden of Geth-semane, and he led an illegal occupation of the temple."

"The last thing we need is for Christians to think Christ was a nationalist insurgent fighting the evil empire."

"Well," Josh said, "he was killed like one, he and all the other Jews who fought the Roman occupation. Crucifixion wasn't used for common criminals. It was saved for those who opposed the Roman state, so obviously they considered him an insurgent. Why shouldn't Christians know that? Why not let history speak?"

"You're being naïve, Josh."

"What do you believe, Elena?" he asked.

"I don't know enough to say. I'd make a fool of myself."

"Since when has ignorance deterred anyone from speaking about religion?"

"I didn't say I was ignorant. I'm not ignorant."

"So don't pretend you are."

"Josh and my father should meet," Elena said. "They could wear each other out."

"But what *do* you think?" Josh said, pressing. "You don't have to shout, but you should have a voice of your own."

Elena was stung by his words. She would have liked to explain her thoughts. How these questions were somehow linked with the shortness of her mother's life and the pain of its lingering ending. How her responses had been shaped by the frustrating futility of her father's searchings. She wanted to explain, too, that when pregnant she secretly prayed equally to God and her dead mother for the health and happiness of the baby inside of her. And that those prayers had been granted — miraculously or not — and to this day she was grateful, but not exactly sure to whom. She wanted to explain how she believed and disbelieved simultaneously. She just didn't know how to put it all into the right words.

"Why do I need a voice of my own?"

"I wasn't looking to be impressed," Josh said. "Just to hear your thoughts."

"Sometimes I say prayers at night to Sharon. I don't believe them, but I remember my mother saying them to me when I was young and I remember how comforting they were. So I say them, partly as habit, partly to remember my mom, partly in the hope they might be real." Elena stopped abruptly, then continued when she realized that no one was judging her harshly. "You know, I don't think religions are about the past. Not really. I don't think any of them are about facts in the past, although that's how we present them. They're about hopes. The past is told to us in a certain way to guide us to the hopes that are important, the hopes worth protecting. There will always be religion, if we call it that or not, because we'll always need hope."

"When you say hope," Josh said, "what do you mean: life after death? Next year in Jerusalem? The presence of a divine and just God?"

"All of that. All of them are just hopes, aren't they? And if they ever turned out to be real, then we'd begin to hope they weren't."

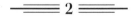

2

THE CAR ROLLED to a gentle stop at the red light at the corner of University and Pine, the momentum of the vehicle being momentarily equalled by the pull of the hill being climbed. Rachel braked gently to ensure the car didn't slide back. "Elena is surprising, isn't she? Sometimes she appears nondescript, mild mannered, and then all of a sudden she comes to life, opens her mouth and surprises you."

"You like her?"

"Yes, quite a bit. I have a grudging respect for her."

"Why grudging?"

"In the sense that she's earned it."

"That's good."

"But I don't like being her boss. Maybe I don't really know how to do it. Sometimes I'm tense and unpleasant, hard on her for no reason."

"You're a good boss."

"Then why did we have such a rapid turnover of sales assistants before her?"

"Because the pay is terrible, because it's boring, because they're young and can make a lot more in a bar on Crescent Street flaunting their assets."

"Why did you lead her on, about Christ being an insurgent?" asked Rachel. "I don't understand why you do that."

"I wasn't leading her anywhere she shouldn't go. I could have pushed much further. I could have quoted all the evidence for the disciples being Zealots."

Rachel stepped on the accelerator, her eyes sweeping left as they passed the underground reservoir with the playing field on top. All of a sudden the side of the mountain seemed to fall away and... yes, there it was again, the magic of clustered buildings at night, seen from a height. Such a pretty city, Montreal.

"You know," Josh began, "in spite of how she presents herself, she's a sophisticated thinker with the benefit of an unusual background."

"That's a high compliment from you, Josh."

"I guess it is."

"Tell me, do you still think every intelligent young woman is attracted to you, or should be?"

Silence in the car.

"You have to let it go, Rachel, if we want to move forward."

"Alright. I've let it go. It's gone. Let's move forward."

"I enjoyed being with you tonight," he found it necessary to add, after another pause.

"I liked your company, too." They were crossing Cote des Neiges, turning onto Westmount Avenue. "Do you know why her boyfriend went to Egypt?"

"Nobody's told me. I didn't even know he'd left."

"He's trying to structure some sort of deal to import fragrances."

"I can see why he'd prefer a different business."

"They seemed busy enough."

"It's a small place with low prices. It can't be easy."

"I've agreed to sell the fragrances in my store. I mean, what harm could it do to try? They'll hardly take up any room and will, at the very least, be pretty bottles with suggestive names."

"What kind of suggestive names?"

"They don't know yet. They're looking for something that will work equally well in French as in English."

"They've started the marketing?"

"They're working on it."

"Why not a woman in a hijab, dark eyes over the veil?"

"Is that what you think is needed?"

"Not necessarily. It's just that it... well, it kind of goes with the territory."

"In your mind."

"Yes, in my mind. Tell me, do you think it's just a reflection of 20th century feminism, what you said about Abraham."

"I think mothers have known for thousands of years that the Abraham story meant the fate of their children wasn't theirs to decide."

"Where's the evidence for that?"

"I'm a mother, I think it, I'm your evidence."

"Alright, is there other evidence?"

"What do you want, a peer-reviewed reference?"

"I'd accept that."

"Perhaps no one bothered to ask any women, or to record their answers if they did."

"Convenient."

"That's how power works, Josh. It extinguishes all trace of contrary thoughts."

"No, real power is when contrary thoughts don't arise. I'm not suggesting patriarchy isn't real, I'm suggesting that it was powerful enough that not even the mothers noticed."

"I can't imagine that. It strains my imagination to think the women wouldn't notice."

"Right, it strains your imagination."

"I have a healthy imagination."

"I don't think the Abraham story is about establishing patriarchy, as you claim, rather it's a story about faith set within a patriarchal society. That's what I'm thinking. There's a difference."

"Why can't you accept the fact that a founding myth, wrapped in the guise of faith, is about establishing patriarchy as commanded by a male god? Where's your intellectual difficulty in grasping that?"

"Who said God is male?"

"I know you Josh, you hope we can get rid of the patriarchy without getting rid of the faith. But the faith and the patriarchy are, and always have been, totally entwined."

There's a pause as he considers this. Finally, "Maybe we no longer agree on the fundamentals."

"I've been saying that for a while."

"But we could work through it, to the more fundamental fundamentals."

"You're the one who won't come with me to my mother's in Haifa. You're the one who had the affair with a girl younger than our daughter and lied about it. You're the one who always disagrees with everything I say."

"You're the one who moved out."

"What you did changed our relationship."

"I never meant to hurt you."

"What did you mean?"

"I didn't mean anything."

"Nothing gets me angrier than hearing you say that you didn't mean anything. You're either lying to yourself or you're lying to me. In either case, there's a lie somewhere."

"Sometimes things happen that don't mean much."

"How you can say that? How can you? If there are repercussions then it means something. That's what meaning is! We're not talking about how you sometimes forget to wear matched socks!"

"I don't know how to discuss this with you, Rachel. I can't find the words."

"That's the problem, isn't it? There are things we both want to discuss and neither of us knows how to begin."

"We have to give ourselves time."

Alright, she thought, let's give ourselves time. And so they sat in the silent car immobile in the driveway. Finally

Josh moved to get out, placing his hand on the inside handle. "Thanks for the lift," he added ironically.

"It was my pleasure."

"Do you want to come in for a nightcap?"

"Not tonight."

"Sometime this week?" He was being serious.

"Don't push, Josh. This is hard for me. Don't try to make me feel worse than I do. You have no idea what it's like not to just get out and go into my own house."

"I'm sorry. I'm trying to act reasonably."

"Yes ... yes, you are."

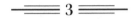

3

ELENA STOOD BENEATH hundreds upon hundreds of hanging plants blossoming under the outdoor canopies at the Atwater Market. She looked up and attempted to be critical, trying to choose the healthiest plants just beginning to flower.

Josh, from a distance, was charmed by the image. He inhaled the freshness of the morning air, then came forward to help her carry the chosen plants to his car. He gently scooped up the trailing branches and arranged them within the capacious trunk.

"Rachel asked for something colourful and hard to kill," Elena said.

"What's not to like? They're exquisite."

They drove west along Notre Dame, passing through an area that gentrification couldn't quite conquer. An upscale retailer had remodelled a deserted *dépanneur* across from a building gutted by fire. Josh imagined the anxious entrepreneur behind well-washed windows gazing expectantly at the ruins of his burnt out neighbour.

"Are you opening the store this morning?"

"Yeah. She calls me the assistant manager and gave me keys."

"You're moving up the ladder quickly."

"It's a short ladder."

They turned right to climb *rue De Courcelle* and passed a large home improvement store before driving beneath an impressive stone arch, after which the neighbourhood transformed.

Josh eased the car into the back alley and parked close to the wall, forcing himself to shuffle out of the passenger side. They carried the plants in quick trips. Josh returned for books from the back seat and placed them on the counter in the store. Elena turned on the lights and began to arrange the plants where Rachel wanted them: two hanging on the left side of the picture window, staggered in height; the third sitting on the right side of the low table. The effect was asymmetrical but balanced.

Elena took the two remaining plants outside and hung them from a pair of hooks already in place. She stepped back. Pale green leaves with small salmon buds waterfalled on both sides of the dark green door. She motioned to Josh through the window to come outside. "It's very pretty," she said, "in the sunlight like this."

"Very."

They stood quietly for a moment, sharing the accomplishment. Josh looked up and down the street before wondering aloud if she might like a juice or coffee and something to eat. She said yes then re-entered the store, switched on the music and set up her cash. When she looked to the window a group of cyclists flitted by in form-hugging span-dex, exotic and colourful.

Josh re-entered with two cappuccinos, two juices, two muffins and two sandwiches. He set it all on the counter near the books. "You didn't specify so I had to cover all the bases. I'm happy it's Saturday."

"Thanks. Me too. I like Saturdays at the store."

"What am I listening to?"

"It's a compilation I first heard in Rachel's car. She calls it her Sufi music but it's really just New Age with a Mideast influence. I convinced her to play it in the store. It's better than that radio station."

"You didn't like thinking you were at the dentist's?"

Josh stepped forward to look more closely at the clothing from the featured Quebec City designer. It was a clear depar-ture from anything he'd seen in the store before, mixing skin-tight stretch material with loose furs. On one mannequin the left breast was clear beneath the tight material while the right breast was well hidden by fur. All the mannequins were exposed in some places and heavily draped in others.

"Provocative," he said.

"I like it."

"When would you wear it?"

"I don't know, but it says something."

"What?"

"It says I'm not one or the other and neither am I who you think."

"That's projecting an awful lot onto a confused design."

"What's confused about it?"

Josh put on his reading glasses to read the attached note, written in French and English, claiming that all the furs were synthetic and all the cottons organic. It added that the designs were inspired by the four hundredth anniversary of Quebec City.

He whistled when he noticed the price. "I understand why she features these. After checking them out anything else in the store is a bargain." Then he crossed over to the counter and placed his hands on the books. "These are for you. I'm lending them to you. There's no rush to get them back."

She leaned over and took a look. The authors were Jabotinsky, Ahad Ha'am and A. M. Klein, writers she'd never heard of before.

"I think maybe I mentioned them to you but I'm not sure. Perhaps I just thought I did."

"No, you didn't mention them."

"I meant to. My wife tells me you read all the time, and then, after our conversation in the restaurant, and you being with Mahfouz ... I don't know why exactly, but ..."

"You want me to read them?"

"I'm just making them available. They weren't doing anything at home."

"Why these books, as opposed to any others you own?"

"They're all written by Russian Jews. Well, not just Russian Jews but Russian Jews from Ukraine. My people, I guess. My grandfather came from Odessa in the early twenties, which was a good time to leave. He was a Bundist."

"A Bundist?"

"A member of the Bund, the Jewish workers' party that spread throughout Eastern Europe. It played a major role in the Jewish resistance against the Nazis, especially in the Warsaw Ghetto. Jabotinsky hated it with a passion."

"Who was Jabotinsky?"

"Here." Josh touched the oldest volume. "The introduction to his novel covers him pretty well. I remember discussing his hatred of the Bund with my father. We were walking along the Boulevard that bears his name."

"In Montreal?"

"No, Tel Aviv. My father and I went there together. More streets in Israel are named after Jabotinsky than after anyone else. That's surprising but true. Not Golda Meir, not Herzl, not even Ben Gurion. Anyway, the boulevard I'm thinking of is in Ramat Gan, which was originally a *moshav*, an agricultural co-operative, but you wouldn't know that now. Now it's the centre of the world's diamond industry. The tallest building in Israel is there. I think my grandfather would have been appalled, but my father saw it as great progress."

"And you?"

"Jabotinsky was always a militant on the right," Josh said, ignoring the question. "He was also the writer who translated *City of Killings* into Russian. Do you know the work of Bialik?"

"I'm sorry."

"Don't be sorry, just remember the name and read him. He's considered Israel's national poet, although at the time of *City of Killing* he was just another Russian Jew adrift in Odessa. The poem is filled with the horror of the pogrom at Kishinev, but it's also about the shame of being an unnecessary victim."

"I'd like to read it."

"I'll find it for you. The press that published it was called Kadima, which is now the name of the ruling party in Israel, although I think that's just coincidental. The best translation into English is by Klein, whose books I'm also lending you. I know, I know, you've never heard of him either, which is sad, because he was Canadian, lived almost all of his life here in Montreal. He was a man full of contradictions—what we now call contradictions. Back then it was called 'wide experience' or 'great personal breadth'. He was a socialist and a Zionist, a founding member of the New Democratic Party as well as the public relations writer for the Bronfmans."

He looked over at Elena, who appeared unimpressed. "Do you know who the Bronfmans are?"

"No."

"Really? You really don't know?"

"Should I?"

"I guess not. There's no real reason. I kind of enjoy that, the Bronfmans as a footnote to Klein." Josh put his hand first on one book, then the other. "This is his novel, right here, actually his second novel, these are his collected poems, and this is a collection of his essays."

"That's a pretty thick book."

"They're all first editions. Be kind to them. Don't take them into the bath."

"You don't want Sharon to illustrate them?"

"I hadn't considered that. In 1954 Klein tried to kill himself. No one knows why or in any case will say. From then till his death seventeen years later he didn't write, which is a great shame because I would have liked his opinion on what was happening. He went from being very prolific to very silent, and there was a visit to Israel in between."

Elena was unsure how to respond. "I'll try to read them, Josh, but I was trying to get away from all the religious stuff. It's depressing. For a number of years all my father wanted to do was talk about the historical Jesus. The question meant a lot to him and he thought, he really thought, that he could get to the bottom of it. He even learned Aramaic. It drove me crazy. Other kids had a dad who fell asleep after work watching the news or hockey. My dad fell asleep while trying to read the Eastern Bible out loud in the original. It was hell."

Her delivery was dry but Josh couldn't help but laugh. "Your father learned Aramaic? That's not so easy, especially if you don't have Hebrew as a starting point. It must have driven your mother crazy."

"No. She had already died."

"Oh, I'm sorry."

"When I was eleven."

"I didn't know that."

"It's okay. Cancer. You can never tell who or when. Anyhow, my dad tells me my mother thought religion a curse. He says she didn't do religion, she did yoga."

"Your father really learned Aramaic?"

"It was the language of Christ's time, wasn't it? It's what Palestinian Jews spoke, so he thought it best to start there."

"What does your father do in Brandon? I don't think I've ever asked."

"Mufflers and brakes."

Josh considered the fact that somewhere in southern Manitoba an ex-Hutterite mechanic working on mufflers and brakes had taught himself Aramaic.

"Have you ever done yoga?" Elena asked.

"I'm saving that for my next life. I chose those books because I want you to know that Zionism didn't always speak with the same voice that it does now. Once it had lots of different voices, some with hope, some with anger. Some wrote about race, others wrote about social justice. I mean, there are huge difference between Jabotinsky, Ha'am and Klein, and I want you to get a feeling for that. People have a hard time remembering but during my grandfather's day, when I was young, when people were anti-Semitic it was most likely they were right-wing bigots who objected to the Jewish organizing influence on the left."

"Is that true?"

"Yes."

"You know," Elena said, "I'm flattered by this, I am, but I'm probably not the person you imagine."

"No?"

"I dropped out of university and work in a clothing store. I'm not exactly a budding scholar."

"You told me you're already an assistant manager. You're an up and comer."

"Yeah, right."

"Did you really drop out? Now I admire you all the more. I wish I'd had that kind of courage."

"You're teasing me again."

"No. I stayed in school because I was always good at it. I joined a law firm and stayed because I was good at it. I joined a film production company as legal counsel straight out of the law firm and now I realize I've been limited by my own success. I think that was true of Klein, too. It happens. You'll understand better as you get older. Early success can be a curse."

"That's something I'll never know."

"You're too young to say that convincingly."

"Can I give you books to read, or is this all one way?"

"I hadn't thought about that. What would you suggest?"

"Do you only read books by men?"

"Of course not."

"Do you know *History, A Novel*?"

"No."

"Elsa Morante. Italian. I liked it a lot. I was reading it when I met Mahfouz. You should read it." Elena noted his dubious expression. "When was the last time you read a woman author, Josh?"

"Morante?"

"I can bring it to work tomorrow."

"I'll try but I might not finish."

"That goes for me, too."

Chapter Five

═══ 1 ═══

O mar would again spend his day assisting Mr. Abdul-Naeem in the fragrance store, as he had for the past two months, and so made his way there as he usually did, winding past the Court building on Champollion Street, turning right on Avenue of July 26th, and then immediately left on Imad el-Din.

For some inexplicable reason he felt on edge. He stopped to light a cigarette, expecting it to help calm his nerves. He inhaled the rough, unfiltered smoke in a series of quick draws, then exhaled it slowly through his nose. The smoke dissipated, the unease remained. Again he inhaled.

In Somalia, he admitted, he had lost control of his family's destiny. Hardly unique. The whole country had lost control of its destiny, although they had fought to get it back. Was he right to have left that struggle to start again? Should he have stayed? But how could he provide for his children if dead? Better, then, for his sons and daughter to face the challenges of life on the margins in Cairo than in Mogadishu or, heaven forbid, back in Baidoa.

He carefully crushed the end of the half finished cigarette and put it into his breast pocket. He slipped down easily onto his haunches, his back against a building, and then silently studied the people who passed.

Omar thought himself reasonable, cautious, and committed to his family, certainly not as either ignorant or extreme. Although not well read, he considered himself as well informed as anyone on his home country, certainly more so than those academics, journalists and politicians on the television. He at least knew how much money was needed to hold the allegiance of a certain number of fighting men for a month, and under what conditions, and how that money would actually disburse on the street. He knew, too, that to impoverish a people was to make war cheaper, for it lowered the purchase price of a soldier's life. He even knew that while starvation is a strong motivator, it's not the deprivation of a single day nor even of a single week. There was hunger and there was starvation. Hunger must endure for starvation to set in, and he had seen that transition too many times.

He had also seen diarrhea drain the life from the weakest. He believed that losing only one child of four in a time and place where more than half of all children perished was the result of his and his wife's good planning, as well as the mercy of Allah. He had held the lifeless child in his arms and then passed her back to his despairing wife. He wasn't bitter, but his resolution grew. He understood the motivation of rage but had no sentimental attachment to it. His idea of winning was to change the conditions in which his life was lived. He was extremely suspect of anybody who defined winning differently.

He vigorously supported the Union of Islamic Courts, as did all those whom he trusted and respected, welcoming them as infinitely better than the warlords who had ruled since the government's collapse in the year of Fadumah's birth. With warlords, the word justice, if used at all, only meant the excuse of the moment. Justice in the Islamic Courts might be swift and rough, but the principles were time-honoured and known, and he believed them appropriate.

It seemed obvious to him that if anyone wanted peace for Somalia they wouldn't support a foreign occupation. But that's exactly what the West had done, supporting the Christians of Ethiopia as they invaded and occupied his country and rolled back the incremental improvements of the Islamic Courts. And of course they and their puppets had everywhere repeated the idea that occupation equalled freedom. Could they really believe the Hawiye people that stupid?

He trusted the Qur'an and the words of the Prophet, peace be unto him, but didn't trust all who presented themselves as believers or spokespersons. He was convinced that the compassion of Allah transcended the differences among warring tribes and individuals. The genius of Islam, as he saw it, was its insistence on compassion. It took the long view, as it should. The logic of the invaders, other than immediate domination and a collapse of moral standards, eluded him.

Given his experiences, Omar had concluded that the nation state was a construction that claimed both the purity of the tribe and the transcendence of Allah, but in fact delivered neither. He did not take American words seriously. They were forever drowned out by American actions. They said they were fighting terrorists but killed entire families for reasons never made clear. They fought from a distance with missiles and drones, or through paid proxies, and were a cowardly people.

Omar loved his wife and daughter and did all he could to protect them. He was aware of the roving gangs in Somalia who rape women, the same young men in pick-ups that his sons would inevitably become if he had remained. For the women the Courts had brought desperately needed relief. Could anyone deny it? They had been the answer to prayers said five times a day.

When in 2006 he realized the Courts would fall he chose to leave the country. After discussions with his wife and members of their respective families, aware of what was brewing, he arranged for his family to be driven close to the Kenyan border. They crossed it on foot carrying nothing, like many hundreds of thousands before them.

For two years they had lived in the world's largest refugee camp, time that changed all of them. Perhaps that is what continued to bother him: he was unsure who he had become. What had two years of subsisting on a thin but consistent trickle of international aid done to him? Was he right that living in Cairo would prove better for his family? Or had he run like a coward, and if so, how would he ever fit in anywhere?

Omar, bothered by these precise doubts, removed the cigarette from his breast pocket and, still crouching, lit it again. A small group of Japanese tourists passed before him followed by a well-off couple. He studied the woman's chador, the man's movement, and concluded they must be Yemeni. Before arriving in Egypt he had never seen a tourist, not one, let alone the organized groups and steady streams that congregated in front of buildings here. Such a phenomenon was inconceivable in his homeland. If they had arrived and managed to hire armed guards so as not to be immediately robbed or abducted for ransom, what would they have done? Where would they have gone to take pictures? There were historic buildings of interest in Mogadishu, but now most were of interest for the rubble they had become. It didn't really matter who had destroyed what, whether through direct violence or the more consistent thoroughness of scavenging, the results were everywhere the same. The tourists could, he thought, have gone to the game reserves, although many of the larger animals had long ago been poached for food.

But here, in Cairo, scavengers had been held at bay for centuries upon centuries and people from all over the world flocked to see what had been saved. He saw them daily; well fed, laughing and safe. Were they really thinking of pyramids, sphinxes, bazaars and belly-dancing? That couldn't possibly be real. They must be thinking of something more substantial than that, but what?

To Omar the tourists were visible but opaque. And yet it was among them he was supposed to find the clients for the perfumes. To the tourists, Omar was invisible in plain view, an unfortunate shadow marring a photograph of the scenery behind.

Sensitive to the foreignness of the place, he everyday tried to learn the signs and symbols that were now his to decipher. He knew how fortunate he was, for many refugees from Iraq had also flooded in. Surprisingly numerous, they were each trying to make connections and discover paths to a more secure future and yet he, Omar Hassan Addi, already had the support of Ibrahim.

He stood up and began to walk quickly, convinced he'd make up for the lost time. He again considered the coming of Ibrahim's young nephew. What was it like for him living in Canada? Was there any reason why his daughter shouldn't live there with him? She was at an age ripe for change. And since neither uncle nor nephew were fools, they must have discussed the fact that business relations joined by marriage were more stable than those that weren't. He himself had pointed that out to Ibrahim, who had said nothing in reply.

Omar decided that he'd watch them both closely, to see in which direction uncle and nephew would lean. Of course, they would also be watching him; the evaluation and considerations going both ways. The uncle would not approve of the nephew marrying Fadumah if he didn't approve of the father as well. They'd weigh his words carefully, as they should.

But Omar, in his pride, concluded that Ibrahim would recognize his seriousness and hard work, and that Mahfouz would not long resist the intelligence and beauty of his daughter. If the negotiations went well, then it would be appropriate to arrange for the couple to see each other again. They would not be alone, but could be ignored sufficiently to feel as if they were.

Omar briefly imagined his capable daughter as she worked in the back of the second hand appliance store in Manshiet El Sadr. The used stoves arrived encrusted with the grime and burnt offerings of an anonymous past and his daughter scoured them in all their parts until they shone with the promise of eternal youth. She worked all day; scraper and metallic brush in hand, a bucket beside her thick with detergent and crud. It wasn't ideal, but the owner was a Muslim Brother and didn't take advantage of her.

Omar turned right again, now left, and began to walk towards the end of the street on which the fragrance shop was located. There were too many such stores throughout downtown, and although this store was freshly painted and close to hotels, where were the clients? Omar hoped a minimal purchase price could be negotiated, for it was obvious that the store's survival could hardly be guaranteed. Yet he, too, understood that the owner must receive some financial reward for his many years of persistence.

Curious about a car parked on the other side of the road, about twenty meters away and with two men sitting within it, Omar crossed the street and approached the vehicle. He walked beside and past it. Neither of the men paid him any attention, but Omar placed their faces into his memory. One never knows.

He re-crossed the street and entered the store, relieved to see the colourful bottles still ranged in order against the walls, relieved to hear the water boiling. Was this space not a welcoming oasis in a noisy city? Thinking about it, there might be a market for *shushumoo*, *xalwo*, or *sambus*, the desserts he enjoyed—and if a range of spiced teas were served, rather than just the mint or black tea found everywhere—how many more people might find their way in? He could imagine, too, bolts of cloth available for purchase on the back table. His wife, who had a way with strong patterns and knew what women needed, could choose them. But really, wasn't it obvious that the store should carry only the more popular fragrances mixed with other items of broader appeal? If that had been done, then perhaps he and the owner would not be there alone.

Omar and Mr. Abdul-Naeem greeted each other courteously. Then Omar sat beside him.

Chapter Six

―――= 1 =―――

Mahfouz and Ibrahim had, after dinner, moved into the small, unadorned living room of Ibrahim's apartment. The chairs were old but comfortable. Mahfouz resisted the impulse of putting his leg over the upholstered arm, as he certainly would have at home.

"What did you study? My father told me you went to Cairo University but I don't think he told me what you studied." Mahfouz wriggled as he asked, trying to settle.

"Economics. I have a Masters Degree."

"I didn't know that."

"It's not as if I followed an academic path, and it was a long time ago."

"It interested you, economics?"

"At the time? Yes. Oh yes, definitely."

"I didn't study what interested me. Not really, I mean …" Mahfouz's was a bit confused as to what he did mean.

"You did what made sense," said Ibrahim, wanting to help the boy.

"Yes," Mahfouz agreed, although not quite sure that was it. "You wrote a thesis?"

"On Egyptian-American trade during the period of Al-Nasir."

"That's interesting."

"I had thought so." Ibrahim found "interesting" a rather unenthusiastic endorsement and tried to explain himself. "I believed if we could get the economic analysis right we could make the changes we needed."

"You don't believe that anymore?"

"No. At some point I realized that economic analysis by itself was not enough."

"Not enough?"

"Like a sand castle on a beach. Doesn't last long, doesn't mean much. You need a political organization to back it up."

Mahfouz was more interested in his own future than Ibrahim's past. "Is it true, uncle, that you told my father you found someone you think I should marry?"

Ibrahim was surprised by the question. "No! Not at all! Is that how your father understood it? I didn't mean that. There's a family I've met and among them there's an attractive young woman. Her father told me she was of marrying age. That's all I said to my brother. That's all I meant. Nothing more."

"Does she want to live in the west?"

"I've never had that conversation with her. In fact, I've rarely spoken to her. I talk to her father, who's trying to make it work for his family in Egypt."

Mahfouz considered the curious implication of this. Hesitantly he queried, sitting up a bit straighter: "She's not Egyptian?"

"No, they're from Somalia."

"Somalia?"

"You're surprised."

"Well . . . yes."

"In fact, the business proposal I've suggested is not for my benefit, but for theirs. I'm happy to make do with my small salary as a teacher and I like my work. But they're refugees and are suffering. I'm committed to helping them."

"Did you tell my father this?"

"I told him I had a business proposal and I do. I told him I had met a fine family and I have. I was definitely not trying to broker a marriage."

"But you didn't tell him that the business proposal was for another's benefit."

"I will take full responsibility for their actions."

"Nor that they're from Somalia."

"Surely you don't share in any anti-African prejudices?"

"No, of course not."

"I detest such prejudice. It's common here in Cairo and it's wrong. There are five of them."

"Five?"

"Three children. Fadumah is the eldest. Five in the family."

"And they're all here?"

"Yes."

Mahfouz said exactly what was on his mind. "My father thought you had become destitute, or almost destitute, and needed our help. He hadn't considered this."

Ibrahim laughed. "You can tell him I'm not destitute, but I would like his help."

"But not for yourself."

"What's a self, Mahfouz?"

"What do you mean? You're not asking me seriously, are you?"

"I am. That family is in my thoughts, in my heart. Is that not part of my self? Isn't your girlfriend part of your self in that way?"

"I don't think about it like that."

"Mahfouz, just as you and my brother are willing to work long hours in Montreal, so this family will do whatever is necessary in Cairo. They need to make this work. They're not looking for a vacation."

"So uncle, given this spirit of frankness, why fragrances?"

"People buy them, Egypt is famous for them."

"Yes, but . . ." The question lingered.

Ibrahim wondered whether this was the right time. "Are you sure you want this conversation now?"

"Yes. It's a good time."

"There's a shop available. The location is not perfect but it will do. The owner is not well and wants to sell. So there's an opportunity."

"And the Somali family would buy it?"

"So much down and the rest spread out monthly over three years. That's the proposed terms of purchase."

"And you're looking for the down payment?"

"I am seeking an initial investment, yes. The larger the initial payment, the smaller the monthly fees."

"But how, really, is this a business opportunity for us? I see how it's good for the ailing owner who wishes to sell, and good for the Somali family who wishes to buy, but how is it good for you, or your brother, or for us as a family? Aren't you just asking us to make a loan to the Somali family? We're hardly bankers, let alone bankers to refugees."

"You could see it that way but it's not what I'm suggesting. Our family puts in money and the Somali family puts in labour. The profits and ownership are shared."

"Is there money to be made in fragrances in Cairo?"

"Perhaps a little if you can get hotels to direct people your way. But wholesale in Egypt is very cheap in western terms. The Cairo store could ship fragrances to Montreal at cost, where you could sell them at a premium. That's what I was thinking."

"We can buy wholesale fragrances without investing in a store in Cairo. Why do we need the store?"

"But it's to your advantage to be associated with a store here. Do you have a history with the wholesalers? Can you negotiate with them? Do you know what to buy? Do you know what will sell?"

"And the Somali refugees know this?" Mahfouz was gently incredulous.

"The current owner, Mr. Hassan Abdul-Naeem, is very experienced, which is why I want the payments to him spread over several years, to ensure he continues to advise. We need him to stay interested."

"But you said he wasn't well."

"I didn't say he had one foot in the grave."

"How do you know him?"

"He's a colleague."

"A colleague?"

Ibrahim was surprised by the rapidity and thrust of Mahfouz's questions. It was an intelligent choice, he thought, for his brother to have sent this young man; someone sensitive to the nature of obligations but who feels none himself.

"Mahfouz, I think that if my brother had no desire to

help me then you wouldn't be here. Of course he thinks it a duty to be charitable but I'm not seeking charity. I'm asking him to help me help another family, and by helping them I'm confident they will find a way to help us. We just need the imagination."

"I think I'm beginning to understand."

"Good."

"It's not what we expected."

Ibrahim shrugged. "Nothing ever is."

"I would like to see the store, go over its records, meet the owner and the family from Somalia."

Ibrahim nodded. He had expected that, at the very least.

"I did some preliminary analyses in Montreal and came with figures for comparative pricing of wholesale fragrances."

"You did that?"

"It wasn't difficult. I looked into shipping costs as well. What you suggest isn't out of the question, but it isn't . . ." —looking for the right words Mahfouz slipped into English —". . . exactly a slam dunk."

"I'm sorry, I don't know that expression. What does it mean?"

"You can't assume the result."

"I understand."

"It'll take time before there's a decision."

"Of course."

"Everyone will have to be patient."

"I'm grateful for your diligence."

"Yes. That's the right word. Diligence. Due diligence."

"Whatever your decision, Mahfouz, I appreciate the effort."

"I've done nothing yet, uncle. But I confess the problem is interesting. The challenge isn't the price of the raw materials. Really, it's not. It's a marketing problem: how to create demand in Montreal for a brand they know nothing about of a product they don't really need."

"I hadn't thought about it that way."

"When you studied economics it was about modernizing the state and grasping the levers of change, that's what you said, isn't it? But I studied business, which is about how to profit from selling a commodity."

Momentarily taken aback, Ibrahim wondered if that was sarcasm from his young nephew or an innocent statement on the difference between generations.

Mahfouz continued: "I'm beginning to wonder how the previous owner, or even the family from Somalia, can help us in our marketing. Maybe they can. There might be a way. As you say, if we have the imagination."

"Your first day here and already you're talking marketing?"

"Why waste time?" the young man replied, somehow forgetting his recent plea for patience.

"Exactly. Exactly so." Ibrahim leaned back and crossed his arms. "Why waste time? When my brother calls, I'll tell him that I found you just as he described."

"Don't do that. Tell him in no uncertain terms that I'm lacking in judgment. Then he'll not only appreciate your honesty, he'll trust your perceptions as well."

Both men laughed, the younger and the elder.

"I feel happy about our venture," concluded Ibrahim, standing. "It's exactly the kind of collaboration our *umma* requires. Shall I make us some tea?"

THE WIZENED OWNER of the fragrance store, Mr. Hassan
Abdul-Naeem, compensated for the shortness of one leg by
a shoe with a much thickened sole, and in spite of the heat
wore a two-piece western suit with a white shirt and a properly knotted tie. He stumped about his domain offering
sweets. He chatted easily with everyone, whether they answered or not, assuring himself that all were welcomed and
comfortable, teasing the children who, out of practiced respect, were quiet in return.

He made fun of himself for having set out nine chairs
when there were only eight people present, complaining
mock-bitterly about the mental lapses of old age and loudly
suggesting that, should anyone not like where they were
sitting, there would always be another chair available.

Mahfouz concentrated his attention on Omar, who was
leaning forward to hear each word the owner spoke, apparently finding the Cairene Arabic and jumps of logic difficult
to follow. He appeared to Mahfouz as gaunt and permanently anxious. His teeth were prominent, his hair thin-
ning, and his long body slightly bent like a well-used rake.
He wore plain brown pants and a yellow printed cotton
shirt open at the neck. Sitting on one side of him were two
boys, one strikingly handsome, about twelve years old, the
other a spitting image of his father, perhaps fifteen. As with
their father, the simple pants and printed shirts were loose
on their slight frames.

On the other side of him sat his wife, large eyes and high
cheekbones in a calm face, her body covered by a cotton
outer garment that rose to a loose head covering over a
tight, pale blue headscarf. Sitting beside her mother, wear-

ing similar clothes cut from different cloth, and with a golden headscarf pulled low over her forehead, was their daughter, the eldest child, Fadumah. Mahfouz looked at her and recognized that, like her mother and younger brother, she had beautifully proportioned features, dramatic cheekbones and striking eyes. Yet he felt nothing for her, just a sense of the absurd in how he had briefly imagined her while in Montreal.

The fragrances themselves, in small bottles of various colours and shapes, were neatly placed on three rows of narrow shelves running along both sides of the rectangular shop. Along the back wall was a small desk with the cash register on it, a longer table on which were set two platters of sweets beside a warming plate for tea, and a door which must lead to the storeroom and back exit.

The fading walls of the room were pale rose. The desk and the door to the backroom had been painted a bright yellow. The floor was tiled blue. The long table was an ageing but still serviceable white enamel. The colours clashed, but with an undeniably warm enthusiasm.

At the front of the shop, carefully positioned on multiple glass shelves, framed by two large picture windows, were rows of intricately shaped and variously coloured bottles, through which the light diffused and refracted.

The introductions, led by Ibrahim, were brief. Mahfouz rose to shake Omar's offered hand. He found the grip pleasingly relaxed and friendly. Omar introduced his family, each by name. Somehow it was understood that, as supplicant, he would speak first. Everyone but he sat before he began.

"My family is together and in good health. This is a miracle for which I thank Allah. There were many times, in our homeland and on the walk, at the border of Kenya and then again in the refugee camp, when I thought our plans wouldn't work. But here we are, safe."

He looked around at the people listening to him, as did his wife, and in that unsought coordination Mahfouz dimly recognized an aspect of their perseverance.

"Allah is merciful," Omar said, setting firmly behind him the many narratives of misery he could have told. Mahfouz had heard the phrase countless times, but had never understood it quite this way: a radical sweeping of the table, a call to look forward not back. "Allah is merciful," Omar repeated much more softly, thinking of his lost child.

"In Cairo we met our brother Ibrahim. We are grateful for his understanding and support. And through him we have met Mr. Abdul-Naeem, whom I have been fortunate to assist in his shop. Now we are meeting you," he said, turning to Mahfouz, "who has come all the way from Canada. For the kindness of all of you, my family and I are deeply grateful. We ask that the merciful creator bless you."

He then summarized his desires as both a personal conviction and a public plea. "This city is a place where my family can live safely, where my children can be educated, and where I can earn what is necessary to support them. I do not want our family to be vagrants passing through, I want us to set roots here. But to do that we need your help, and will be most grateful for it. We intend to earn your assistance, and to pay back any debts which are owed. I am confident that if we work together it will be good for both families."

Omar sat, indicating he had finished. Mahfouz, surprised by his formality and brevity, realized that the presentation had been considered, perhaps rehearsed. But why treat it with any less respect for that?

Mahfouz stood. There were so many questions he

wanted to ask, needed to ask, but how could he closely question a man older than himself in front of that man's children? It wouldn't be right. It would be better to accept this event as fulfilling certain functions, in the knowledge that a more informative meeting would take place later. He stole a quick glance towards the front of the store, his attention caught by the entangled colours streaming through the veil of empty fragrance bottles. He then turned his gaze to the two older men, whom he addressed modestly. "I thank my uncle Ibrahim for his guidance and advice. And I thank Mr. Abdul-Naeem for his warm hospitality. I thank, too, my father in Montreal for supporting me to come here. I know that I carry his best wishes for all who are present."

Ibrahim smiled. It was an appropriate beginning.

Mahfouz turned to face Omar. "I'm happy to meet you and your family. In some ways, I'm like one of your children, for my father, too, brought me to a strange country when I was young. I remember knowing that as long as I was in his care nothing bad could happen. I imagine that's what your children also think as they sit in this room. As long as you're here, they're well."

A smile flickered on Omar's lips.

Mahfouz looked towards the two boys and was surprised by their attentiveness. Did they even understand what he was saying? Did they speak Arabic? Did Fadumah? Of course he had assumed she would, his uncle had said he had spoken to her, but was it true? He looked at her and she diverted her eyes. It struck him that while he had left his home in Montreal only a week before, she and her family had left their home in Somalia years earlier, and somehow, unbeknownst to either of them, they were destined to meet in this small fragrance shop on exactly this day at exactly this hour. But isn't it always like that, he wondered, if only we noticed, fate and fortune operating well beyond our brief calculations of awareness.

He turned back to Omar. "The question we have to answer is actually quite simple. How can we best help each other? If we begin by imagining a future which is good for all of us, fair for all of us, and then move towards it, we can fulfil our duties."

The use of the word "duties" delighted Ibrahim. He murmured *Inshallah* and Omar and Mr. Abdul-Naeem dutifully repeated it.

Mahfouz knew there was a rising anticipation in the room for him to commit, to say something positive and clear. Yet he couldn't give a definite yes. He couldn't. But perhaps he could indicate a general orientation, at least pledge his family to a serious evaluation of the opportunity that had brought them all together.

"I want you to understand that my family's business in Montreal has only grown through hard work and patience. We have learned not to be rushed into any decision, and to move forward only when the conditions are right." It's as if he heard his father speaking, choosing words like that. "However, I will do everything I can" — an irrevocable sentiment if intended, a common enough phrase if not— "to ensure that you and your family will not remain refugees forever, to work together so that your family may grow roots in Cairo as my family has grown roots in Montreal."

There, it was done. A mutual destination had been announced, although the actual path remained unknown. He had stated his intentions without defining any action. He sat.

Suddenly serious, as if warned by an inner doubt, Omar

leaned forward and then stood, again claiming everyone's attention. He addressed Mahfouz directly and spontaneously.

"Thank you for your words and the good wishes of your father. I understand that there is much to be discussed before we can go forward. I do not assume the future. That is why I hope we will meet again soon and talk at more length. I look forward to that, and am prepared for it."

A wave of gratitude swept through Mahfouz. He suddenly wanted to meet with Omar alone, away from the others. Between them, speaking directly, something would be possible; if not the deal at least an understanding from which something else might emerge. Okay, he thought, Omar and I can work together.

Mr. Abdul-Naeem bounced to his feet and quickly returned from the back of the room with a refreshed plate of sweets in one hand and a pot of tea in the other. The mood of the room relaxed. A current of celebration began to ripple through it. Ibrahim moved forward to share a few words with Omar. The mother turned to her daughter and placed a hand on her shoulder, saying something in a fluid and beautiful language incomprehensible to all but her family. The sons, having put more sweets into their mouths, stood up and wandered about staring at the all-too-precious bottles of fragrance.

Watching the boys, Mahfouz suddenly felt a great shame wash over him, the source of which he couldn't place. He looked to the ninth chair, as if it would inform him. But of course the empty chair said nothing.

Mr. Abdul-Naeem beckoned Mahfouz over to a shelf where there were three small bottles of pale blue glass, each with a cut glass stopper in its mouth.

"These are among my most precious."

Mahfouz inhaled directly from the first — sharp and strong, certainly not sweet. "Do you like it?" asked the owner. "Does it remind you of something? Don't tell me, just think about it."

Mahfouz didn't want to admit that it reminded him of fermented bananas and soap powder mixed in equal measure — fruity and stringent — but he supposed that some might like it.

The owner dipped a little stick into the second bottle and then withdrew it to shake it lightly in the air. "Maybe this."

Mahfouz was taken by the second scent. It was much lighter, perhaps with almond oil, but something else, too. He could have sworn it had a faint trace of black chocolate.

The owner laughed at Mahfouz's expression. "Nice, isn't it? Quite different from the first. But people want different things and we have to have something for everyone. You, clearly, don't like the more fruity tones. Here, smell this." He handed Mahfouz a fresh stick with a third scent on it.

Before inhaling Mahfouz closed his eyes and tried to banish all preconceptions of what the fragrance would arouse within him.

"Do you like it?"

Mahfouz chose one word to capture the mood he felt. "Intimate."

The owner was pleased. "I've heard it described many ways. I think that the most eloquent yet."

Thinking of Elena, Mahfouz added: "When I go back to Montreal, I'd like to bring a small bottle of this with me."

"Of course," Mr. Hassan Abdul-Naeem said promptly. "I will put it aside for you. It's my gift to you. In fact, I intend to give you samples of a number of the better scents."

Omar's wife gathered her sons and Fadumah joined them at the door. Mahfouz went over to again shake Omar's hand. He hesitated, then asked: "How did you meet my uncle?"

"Through my work with Harakat Al-Islah. It is they who have helped me thus far. One of the Egyptian doctors in the camp was also a member. He introduced me to your uncle."

Mahfouz realized he was at a loss as to what that might imply, but wasn't prepared for the other to see his uncertainty. It would be a question for later. He nodded his head again, as if understanding. "We'll meet again soon," he replied, smiling.

The family having left, Ibrahim and Mahfouz spoke briefly to Mr. Abdul-Naeem who appeared suddenly tired, if content and relaxed. "Yes," he said, "yes, the meeting went well. Better than I expected."

Finally outside, Ibrahim congratulated Mahfouz. "You spoke well. You put everyone at ease. You handled the situation just as I had hoped."

Mahfouz's reply surprised Ibrahim. "After I spoke I felt ashamed. I was ashamed of myself. I don't know why."

"Why? You shouldn't feel like that. You managed to tell them where your heart is without promising anything in particular. That's what you had to do and you did it well."

"I spoke like a politician."

Ibrahim laughed. "Maybe you have gifts that way. Don't be ashamed, I've thought of that path myself. Besides, everyone understands that nothing will happen quickly. Let's walk for a while. It will do us good."

"Yes," Mahfouz replied, not moving. He looked down the street, up at the skyline, felt through the pores of his skin the assault of downtown Cairo's unending noise and viscous air. Then he looked back into the small shop through the window of coloured bottles: another small shop, this one selling smells; another lease attached to impossible monthly payments; another set of books with small numbers; another precarious dream of solvency; another family depending on an unlikely success.

"Mahfouz?"

"Uncle?"

"Are you okay?"

"Yes, just a bit ... Where are we going?"

"This way," his uncle said, "to the el-Abd bakery."

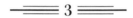

3

"WHEN NAPOLEON INVADED," Ibrahim said, "he claimed to be liberating the country from the Ottomans. That was kind of him, don't you think? His initiative, which we Egyptians resisted, apparently awakened a moral indignation among the English, because they followed with an invasion of their own."

Mahfouz didn't want to listen. None of it made sense and besides, it was all so long ago. He was fascinated that almost all the young women passing him on the busy sidewalk were wearing hijabs, often of a vibrant colour, usually above fitted shirts and very tight jeans. While their heads might be covered the word modest didn't spring to mind. Burqas were for sale in one window and thong underwear in the next, and the same women could be seen stopping at both. It occurred to him that those not wearing hijabs were probably

Copts. He wanted to question his uncle about them, but Ibrahim was too much in the thrall of his own wit to notice the unspoken query on his nephew's face. "And that, of course, eventually led Mohammed Ali to invade, claiming he needed to pry our country loose from the English infidels. He's called the father of modern Egypt, in spite of the fact that he was an Albanian who didn't speak Arabic and fought for the Turks."

"Ah," said Mahfouz, having now forgotten whatever it was that had interested him. "Mohammed Ali was Albanian. I had forgotten that." Although, in truth, it was a fact he had never known.

"Have you ever seen a picture of King Farouk?" Ibrahim asked. "He was a direct descendent of Mohammed Ali, a handsome man when young, but extraordinarily fat when he abdicated. Not just fat, but really fat, round like a beach ball. It turns out his only interests were eating rich food and collecting pornography. His sister was extremely beautiful, which was her misfortune, as she ended up the first wife of the Shah of Iran."

The amplified voice of the muezzin suddenly haunted the late afternoon, overwhelming his uncle's historical wanderings. Small carpets were rolled out in sheltered areas for the believers to pray. Mahfouz flushed with the momentary cleverness of comparing the actions of the faithful to Pavlov's dogs, but in the very next instant found himself irritated by his uncle's indifference to the call.

They entered the bakery and Ibrahim selected a few pastries to sample. Mahfouz took the first one offered and bit slowly into ground pistachio mixed with lemon juice and cinnamon, all tightly compressed between exquisitely light layers of buttered phylo soaked in honey.

═══ 4 ═══

"JUST COME HOME," Samih said when Mahfouz phoned him. "Keep all the money and come home."

"I can't do that."

"Why not? Is anyone stopping you?"

"My return ticket isn't until next month. I would have to pay a change fee to the airlines."

"That's not a real reason. It wouldn't be a lot and you have the money."

"I have a responsibility here."

"No, you don't. Not a responsibility. You would like to be a nice guy, I understand that, but that's different from a responsibility."

"You told me, when I was leaving, that I had a responsibility to do the right thing."

"I don't feel good about this."

"You don't trust me."

"It's not that."

"No?"

"I thought my brother needed financial help. I thought it would be good for you to get out of the country for a while, clear your head and see your girlfriend through fresh eyes. I thought you had worked hard and needed a break. I thought a lot of things, but now I think I made a mistake."

"You can trust me."

"I do trust you. You'll do what you think right, not what's obvious. Sometimes it's better to do the obvious."

"That's an odd way of putting it."

"You know what I mean."

"You don't want me to give your brother any money."

"I don't want you to give his friends any money. Tell

them you're glad to have met them but that our restaurant burnt up in a freak fire. Tell them a meteor hit it. Tell them anything you want, just don't promise anything."

"I didn't promise anything."

"Good."

"You're being paranoid."

"Call your girlfriend. Maybe she can convince you to come home. The weather's beautiful here. Sunny."

"I'm in Egypt. The sun shines here, too."

"I'm not trying to be subtle."

"I noticed."

"I want you to come home."

Having his wings clipped hurt, and Mahfouz resisted. "I can't do that. I just got here and Ibrahim wants us to go to Alexandria to visit the new library. He wants us to spend time together. I'm staying at his house as his guest. I'm speaking on his phone. I can't just turn around from one day to the next and leave."

"Okay, go with him to Alexandria. Walk around the harbour. Be a tourist. Look at some sights."

"I haven't promised anything."

"Tell them you have to return to Montreal to consider, and then you and I can talk."

"Will you be open to what I have to say?"

"I doubt it."

"You know," Mahfouz said, "I think I could make it work, the fragrance business. I get ideas. I see marketing images. There's a way of approaching this where the numbers make sense. Do you want to hear about it?"

"When you come home."

"Didn't I go to school to develop these skills?"

"Listen, I can't talk long, I'm at work."

"Is everything okay at the restaurant?"

"Some outfit in the States is wholesaling tomatoes with salmonella and people are getting sick."

"From our restaurant?"

"No, no, not from us, not here. But it was on the news and now everyone asks where we get our tomatoes. It's like when we had the scare with the California spinach that was irrigated with diluted pigshit. Everybody wants to eat local organic produce but no one wants to pay for it. A few of the regulars have asked where you are."

"What do you tell them?"

"That you're in Cairo on business."

"Are they impressed?"

"How would I know? I doubt it."

"I had a dream the other night. I've had it twice now. You were in it."

Dreams were not something the two ever discussed, and the father found it odd to hear those words. He remained silent.

"We were carrying heavy furniture down three flights of stairs and onto our old truck," Mahfouz said. "A hot day like today. My shirt was drenched in sweat."

"We had lots of days like that," Samih finally replied. "Big, ugly sofas caught in tiny stairwells with impossible corners. It would have made more sense to throw the pieces out the window and sell what landed as firewood."

"Maybe not a good way to get repeat customers."

"Some customers you don't need. Did the truck have the automatic lift?"

"No. It still had the ramp, but we couldn't use it because we were parked in an area that was too tight. Everything was tight, we never had enough room."

"How did we do, in your dream?"

"You were swearing up a storm."

"A bit of enthusiasm lightens the load. I'm glad we don't have to do that anymore. In the mornings I'd be so stiff I could hardly move. But no matter how I felt, I started again. Fourteen years my life was like that, carrying heavy things up and down narrow staircases."

"It can't have been all bad."

"It was all bad. If they had nice furniture then they could afford a bigger company, and if they had light stuff then they did it themselves. We had the heavy stuff of people who were broke. Inevitably they lived on the top floor of apartment buildings without elevators or in basements behind the furnace."

"I remember when you first showed me the automatic tailgate."

"We only had that for the last two years. You were a good helper, Mahfouz, skinny but willing. Your mother was always worried that something would fall on you or that you'd collapse under the weight."

Mahfouz suddenly felt close to his father. "Hey, have you ever been to Alexandria?"

"Of course."

"Anything I should do there?"

"I don't know. It was a long time ago. I can't imagine what it's like now. I used to swim in the Mediterranean. We would go there to see the European women. It was like two different countries, Alexandria and the rest of Egypt. We thought the city pretty wild back then. I imagine its different now."

"You went there to see the European women?" Mahfouz asked, laughing.

"What's so amusing? That I was young once or that I still remember it? There was a particular evening—I'm sure I went to the beach for the women—but what I remember is this boat in the distance. It was a big oil tanker. The water was so smooth that the reflection of the boat was as clear as the boat itself. It was as if there were two identical boats connected at the water line upside down to each other. Behind it the colours of the setting sun were spectacular. Or perhaps it was at Port Said, not Alexandria, I can't remember."

"I should get you a gift while I'm here." Mahfouz couldn't restrain his sarcasm. "You want a T-shirt?"

"If you have to get me something get me a book about the new Library. I'd like that, one with drawings of what they think the old one was like before it burned, and pictures of what the new one is like now. Don't get it in Arabic, get it in French or English, so that guests coming to our house can read it."

"You should be here with me."

"There's no reason for us both to be away."

"I guess not." Mahfouz paused. "One day we should travel somewhere together."

"Your mom's well. She likes your girlfriend and her daughter."

"That's good. Have you finally spoken to Elena, said more than hello?"

"She invited your mother and me to her place for dinner, to thank us for when we take care of Sharon."

"She did that?"

"She's a decent cook, your friend. Well, the meal was so-so, but not bad. The salad was good. She used grapefruit sections and walnuts on top of arugula."

"And? What do you think? Do you like her?"

"She seems nice enough."

Ha! His words were grudging but clear. He liked her. He liked her and didn't want to admit it. "She's beautiful isn't she?"

"She looks okay."

"I didn't mean looks, I mean who she is."

"Alright, alright. You're a lucky man and I don't know what you did to deserve it. I like the kid, too. Very much. She reminds me of you when you were young."

"I'm glad you like them."

Samih again tried to end the call. "I have to go."

"I'm not holding you."

"Call me when you get to Alexandria, can you do that?"

"I'll do that."

Chapter Seven

The road continued to rise and fall, curve and straighten, reflecting the travel habits of centuries, perhaps millennia, along the north shore of the great river. Elena gazed through the window, her thoughts led by the curiosity of her eyes, her body subtly swaying to the music.

"Do you think," she asked Rachel, "that different tribes live on the south and north shore?"

"Tribes? You mean natives? I don't know. Why?"

"The Assiniboine runs through Brandon. North of it were the Cree and south of it the Sioux. Traditionally, I mean, now it's all mixed. The land of the Cree was called the land of small sticks and the land of the Sioux was called the land of no sticks."

"Poetic."

"Kind of describes the geography."

"I guessed that."

"The St. Lawrence is so much wider than the Assiniboine. I mean, you can almost always ford the Assiniboine, or think you can. You couldn't even consider that here. Look at it! I think there must have been different tribes."

Rachel looked over. "You're right. A big river."

"You'd really, really, really need a boat to cross."

"I know almost nothing about the tribes that were here," Rachel said after a pause. "Montreal used to be called Hochelaga, I know that. The name of Quebec City comes from Kebec, which means the place where the river narrows. I don't know in which language."

"Algonquin?"

"Is that it?"

"Maybe. The Algonquin fought for the French and the Iroquois fought for the English. That's what we were taught."

"I think that's right."

"In Manitoba, the native-white thing is so much more intense than here. Here all you hear about is French and recent immigrants. They even have a commission to study it."

Rachel was surprised that Elena was aware of the Bouchard-Taylor Commission, but then again, why not? It was the talk of the town, and her boyfriend was an immigrant. "Hard to see what effect all the words will have, isn't it?"

A small market town sprouted in view boasting a rather imposing Catholic Church. The prominent spire, once the symbol of a meaningful future both for the living and the dead, was now not much more than a photo opportunity for drowsy tourists who themselves came from not too far away. On the outskirts of town they drove past an industrial park with unleased buildings and yawning lots, more than sufficient room for the anticipated, often announced, but once again mysteriously delayed, future industrial development.

The road cut away, feinting a new direction, only to take

advantage of a shortcut and again keep pace beside the relentless river. Between towns once broad tracts of granted land had been divided and re-divided by subsequent generations until each farm unfurled like a thin ribbon behind a single family residence.

"Would you mind if your daughter went out with a Native?"

Rachel didn't want to get dragged into this discussion. Nonetheless, she was curious why Elena asked. "I'd prefer if my daughter went out with one of her own. Maybe that's old fashioned of me, but I think it makes for a better marriage and a more stable family. Why do you ask?"

"How about if it isn't marriage? If it's just sleeping together?"

"Should I separate sleeping together from marriage?"

"I guess that's implied."

"Same answer. I would prefer if she slept with someone with whom she could share essential values."

"So you'd be upset?"

"Does that surprise you?"

"No. A lot of people think like that."

"The relationship wouldn't make sense to me. How can you really love someone you don't understand and who doesn't understand you?"

"You don't think she could share essential values with a Native?"

Rachel hid her irritation. "At the end of the day it's her choice, but I'd prefer if she did the right thing."

"Sometimes I wish I were Native."

"Really? Why?"

Elena, not feeling the need to answer, again let the music

fill the silence between them. She became absorbed in tracking the distinct layers of clouds racing at various speeds across the sky. Then, "Canada produces about a quarter of the world's uranium. Did you know that?"

"No, I didn't," Rachel answered, having given up on trying to follow Elena's line of thought.

"Yeah. It's surprising more people don't know."

The music ended, a new song began, and the singer's voice repeated over and over, mantra-like, a seemingly hopeful but strangely melancholic refrain — "remember the loveliness inside you."

"I don't want you to think that I've got anything against Natives," Rachel said, hoping to clarify. "I don't. I'd also be upset if my daughter wanted to marry a Christian or, God forbid, a Muslim. I'd think that something was wrong, that she was denying a part of herself."

"What do you mean, denying a part of herself?"

"Don't you know what I mean?"

"Couldn't she be finding a part of herself?"

"I know that not all Muslims are sexist, but they tend to be, don't they? Isn't it standard in their culture?"

"I only know Mahfouz and a few of his friends. He isn't sexist. Not to me, anyhow. Or not that I notice. Does it bother you that I go out with him?"

"No."

"You sure?"

"You're not my daughter."

The river receded, then re-approached.

"Josh once told me that he studied the Reformation," Elena said, again seemingly out of the blue.

"When did he tell you that?"

"I can't remember. I think he came in looking for you. A while ago."

"That's how I met him, in that class at McGill."

"What was he like then?"

"He had lots of hair."

They both laughed, and then laughed again, enjoying the release of it.

"He was very attractive back then. Not just his hair, his confidence. He was going to change the world."

"And did he?"

"He's done well for himself, but no, he hasn't changed the world."

"My father wanted to change the world, too."

"It comes with the testosterone. It makes them crazy like that."

More laughter, which bound them closer.

"Don't you ever want to change the world, Rachel?"

Enjoying the question, the older woman looked over at the younger, whose body continued to sway slightly within the loose embrace of the music. I used to be slim like that, she thought. "Perhaps once or twice I've thought about it, changing the world, but never seriously. It's not something I consciously try to do. I'm not like Josh that way. And I doubt if you're like your father that way."

"But we do change the world, all of us. I don't think we even have to try. I change the world, I know that."

"How do you change the world?"

"I had Sharon, that changed the world. I left my dad to go to school. I'm in the car with you listening to this music."

"Isn't there a difference between changing your world and changing the world?"

"Why? The exhaust from this car changes the temperature of the whole earth, your thoughts change mine and mine change yours and where does that end?"

"I don't know, Elena. That attitude's a bit flakey."

"Why flakey?"

"It's trivial."

"Why trivial?"

"Because it's always true. I mean, what are you saying— we change the world with every breath we take?"

"Why is something trivial if it's always true?"

"It doesn't really tell us anything. It lacks the power of distinction. But I understand the paradox."

What paradox, wondered Elena. But her thoughts, like the incessant flow of the river, the blur of the countryside, the layering of clouds, slipped by undefined.

"Who's taking care of Sharon now?" Rachel asked.

"She's staying with Mahfouz's mother for two days. He's still in Egypt so there's a free bed in his house. It's all working out. They were both pretty excited. Sharon hasn't slept over at anyone's place since we moved. I told her I'd call tonight to see how it was going. I gave them your cell number, too, in case of an emergency. I hope you don't mind."

"You don't have a cell?"

"Not yet, maybe next paycheque."

"Of course I don't mind. It makes sense. How's it going for him in Egypt, do you know?"

"He's hopeful."

"Have you told your dad about him?"

"About Mahfouz? No, not yet."

"Will he be upset when he finds out?"

"You mean 'cause he's Muslim?"

"No, I meant because he's a man. You have a man in your life."

"He wants that. He thinks that's the natural thing."

"Well, since you bring it up, will he mind that Mahfouz is a Muslim?"

"No. He might ask him a lot of questions, but other than that ..."

"Why haven't you told him, then?"

"I don't know."

"You should, don't you think?"

"I should do a lot of things."

"I wasn't admonishing you."

"I'll tell him soon."

"Does Mahfouz ever talk about Israel?"

"Not much."

"What does he say?"

"I don't know."

"What do you mean you don't know?"

"I mean I don't understand the history of it."

"Like what?"

"He says it should go back to its pre-1967 borders."

"Does he say that Israel shouldn't exist, that he thinks it was a mistake?"

"I've never heard him say that."

"But he thinks it?"

Elena replied to the question she thought Rachel wanted to ask. "He says that what's happening to the Palestinians is a crime."

"Is that what you think, too?"

"Yeah."

"Maybe you don't understand the whole story."

"I said I might not," replied Elena.

"That's true. You did say that. If the media weren't so biased you'd get better information."

"He said that what's happening in Gaza is collective punishment, and not all that different from Nazi crimes." Elena wondered how to extricate herself from a subject while simultaneously tumbling in at the deep end.

"People who say that are extremely ignorant."

"Well, he said it."

Rachel leaned forward and turned off the music, preferring silence as the setting for her words. "The best the Palestinians could do, should do, is to find some dignity as they concede defeat, but they can't even get that right. They just insist on bringing more violence upon themselves."

"That's not fair. I mean, the Israelis came and kicked them off their land. How can you describe that as Palestinians bringing violence upon themselves?"

"It's our land."

"Not from their point of view. They've been living there an awfully long time."

"I'm bored by that debate. The point is, who controls it? We do, so they lost. They have to deal with it."

"I guess they don't think it's over."

"That's just what I said, they refuse to admit they're defeated. And that's the problem, they go on fighting."

"They have something to fight for."

"But they're defeated, and until they deal with that, they are their own worst enemies."

"You don't think they have a right to resist?"

"They can resist if they want, but then they can't complain when they suffer the consequences. Do you understand? They have to recognize and admit that Israel is and will remain a Jewish State. If they don't like it they can go elsewhere. There's lots of room in the Arab countries."

"No one would dream of asking the Sioux or the Cree to officially recognize Canada as a white state where white people have more rights, and if they don't like it to go elsewhere."

"It's not the same."

"Don't you think your position only creates more hate: 'Please sign here to agree you have less rights than the people who have taken away your country'?"

"History proves it's better to be strong and hated than weak and hated. And the Muslims have always hated us, believe me."

"So that's the only choice, between being weak and hated or strong and hated?"

"What are you suggesting, universal love? Seriously? Look me in the eye and say, oh yes, I am suggesting universal love, brotherly understanding . . ."

"I don't have a solution."

"Right, you don't."

Elena tried to let it go, but couldn't. "What you're saying surprises me."

"Life's full of surprises."

"Aren't you being patriarchal?"

"I'm against patriarchy."

"I know, that's why I'm asking. War, hatred, no compromise, isn't that all patriarchal? Aren't those all part of the tough guy thing? You can't exactly call it maternal and nurturing."

"Just because I don't think males superior to women doesn't mean I don't support a strong military. Look at Margaret Thatcher, Golda Meir, even Hillary Clinton. I don't have a lot of time for people who assume women are pacifists with smoke in their heads instead of brains. Are you a pacifist?"

"Yes."

"You wouldn't be if you or Sharon were in real danger. History is a jungle, and it's every people for themselves."

"You believe that?"

"I don't *believe* it, I *know* it. And so do you. You just can't acknowledge it."

Elena was piqued. "I'd acknowledge it if I thought it."

"Maybe not. You've been trained to be a hypocrite. It's not your fault. That's what Christianity does. There's reality and then there's this layer of false sentiment which is what the Christians always talk about."

"I don't understand."

"Look, I don't live in a world where a defeated, crucified man is a god and everyone pretends to love their enemies and turn the other cheek."

"Anyhow," said Elena, "I'm not a Christian."

"Yes, you are."

"I have no choice?"

"You can pretend you do, if you like. But it's not so easy. It's how you were brought up, how you see reality. It's deep under the skin."

This provoked Elena. "Saying Christianity trains people to be hypocrites is like saying Judaism trains people to be racists. You know, chosen people, only one people loved by god, which is why you don't think twice about forcing another people off their land and treating them like sub-humans."

"That's what people really think, isn't it?"

"Why shouldn't they?"

"But it doesn't make sense. Jews can be of any race, so how can that be racist?"

"What word do you want to use then?"

"I don't want to use any. I want you to wake up and smell the coffee."

"But Israel is racist, or whatever word you want to use. A Jew born in Brooklyn has more rights in Israel than a Muslim born in Jerusalem."

"It has to be that way to remain Jewish. It's only realistic."

"That's the word you want to use? Not racism, realistic?"

"Listen, Elena, I support Israel because that's the most direct way to be loyal to who I am, to who my parents were, to who my grandchildren will be. I support it in every way possible and if I don't agree on a particular action or strategy the Israeli government takes, I'm quiet about it."

"So you refuse to condemn the crimes?"

"Maybe I regret them in my mind but I wouldn't say anything out loud. It's not for every foot soldier to condemn day in and day out what others who know more are doing. It's not for me, or Josh, as smart as he might be, to always question the decisions of others made in circumstances we know nothing about. It's disloyal."

"You put a lot of confidence in those at the top."

"What should I do, support my own people or go with the opinions of self-righteous gentiles? Forgive me, but why would any sane Jew trust the Christians?"

Elena doesn't reply.

"Right," said Rachel. "You can't explain why. Let's face it, if Israelis were really like the Germans there wouldn't be any Palestinians to talk about."

Elena remained silent.

"Our future won't depend on the charity of Christians. We won't let it. It has to depend on our own power. That's reality. If Christians don't want to understand that then they're just fooling themselves, which wouldn't be a first. Do we understand each other?"

"Not really. I don't understand the ethnic cleansing, or the insistence that people can't have equal rights, or the blockade of Gaza. You'd have to explain that to me."

"I don't have to explain anything to you," Rachel said, her hands tight on the steering wheel. "You want me to think this is all a debate where the best argument wins. It's not a debate, it's about our survival."

"How can you say that? You don't live there! No one's threatening you! You live in a big house in Westmount!"

"You see, you don't know what I mean! You can't understand!"

Only the sound of the wheels and the slight drone of the car.

Both sensed the conversation had been waiting to happen and that it remained unfinished. Neither knew when it would begin again or where it might lead. Neither felt a desire to reconcile, or at least, not yet.

"Do you want the music back on," asked Rachel eventually, respecting the fact that Elena had been refreshingly direct with her comments. You had to give her credit for that.

"No. The silence is okay."

Ten minutes later Rachel spoke again, her affection for Elena coming through. "Why do you want to be Native? I think that bizarre. Don't you like who you are?"

"Who am I?"

"You're supposed to know that, not me."

"What if I don't want to answer with the old words? I'm

White. I'm Christian. I'm English. What if I don't like those words?"

"You can't deny who you are. You'll only hurt yourself."

"They feel wrong. They feel like pretend words."

"What words do you like?"

"I don't know yet."

"I don't understand why you think you have a choice, Elena. Honestly, you're losing me on this."

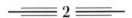

2

IRRITATED BY THE typical out-lying pattern of urban sprawl and big-box stores, Rachel decided to change plans and approach downtown Quebec City from the water. It was an indulgence, she knew, to follow the south shore for a few miles and then cross back on the ferry at Lévis, but they weren't in any hurry. If they had been she wouldn't have taken the north shore in the first place. It makes a difference, she thought, to approach a destination the right way.

They entered Ste. Foy and followed the signs for the Pierre Laporte Bridge. It was, she knew, named after the minister in the Quebec Government who had been kidnapped and killed by *Le Front de libération du Québec*. But she had been only a child when that had happened, and knew little about the time. Hadn't the FLQ claimed to be patterned on the Palestinian Liberation Organization? Why had they said that? What could they possibly have meant other than a preference for irrational violence?

Her thoughts jumped as two bridges loomed in front of her: one offering a slightly arched surface cradled by sloping, coordinated, steel cables; the other presenting a flat road bound in place by an intricate pattern of steel trusses riveted into repeating triangles.

Then they were high in the middle of the bridge, the mottled water far below them.

"I want to tell you something," Rachel said quietly. "I'm not living with Josh anymore. I have my own apartment. That's what I've been doing recently, finding an apartment, fixing it up, moving out. You might as well know."

"I'm sorry," Elena said, thinking that appropriate. Then, doubting herself, she quickly added: "I mean, I'm glad for you if that's what you want."

Rachel, caught by a wave of unexpected emotion, was momentarily too distraught to answer. Tears sprang to her eyes. Elena touched her forearm gently.

"It's okay. I'm fine. Thank you. It was hard. I'm surprised how hard. It's been hard for a while." She smiled wanly.

"How long have you been married?"

"Twenty-six years. But sometimes, perhaps, you just have to let go." Rachel paused, then explained: "I have to follow my instincts, listen to my heart. Self-respect, I suppose, when it comes down to it. On one hand I feel like, okay, I want this, but on the other hand I think, no, I can't do it. I don't want to believe that my past was all somehow misguided, that it ended in failure. I don't have the energy to sustain that."

"But you think it's the right decision, to move out?"

"Right now I do, at least for a while. He had an affair but won't talk about it. He says it didn't last long but I can't help feeling that it did, and that maybe he's looking for another. We have trouble discussing things we used to agree about and when we talk, we argue. It's not the right way to live."

They arrived at the ferry terminal and were waved forward onto the boat. They exited the car, relieved to climb the stairs to the open deck and enjoy the fresh air upon their faces. They moved as close to the bow as they could and gazed across the broad river to the city rising at the high end of a long, lifting cliff. To their right the river opened dramatically, wide enough to hold in its palm the gently rising *L'île d'Orléans*. To their left, beyond the petroleum storage tanks, the sky was layered in shifting gradients of salmon and ochre, the sun falling behind a shore of silhouetted trees.

"I never knew it was so beautiful," exclaimed Elena.

"Living in Montreal it's easy to forget that this is the capital. It's like Jerusalem and Tel Aviv, the capital goes with the history, not with the size. Odd isn't it, Israel and Quebec have about the same size population. One depends on nuclear weapons for its security and the other has no army at all."

"I'd never thought of it like that."

"I want my mother to live with us, but she prefers to live in Haifa. I go every year. Recently she's been telling me I need to buy a funeral plot there so that she won't be alone when she faces eternity. She's a bit of a character."

"Will you do that? Buy a plot there?"

"I don't want to. There's a small cemetery on the Outremont side of Mount Royal. I'd prefer that."

"When my mother was ill, she said she wanted to be cremated, but my father insisted he couldn't do it. I remember him saying: 'We burn trash, not bodies.' That kind of phrase sticks with you. Anyhow, she told him later it would be okay and he could do what he thought best. I was surprised she gave in, but she did."

"It meant a lot to your father and so your mother accommodated. It's what women do."

"He bought two plots side by side. The other is still waiting for him. I used to visit my mom there. It was pleasant enough."

They heard the thick plaits of the mooring ropes being thrown back onto the lower deck. Somewhere in the bowels beneath them the engines throbbed to momentary life. The ferry nudged forward. Out of the protection of the quay the vessel immediately slipped sideways, gripped by the encompassing current. The captain permitted the quickening drift and the heavy boat, now but a cork on a surface, was drawn farther into the river. Then, of a sudden, the engines re-engaged with a groan, the propellers churned in earnest, the hull shuddered, and the boat corrected itself, struggling for the opposite side.

"Can you see the wall that goes around the Old City?" asked Rachel, pointing. "The French built it to keep out the British. Of course, it didn't work." She again thought of Israel: "Walls don't work in the long run."

They discussed their schedule. The next day, in the morning, they'd meet with the fashion designer and his cutter to see the new work. In the afternoon they'd visit other boutiques, and late afternoon they'd return to Montreal via the south shore. But tonight was theirs. Rachel proposed they go for a walk. They could start in front of the fairy tale castle with the verdigris roof and go all the way along the cliff to the Plains of Abraham. Then they could make their way through the park to a street called *Grande Allée* that had any number of excellent restaurants along it. It'd be fun.

Elena described the new earrings she had brought with her, large and looped, like none she had ever worn. Rachel asked her to put them on. Elena shuffled around in her small bag until she found them and, laughing, managed to get them through the piercings.

Rachel told her they suited her.

Standing close, aware of each other's vulnerabilities, they spoke loudly into each other's ears, struggling in the wind against the quick decay of their voices.

Chapter Eight

=== 1 ===

Mahfouz considered his uncle to have mastered that most infuriating tactic: bewildered incomprehension when faced with straightforward but uncomfortable questions. Ibrahim, however, relaxed and philosophic, leaned back on his chair and enjoyed the broad view of the east harbour of Alexandria. He noted that his young nephew preferred statements, and considered that no question had as yet been asked.

Mahfouz began again: "Uncle, you don't say prayers, you don't go to the mosque, you talk about strengthening civil society."

Ibrahim smiled. What was there to say? Three true statements, all nicely linked.

"You're secular."

And now a fourth.

"Yet you support the Muslim Brotherhood, a religious party."

Ibrahim sighed, spread his hands on the small table in front of him. There it is, a fifth statement and still no question, although the "yet" seemed to indicate an area of dispute in the young man's mind. Ibrahim gave a half nod of his head to indicate that, while closely following the argument, he still awaited the question.

Mahfouz, having paused for an explanation not forthcoming, taunted him by adding: "Which is a banned party, illegal."

"It's not my fault it's banned," Ibrahim said eventually, interlacing his fingers.

Mahfouz was exasperated. "Isn't there a legal party you could support?"

Ah, finally! Ibrahim answered this first question with one of his own, trying to better gauge his nephew's intent. "Do you think any of the legal opposition parties would be allowed to win?"

"No. I understand that, but still, if there's another party that represents you better isn't that whom you should support? They may not win the election but at least your voice will be heard."

Ibrahim now understood: his nephew valued elections for the noise before them, not for the change of government after. But why be dismayed with the young man? Hadn't that become the general view?

"Listen," he explained, trying to find his way to the precise point, "the Brotherhood is banned because it is an effective and organized opposition, and I'm part of it because it is an effective and organized opposition." Mahfouz leaned forward to reply but Ibrahim cut him off. "I haven't finished. Whatever opposition party I support, if it proves to be effective, it too will be banned. Do you understand that?"

Mahfouz rocked back on his chair and gazed about, letting it be known that his intelligence had been insulted, before leaning forward to again pursue his argument. "You say you support the Brotherhood because it's an effective opposition, but it isn't legal, so how effective can it be? And it's not as if it hasn't been around forever, so why would one think it will be any more effective in the future than it has been in the past?'

"We're effective enough that the government feels compelled to round up and detain members. Thousands of us have been arrested. Eight hundred Brothers were recently imprisoned before the local elections, stopping the most prominent among us from being candidates. Eight hundred! That's how it works."

"Is counting members in prison how you determine political effectiveness?" asked Mahfouz, happy with his rhetorical sleight of hand.

"Why not? It's not meaningless."

"Uncle, believe me, a large number of people in prison is not a sign of effectiveness, it's a sign of ineffectiveness. The ten thousand Palestinians in the Israeli jails, is that a sign of their effectiveness? The twenty thousand Iraqis in the American jails, is that a sign of their effectiveness? Get real!"

Ibrahim was unsure how to counter that thought. The numbers surely indicated a popular resistance, but can you have a movement that is both popular and ineffective? Yes, he acknowledged to himself, yes you can. Perhaps Mahfouz was right on that point, but he didn't want to concede it. He said nothing.

Mahfouz filled the silence. "Besides, even if the Brotherhood does form a government, you won't get what you want because you're secular and they're religious. They want *Shari'a*. So how does supporting the Brotherhood make sense?"

"It's a bit ironic, isn't it," Ibrahim replied, beginning to warm up to the challenge his nephew offered, "that America insists that the world recognize Israel as a specifically Jewish state, and then supports our Egyptian dictator who declares that no political party can have religious affiliations. Why is that? Do you have any idea why that might be?"

"Don't ask me to explain the Americans and Israel. I'm not going there. We're not talking about that. It's not related to the issue we're discussing."

"You should think about it," replied his uncle testily, suspecting that his nephew had no intention of understanding. "Many of our supporters are secular. I don't know, a third at least would be a good estimate. Neither they nor I want religious fundamentalism. Egypt isn't about to become Saudi Arabia. We despise Saudi Arabia."

"Everyone despises Saudi Arabia. But that's not the topic either."

"The Americans don't despise Saudi Arabia! They love it! They support it! They support Islamic fundamentalism in Saudi Arabia, Jewish fundamentalism in Israel, and Christian fundamentalism in their own country. And that's the point, Mahfouz, that's the point! When the religion of Mohammed is backwards and repressive, as in Saudi Arabia, the Americans have no trouble with it, but when it organizes to feed and educate people, to liberate them, when it rediscovers its progressive roots, then all of a sudden we hear of the great principle of the division of state and church! Then, my god, it's illegal!"

Mahfouz was surprised by this assertion. "The people in America don't think Islam and progressive can be used in the same sentence."

"That's their ignorance."

"They see our religion as violent, stupid and backwards,

and that anyone who believes in it would naturally support violent, stupid and backwards leaders."

"I'm sorry for their lack of education," Ibrahim replied, enjoying himself. "They are victims of their own propaganda."

"Perhaps, but that's how they see it."

"They are blessed with great ignorance."

"Blessed?"

"Otherwise the shame would kill them."

Mahfouz was astonished. "Shame?"

"Look at Iraq, maybe a million dead, more than four million refugees. Quite the accomplishment."

"You know, that's not how the American people see it. They think they're the good guys, that no matter how many soldiers they send into Iraq to keep the peace the Muslims still find a way to kill each other."

"They invaded to keep the peace? Ah, that explains it! Now I understand! It's all clear! Nothing to do with oil, nothing to do with Israel. No, no, they invaded to keep the peace!" Ibrahim laughed with equal measures of scorn and amusement.

"That's what's said in the newspapers, that's what's reported on television. The soldiers remain there to keep Muslims from fighting each other while the country learns to appreciate freedom and democratic government."

"No one can actually think that! Why are you bothering me with such stupidity? Am I supposed to laugh or cry when you say such ridiculous things? They wanted Iraq weak and divided and supported all sides of a civil war to achieve it. Anything else is ..." — and here he surprised Mahfouz by using the English word, twirling his hand at the same time — "spin."

"Spin?" Mahfouz repeated in English.

"It's the right word, isn't it?"

Mahfouz wanted to challenge his uncle's righteous indignation, not admire his attempt at colloquial English. "Does it ever occur to you that the Americans are right? That we Muslims are only getting what we deserve?"

"What do you mean?"

"Think about it. Sunnis kill Shi'as, Shi'as kill Sunni, both kill Al-Qaeda who, we are told, kill everybody. But that's just the start. Shi'as kill Shi'as, too. The Lebanese kill Palestinians, and the Palestinians kill each other, Hamas against Fatah. The Syrians, of course, fight the Saudis, who fight the Persians. The Turks, how can I forget the Turks, they kill the Kurds, while the Kurds kill on all three sides, the Turks, the Arabs and the Persians ... and we are all supposedly Muslim. No wonder everybody thinks we're savages. And you know, as long as we fight each other, we are savages. Stupid savages. We will never unite. Never. And because of that, all anyone will ever feel for us is disdain. Repugnance. And our enemies will continue to laugh as they walk all over us."

"We're not the only ones who fight amongst ourselves," suggested Ibrahim lamely, "aren't both World Wars full of Christians killing each other?"

"And you, you supported Abd Al-Nasır, didn't you?" asked Mahfouz, probing in earnest for his uncle's self-doubt. "And yet now you say you support the very party that he banned. And why did he ban it? Because it was backwards, because it was violent. How does any of what you say make sense? How?"

Ibrahim was saddened to hear his nephew speak like that. Not only saddened, but burdened, and with a growing sense of defeat. How could he capture what the memory of Al-Nasir meant to them? How could he describe a leader born from among the people who had sufficient energy to fight both religious conservatism and western colonialism, and who did both with sufficient wit to unite Arabs, not divide them, and how rare and precious such a gift had been.

"You're right. I was a follower of Al-Nasir," he said, "even when there was no longer an Al-Nasir to follow. And yes, you're right again, I now support solidarity through Islam. But surely you understand that. Aren't you the one, having spent your life in Canada, having studied business, who prayed when arriving? You saw the city from the air and you prayed."

"I was moved, that's all. It was nothing but a moment."

"Yes, it was nothing but a moment, but a moment when you felt that you belonged. Look, Mahfouz, I don't want to be precious about this, but I, too, used to think solidarity came about through discussion and debate. It doesn't. Debate clarifies division. Solidarity based on self-interest twists like the wind and endures but a second. It's not solidarity at all: it's perpetual war. What we need arises from the compassion and dignity you felt when you saw the sun rise over the city of your birth. You touched the eternal and knew yourself to be a part of it. That's what brings us together."

Ibrahim paused, then braved what had bothered him for years. "Al-Nasir was wrong to outlaw the Brotherhood. It was a mistake. When he did that he outlawed the moral outrage of his own people. What was the effect of that? Did it save Sadat? Not for a second. It ensured his death. The path that Mubarak is following is a lost cause and frankly, even the men who rule beside him know it. They imprison us Brothers even when they agree with our positions. Do you think they believe that polishing the shoes of the Americans will save us? Do you think they believe that being the jailor of Gaza will keep us from harm? How can peace be maintained by starving one's brother for the sake of one's enemy? They would like to stop whoring, but they're paralyzed, hoping to die in leisure before the popular reaction breaks out."

The server reappeared and Ibrahim asked for another tea. Mahfouz ordered a second mango juice. Neither said anything as they watched several families with children weave through dense traffic.

"You were educated in the west," Ibrahim said. "For you movements based in faith are different than those based in social analysis. How would you put it: there is no bridge between idealism and materialism. I thought that once, but now I disagree. They're not opposed. It isn't an either/or. Religions themselves are a form of social analysis. I don't pretend to know how faith and economic thought work together exactly, but they do, and I know that both are necessary to achieve lasting change. Have you ever read Shari'ati? Or Soroush? No, you haven't, have you? You're not aware of the range of Islamic thinking on these problems. You were too busy learning double-entry accounting. Or perhaps you were doing case studies of franchise operations, figuring out how to run a profitable McDonalds or a Starbucks."

Mahfouz was deeply stung. He wanted to stand and terminate the conversation. Yet he knew his uncle was tending to wounds he, Mahfouz, had inflicted. He remained seated.

"I have their essays at home, if you think you're up to a bit of serious reading. I suggest you start with the Shari'ati." Ibrahim himself stood up as if to dismiss the conversation, but just as abruptly sat down again to face his nephew. "I'm not trying to avoid what you said. You're right that wherever you look Muslims fight Muslims. And you're right to ask who benefits. Certainly not us. There are insane Muslims who want us to fight amongst ourselves, I don't deny it, but only a few. The real question, Mahfouz, is this: how can those of us who want to remain sane see within the darkness? For that we need the illumination of our history, which includes our religion. It's not a question of being either modern or anti-modern, but of not being blind. You have no idea how sad your words make me. You tell me that for the people of America we are lesser beings, deserving of contempt. From the depth of my sadness I tell you this: good, let their ignorance be our strength." He looked about, as if to see who was in earshot of his unspeakable thoughts. "You want to be frank? What's a missile or a bomb if not a portable oven? What is the American military if not millions of portable ovens, all set to bake human flesh? Have you ever seen the photos of charred bodies after an attack from the drones or F-16s? That is what we Muslims face as we seek our independence from colonialism. Incineration. Ask all those whose family members have been cooked. Oh, it's unfortunate, everyone says when it happens, but then the next day it happens again: in Iraq, Palestine, Lebanon, Afghanistan, and now in Pakistan. Or for that matter, ask the people of Tehran if they feel good with the threat of being baked. I tell you, Mahfouz, the Israelis and the Americans will eventually bomb Iran, and they will eventually bomb Cairo too, but we, like the Persians, like the Palestinians, will emerge from beneath the radioactive sand having become the mutant cockroaches they fear, and we'll force the Europeans and Americans out and retake our places in our own land. Some things are foreordained."

"Foreordained?"

"You see how useful faith is. It strengthens one."

"Illusions. Fantasies. Nothing real!"

"Commitment!"

"And if they don't bomb Iran? How does your story end then? What if they're intelligent enough not to do that? What happens then?"

"We should give thanks if they don't bomb Iran. We should give thanks if they leave Iraq, if they recognize Palestinians as human, if they leave Afghanistan to the Afghanis, if they no longer protect and defend the worst of our dictators in Pakistan, Saudi Arabia and Egypt, if they stop supporting Israeli expansion. But Mahfouz, seriously, how likely is that?"

Mahfouz was confused, elated and despairing, all in equal measure. His uncle had openly expressed the pervasive anxiety he always felt, the injustice he everywhere saw. Ibrahim had confirmed the unequal powers, yet still expressed the conviction that the struggle could be won; if not in this generation, which was clearly impossible, then in the next; if not by the healthy, then by the sick. All this resonated within him, even as he regarded his uncle's promises of victory as so much nonsense.

He turned his face away from the older man, but Ibrahim even then wasn't finished. He wanted to reveal all of life's hard-earned truths. "Mahfouz, if you really want to understand history, note the differences between what you want to have happen and what actually occurs. The distance between the two is where history becomes apparent, not in a textbook, but in your own life. That is why you, the young, have no sense of it. You neither know what you want nor what has happened. History has to come later for you. And that is why some Westerners claim history is over, because they can't see any difference between what they want and what they have. They've convinced themselves that military superiority and moral depravity meet at the only horizon possible. They're fools, truly a faithless people, but their conditions will change and one day they will open their eyes to see history exploding everywhere at once, as it always has."

Mahfouz could take no more. "I want to walk around a bit, uncle. Do you mind? Who knows when I'll next be in Alexandria?"

"Of course, of course," Ibrahim muttered, suddenly sharing the desire to be apart. He felt despondent, wondering why he had wasted his breath on someone who just couldn't understand. "Let's meet back here in three hours, and then we'll find somewhere for dinner. Does that give you enough time?"

"Yes, that's plenty," replied Mahfouz, his shoulders tense, his mind wound tight.

Ibrahim sat without moving for a good twenty minutes, absorbed in the significance of his life's choices. If things had gone differently perhaps he could have had a child. How would that have changed his life? And when he died, as he surely would, what would be his legacy?

The surface of this reverie thinned and Ibrahim heard again the incessant clacking of metallic tongues along *le Corniche*. He decided to walk to Mohammed Ali Square and find a newspaper with the film listings. It would be a relief for the two of them to watch a movie together, to pay attention to some clever clowning on a big screen. There must be a film they would both like. Perhaps one of Chahine's? The master could always find a way to get everyone laughing in recognition of their shared predicament. Then it struck Ibrahim with a small shock that the great director was, at that very moment, lying in a coma after a brain haemorrhage, hanging between life and death. And this, Alexandria, was his beloved city.

Ibrahim stood and looked over the east harbour to where the façade of French architecture was challenged by the distinct minarets of the Busseiri and Abu Abbas Mosques. Further to the right a strangely isolated fifteenth century castle marked the place where the great lighthouse, the Pharos, once stood. One of the seven wonders of the ancient world, it had risen to a height five times that of the current structure, remaining vertical for almost one and a half thousand years before the settling earth caused it to crumble. He tried to imagine the flame, carefully tended, burning on the top in front of polished metal mirrors. What had that flame meant to the countless generations who had lived within sight of its nightly glare, or had crossed wide, dark, waters seeking it?

Chahine's recent film, his last, *Chaos*, was it still playing?

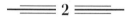

2

MAHFOUZ BOUGHT a cheap guidebook at a street kiosk, then crossed back over the busy street to get closer to the water. He sat on the low wall running the length of the bay. This street, too, officially bore the name of July 26th, although everyone called it something else.

Thumbing through the pages he found a short section on the history of Alexandria. He read that it was founded as a regional capital within an expanding Macedonian-Greek empire. Ambitious in scope, the empire held together only as long as the life of the man who founded it, which wasn't long, the immortal conqueror dying at the ripe old age of thirty-two in what is now known as Iraq.

The guidebook went on to add that some historians believed he was poisoned, others that he died of war wounds, and still others that he had died from medical treatments for non-fatal wounds. Mahfouz noted that there was no logical reason to assume his death wasn't the consequence of all three causes simultaneously. But imagine that, dying so young: what a strange age to live in. Even he'd do better than the great Alexander!

One of Alexander's wily generals, a Greek with the family name of Ptolemy — which means 'warlike' — grasped the tangible rewards of victory by claiming for himself the title of Pharaoh of Egypt, relieving the Persians of a role they had held since their invasion of 525 BCE. The new dynasty, the Ptolemaic, lasted three hundred years, ending with the suicide of Cleopatra, the first of her line to learn the language of the people she ruled. After her death the city fell under the control of an expanding Roman Empire. The conditions were then set for the city to become the turbulent interface of Egyptian, Greek, Roman and Hebrew society, the cultural mix from which early Christianity emerged.

Mahfouz closed the book. It bored him. He knew that Egypt had been at one time a Christian nation. There was no shame in that: the Prophet hadn't yet been born. But if he wanted to understand the city it would be better to wander and get lost. If he did so with an open mind, the ancient voices would make themselves heard in the soft breeze coming off the water. If he listened, the stones would speak.

But half an hour later, convinced that there was precious little evidence to show for all of Alexandria's long history, all he heard was the growing echo of his own loneliness. What did he care what had happened before or the influence it might have had? What did he care about Alexander, Cleopatra, Julius Caesar or Hypatia? They were all dead. Nor were their spirits in the air. They were dead dead, drained of anything fresh or significant. Even their monuments had disappeared. And he was alive — alive! — every cell in his body replicating and his future still unknown.

So he did what he had paced the streets wanting to do: he bought a long distance phone card and located a payphone as far as possible from the impatient traffic.

"I'm kissing you," he said to a surprised Elena at eight in the morning her time.

"I can feel it," she replied, the time of day being of no importance, only the timbre of his voice.

"You're cruel to say that," he said, happily complaining.

"You started it!" she exclaimed.

"Do you want to know where I'm kissing you?"

"No, I don't."

"I'm kissing you all over."

"All over." She paused. "Where all over?"

"What do you mean where all over? Everywhere all over."

"Tell me," she insisted.

"All the right places, behind your ear, on your nose ..."

"On my nose?"

"Hasn't your nose felt neglected since I left," he said, giggling.

"Perhaps a little. I miss you. I do."

"How much?"

"A lot. All I think of is you."

"Really?" He was in heaven.

"Do you miss me?"

"Not much."

"Not a little bit?"

"Perhaps a little bit." And then: "Why aren't you with me? Why aren't we together?"

"You'll be back soon."

"Not soon enough."

"Are you still kissing me?"

And so, with pauses to share the intimacy of hearing the other breathe, they used up the fifteen minute limit on the phone card. After an ignored warning they then shared the poignant anguish of the line going dead.

Mahfouz continued his walk, newly entranced with everything he saw. It was a beautiful city. Yes it was, an exquisite city, an extremely important city, for every sound within it renewed memories of a lithe and willing Elena.

Chapter Nine

═══ 1 ═══

Four men sat around a card table set in the middle of a small fragrance shop, anxious to begin. A small box of Somali desserts, thanks to Omar, lay open in front of them. Tea was poured by Mr. Abdul-Naeem.

Since Ibrahim insisted he had no direct stake in the financial deliberations, he assumed the role of independent and senior counsel, urging everyone to state their desires while remembering to be reasonable and fair. His attitude bothered Mr. Abdul-Naeem who wondered how the uncle of Mahfouz could seriously be considered neutral. And further, what could Ibrahim, secure on a government salary that had just been raised by decree, know of the commercial world? Easy for him to talk when the state ensured his well-being and put him in a position to take gifts — let's be kind and call them gifts — to provide the necessary extras. To him the state gave and gave, but from the small businessman the state only takes.

The three began tentatively, explaining their initial

positions. Principles were introduced and then assumed. According to tradition they didn't discuss interest on money. That didn't deter them from configuring different prices, schedules of repayment and a range of projected earnings. Eventually the discussion gave way to a comparison of numbers which, reconsidered from individual perspectives, appeared to misrepresent agreed upon principles.

The discussion began again. Intensified.

Mr. Abdul-Naeem shook his head and repeated his refrain that no, no, this was not enough for a life's work ... not for a life's work. He argued that, while it was true recent sales were down, the business was cyclical and sales would soon rebound. But when offered a larger percentage of future sales or more as a lump sum now, he continued to prefer cash up front. That amount, however, under the constant pressure of Mahfouz, got smaller as the afternoon got longer.

Omar, initially cautious to a fault, almost subservient, finally realized that he was the only one at the table with the pressing concerns of a family. He looked around and asked that his hands not be tied too tightly. What good was a business if all the revenue went to pay for the past? He must be able to care for his family. If he couldn't support his family now and in the future, then all this would necessarily fail.

Ibrahim felt relief that Omar was finally speaking up. Mahfouz nodded. Mr. Abdul-Naeem sighed.

Mahfouz played his position well, working within the constraints of the capital he carried on him and what he thought would be available, should he be able to convince his father. He refused to commit to any payment beyond three years.

They finally came to the grim realization that there was a proposal on the table equally unacceptable to all and thus, as Ibrahim emphatically pointed out, considered and fair. For the moment, anyhow, it was the best that could be achieved. Time to stretch one's legs, to reflect on the compromise offered, to drink more tea.

Standing, they began to discuss how their verbal agreement might be formalized. Ibrahim offered to write it up for their mutual approval. Mr. Abdul-Naeem insisted that his lawyer see it before he could sign. Mahfouz agreed that this was prudent, and added that his lawyer, too, in Montreal, would need to review the document.

Omar turned to Ibrahim and heatedly asked why they needed the advice of two lawyers, neither of whom had been in the room, one of whom lived in Canada, before they could sign any agreement. Ibrahim solved that problem by offering Omar a lawyer as well, telling him that there were many among the Brotherhood who would consult for free on his behalf. Heartened by this show of unexpected respect, Omar backed down, grateful. Three lawyers. Alright then. Good. Why not?

Ibrahim looked about, satisfied. He considered himself to have worked hardest of all, and assumed credit not only for organizing the meeting but also for the speed of negotiation. Just under two hours. True, money had yet to change hands and documents had yet to be signed, but the heavy work, the agreement in principle, was done. Everyone had gained something. This, he thought, was political work at its roots; strengthening the *umma* through co-operation and mutual assistance. The healthy tree bears good fruit.

Mahfouz was thoroughly relieved. Of course his father had told him not to go to the meeting, but what harm was there in returning with an unsigned agreement as the basis of a conversation? It was, all said and done, a very small investment. His uncle had been right, just the consulting of Mr. Abdul-Naeem on wholesale exports to Montreal might be worth the amounts discussed.

Besides, what wasn't possible now that Rachel had agreed to sell their samples through her store in Westmount? She had exactly the right clientele. And there were many such high-end boutiques in the city, especially along Laurier and Saint Denis. He and Elena could arrange distribution through a select few and, if that were successful, branch out into other cities. Perhaps, if he could keep the concept simple, they would even offer franchises.

He was confident of wearing down his father's resistance. When face-to-face there wouldn't be a question he couldn't answer. He was a man with a plan: marketing, distribution, production and financing. His father would see how all the pieces fit. He would be proud.

Mahfouz began to laugh easily among the older men, his presence energetic and charming. He let himself act the successful entrepreneur. He talked about returning to the business in Montreal without mentioning the apron, carving knife, broom and scrubbing brush that awaited him. He asked a steady stream of questions related to changing trends in the tourist trade. Mr. Abdul-Naeem, flattered by Mahfouz's intense interest and relieved that the process was finally coming to fruition, did his best to answer. He explained how Russian speakers and central Europeans were for a while the new growth market, but were so no longer; how tourists came from Japan but increasingly from China and yet, for reasons he couldn't fathom, the Orientals wouldn't set foot in his store. It was a challenge, he said, worth considering.

Omar enjoyed watching the confident Mahfouz. Events

were unfolding very well. He sauntered to the front of what he now considered his store, looked out the window and scanned the road. Nothing special to be seen. He returned to Mahfouz who was still talking to Mr. Abdul-Naeem and softly apologized for interrupting: would Mahfouz like to meet with his family again before he returned to Canada?

"Of course," Mahfouz answered, not wanting to insult his new partner. "Please. I have been thinking the same thing. It would be my pleasure to invite you and your family out for dinner. Would you accept?"

Omar smiled broadly.

Could it be, Mahfouz wondered, seeing the youthful optimism shining through Omar's habitual anxiety, that this tall, thoughtful, bending rake was not yet forty? Mahfouz suddenly wished he could speak frankly to him, discuss politics in Somalia and his family's time in a refugee camp, speak openly of his own life in Montreal and the importance of Elena and Sharon in it. He suddenly thought Omar's friendship possible.

Omar saw the flicker of genuine interest pass on Mahfouz's face. Yes, there it was, a genuine recognition, an acknowledgment, something to build upon in the coming years. God is merciful.

Mahfouz dutifully extended the dinner invitation to both Mr. Abdul-Naeem and his uncle, insisting that the evening be at his expense, as it was an opportunity to thank everyone for the successful visit. Could they agree on the evening after tomorrow, the very eve of his return to Canada?

The date accepted, the mood in the room grew increasingly fraternal. All future business arrangements were to be co-coordinated through Ibrahim, whom they thanked in advance. They discussed tentative dates for Mahfouz's return.

Omar leaned forward to take the last sweet out of the box.

It was at this moment that both front and back doors were forced open and a brusque authoritarian voice instructed them to lie on the floor with their arms behind their backs.

Ibrahim looked around at the half dozen men with machineguns and batons at the front door and an equal number at the back, all dressed smartly in black, and was immediately resigned to the fact that he was going to be detained. Imprisoning Brothers was a regular occurrence and had became ever more frequent as rising food prices led to greater unrest. He wanted to say something to comfort his nephew but no words came. He lay face down and put his arms behind him, wondering just how long this detention would last and what effect it would have on his teaching position.

Mr. Abdul-Naeem, his face flushed equally with anger and fear, also prostrated himself, his arms behind.

Mahfouz initially didn't understand what was happening and gazed about in childlike confusion before falling to his knees and then lying down, his arms, too, behind his back.

Omar was surprised that his three colleagues had lain so quickly. It didn't make sense to him. Why would they do that? To prostrate oneself and agree to being tied and taken away like a beast only ensured being tortured before being killed. If he was to die he should die quickly, against the enemy in front of him.

The short, confident, middle-aged man with the colouring of the upper Nile repeated the order for everyone to lie down. In his mind, from long experience in exactly this sort of operation, everything was going as usual. The four men in front of him were surprised, unarmed and obedient. The

African, understanding that he stood alone, must soon prostrate himself.

Omar, however, refused to be taken, not in the vain hope of victory, but rather with the rare clarity of those who, assuming death, don't fear it. He moved with deft speed towards the front door and reached below a surprised face to grab an exposed throat. The man he gripped felt the windpipe being pulled out of him and succumbed to the momentum of Omar's pull.

If those at the back dared shoot, they would kill their own.

Batons began to rain on Omar's body. He had, however, incapacitated one man, and was using him both as shield and battering ram. He intended to fight through all six on his way to the door.

A hard blow to Omar's head finally sent him staggering sideways.

There was a brief burst of machine gun fire from the back and Omar's body spun from the impact. Yet against all probability he remained standing, one useless arm hanging limp. In that sliver of silence, Omar raised his other hand in a gesture of committed defiance. He was, in that infinitesimally small slice of time, relieved and proud at who he had become.

The unbearable cacophony of two machine guns shattered any illusion of possible survival as his body jerked and twisted inconsolably.

When he finally settled, his head thrown back, his slender throat exposed, his long legs splayed at unusual angles, it was the pulped and exposed core of him which drew attention: thick blood bubbled and oozed through the splintered ribs.

Thirty-eight years old, lover of God and father of four, his major ambition to support his remaining children away from the fear, violence and hunger he had known so well, Omar was dead.

Ibrahim, Mahfouz and Mr. Abdul-Naeem were hand-cuffed and thoroughly kicked. Then two policemen went to either side and half lifted, half dragged each of them along the floor, through the spreading puddle of Omar's blood, out the back door and into the waiting transport vehicle.

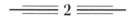

2

MAHFOUZ WANTED TO think of himself as a man who came to Cairo to discuss business, who had done nothing wrong, who was waiting to speak to the proper authorities. He assumed his best defence was poise accompanied by the calm certainty of his own innocence. He sat in the holding room trying to hold himself straight, trying to present an aura of importance and dignity, in spite of Omar's blood on his clothes, in spite of the trembling leg.

His front tooth had shattered in half when his mouth hit the floor of the transport vehicle and the pain of the exposed nerve was sharp. He tried to protect it from the air with his tongue. He was unsure if he could hear properly. One eye was swollen. However, he was alive. Omar, he knew, was not alive, and Mahfouz was traumatized by the repeating vision of his death, the unforgettable and deafening sound of the live fire.

Someone entered, helped him shuffle to a bathroom where he was allowed to wash, to urinate. There was no mirror in which to look at his swollen face. He was given prison clothes to wear. He kept his shoes, but without laces. He was helped into another room where his fingers were printed, his pictures taken, and then to still another where preliminary questions were asked. He attempted to answer fully, in spite of his painful mouth. Those who listened found him incoherent, a profound fear shining uncontested from his one good eye.

Returned to his holding room, he again tried to sit straight, as if at a job interview. He wondered why he was kept separate from both Ibrahim and Mr. Abdul-Naeem. Others were brought into the room, but he held himself distant. His leg continued to tremble. He stood and started to shuffle back and forth, his leg feeling more firm when bearing weight. Eventually exhausted, he went to sit but his leg gave way and he fell. He twisted to look up at the caged fluorescent lights as they flickered and stuttered in their wire cages. Was that a voice yelling in the room beside him, or someone talking to him in this room? He wasn't sure. He sat up only to remove his unlaced shoes. He lowered himself back down on the floor, his arm on his shoes, his head on his arm.

He awakened to a flood of anxiety. How long had it been? Fifteen minutes? An hour? He lay there stiff and unmoving. Why had Omar fought? If he hadn't fought, if he hadn't been unreasonable, then the misunderstandings might have been rectified, the situation cleared up. They would all have been released by now, comfortable in their own beds. Life would have gone on. The problem wasn't that he had been arrested: innocent people do get arrested, and mistakes are made, even if no one seems to know why.

The problem was the moment of violence which forever changed the present. It gave direction to time, for it couldn't be undone. That violence was Omar's fault and it had changed everything. Everything that had happened and was happening was Omar's fault. Fuck Omar. Fuck him.

═══ 3 ═══

EARLY IN THE morning of the next day Fadumah and her mother went to the store in the hope of gathering news about Omar, who hadn't returned. As they approached they saw the police tape over the locked door and the brown paper covering the inside of the shattered front windows. However, the job had been done hurriedly and it was possible, if one bent and shaded the glass from the sun, to see the store's interior through an area at the bottom. The broken fragrance bottles had not been swept, nor the bloody floor mopped. There were bullet holes in the walls, casings on the ground.

Fadumah sought out the eyes of her mother. They were knowing and sad: either dead or imprisoned, and if imprisoned then hurt, for he would not have gone without a fight. So many years of tenacity, cooperation and sacrifice for a shared future yet to come and here, now, peering into the window of a small shop on a small side street, the future was visible.

Not a word passed between them. They assumed that they, too, were sought. They knew women were regularly swept up and abused so that husbands, brothers and fathers would speak. Neither pause nor fear, said the voice in Fadumah's head, trust only those you must. She and her mother turned as one. They neither wailed nor lingered. They did not ask the neighbouring tailor what had happened. They walked away with quick steps, knowing that somewhere someone rejoiced over their tragedy.

Omar's enemies had tried to kill him in Somalia, but hadn't succeeded. They had lost track of him while he lived in the refugee camp under an assumed name, but had found him in Egypt. To his wife and family, if he were dead, he had died a martyr. That the security forces might have come only to pick up Ibrahim never occurred to them.

In the distance sirens wailed as emergency vehicles moved sluggishly through the thickness of the Cairene traffic. Fadumah and her mother assumed, wherever the vehicles may have been headed, that they were bringing reinforcements for the armed, not care for the fallen.

Chapter Ten

Sharon lay in her small bedroom with the lights on. She studied five visible drawings, four of which were held in place by green painter's tape at the corners. She had put up the two beside the dresser without her mother's help. While the bottom one seemed straight enough, the top one slanted. She'd have been upset, however, if anyone had straightened it. When she looked about everything in the room slanted, even the walls, so the picture fit.

The lower drawing was of the mosque that wasn't a mosque which she drew while looking at the poster in the kitchen of Mahfouz's restaurant. The one above was the family portrait with the grandmother whom she had never met in her wheelchair. Although her mother regularly threatened to send both drawings to her grandfather, Sharon doubted they would ever make the voyage. Which was okay. They were fine where they were.

She looked at the third drawing, her favourite of all time, and the only one she had brought with her from Brandon.

It hung in a place of privilege directly over the dresser. Her mother had put it there when they first moved to Montreal. She had used tape carefully folded upon itself on the back, so the picture appeared to float on the wall with no support whatever. Sharon liked that. She liked that a lot.

The image was of several carefully labelled friends holding hands in front of a large square building, which was her old school. She still remembered the friends. She still had dreams of them being with her in that building.

The other two drawings, done only yesterday, were taped on the back of the now almost closed bedroom door. Her mother had taped them so they were pretty straight, maybe a bit disturbingly straight. They were both images of the same dead cat with maggots living in it.

She and Leila, whom she had met at the park near Mahfouz's parents' place, had discovered the cat lying beneath bushes that grew between the fence and the sidewalk. When they had approached and sat on their haunches to investigate, peering through the ironwork, they had seen that it was a grey cat, medium sized, very stiff and quite flattened. In the middle of a large wound in its side was a seething ball of white bugs crawling all over each other.

The cat's eyes were closed and yet, from the tilt of its neck, it appeared to the girls that it was not happy with the situation, that it was distinctly uncomfortable. Sharon had, in fact, posed the question out loud. "Are you uncomfortable?" But of course the cat, being quite dead, and perhaps dead for quite a while, had not answered.

Sharon found a stick about two feet long and then Leila had done likewise, and they had both poked at the porridge-like mass squirming in the nest-like cavity on the side of the dismal animal. Several of the bugs attached themselves to the tip of their sticks. When Leila pointed out what they were doing, clinging there, and even beginning to crawl with outrageous audacity towards the end held in their hands, both she and Sharon withdrew their sticks and beat them on the ground, forcing the white squiggly things to fall off.

Both girls had stood fascinated as the maggots squirmed in unusual isolation on the dark ground. Neither liked the bugs. Both felt sorry for the cat. Leila suggested going home to get a box so that they could bury it, but after an initial enthusiasm they both let the idea drop. Something about the situation seemed too far along to tempt intervention. Also, to bury the cat meant to bury the bugs with it, which didn't seem quite right, an indignity to the cat. Not that nice for the bugs either, considering they weren't dead.

If you buried bugs like that, Leila asked, would they die? Sharon had thought it a good question. She shared the impression that they would just feast below and then crawl up to the surface and continue their lives, fat and jolly.

The two girls decided that the dead cat wasn't necessarily in the wrong place, hidden like that beneath branches at the edge of a park. Almost buried. Close enough.

So they had retreated, found a place to leave their poking sticks beneath a different bush, and then climbed onto the swings to think new thoughts. But the stillness of the unmoving cat, along with the thriving, very busy community of maggots, bothered Sharon, so she said goodbye to her new friend and returned to Mahfouz's parents earlier than expected.

Later that night, in the security of her home, she had drawn the pictures from memory. In the first attempt none of the lines seemed still. The whole picture had a quality of quick, spontaneous movement. In the second, the lines for the cat were heavier and more defined, and yet the bugs still squirmed and danced. It was the contrast that Sharon had liked. It pleased her then, and pleased her now.

In both pictures, for a reason she never thought to question, she had drawn the grey cat in green, and the white bugs were drawn in red, like the people in the other drawing on the wall. And because she had used green for the cat, she had chosen blue for the branches of the bush above. But now that the top of the picture was blue, it could be mistaken for a sky floating above the fixed lines of a large green mountain, on the side of which was a grove of thin red boughs, dogwood perhaps, bending in the wind.

Her mother had called the drawings two beautiful landscapes and immediately hung them up. Sharon had tried to correct her, saying that they were both of a dead cat with white bugs on it that she had discovered while playing with Leila, but her mother had been irritated by the suggestion.

Sharon, having closely considered the pictures on her wall and the slant of her world, eventually fell asleep with her light on, while her mother continued to sit unmoving and awake in a chair in the darkened living room.

Why had Mahfouz missed his flight home? Why had he not immediately called? What could it possibly mean? And what could she possibly do?

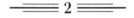 2

THANK GOD HIS father was out there somewhere, working on his behalf.

He could doubt a million things, but not that. His father

would find a way forward. He'd understand that something has gone wrong and would contact the Canadian Embassy and they'd get involved. There would be phone calls. Someone would take responsibility and eventually rectify the mistake that had been made, perhaps not quickly, but necessarily.

His father knew that big wheels turned slowly. His father had perseverance. Patience and perseverance were an effective combination. So he, too, must be patient, and trust his father's perseverance. This would work out somehow. Perhaps, at some point, he would even receive an apology, both for lost time and the trauma of wrongful imprisonment, although that was more than what he wanted. All he wanted was to get on an airplane and never come back.

Why didn't that stupid man lie down as he was told?

Mahfouz had never heard machinegun fire before, never smelt it, never seen the results. It was not what one imagined. He had asked one of his jailors how many bullets a machinegun shoots per second. The man asked if it was an American M-16 or the Russian AK-47. Mahfouz said he didn't know. The guard, clearly surprised that Mahfouz couldn't tell them apart, told him it was between twelve to fifteen bullets a second.

How many seconds did the firing last? Five seconds in all would be a fair guess, even though it seemed an eternity at the time. But there were two guns. So somewhere between a hundred to a hundred and fifty bullets hit Omar in about a twelfth of a minute, churning his torso into melted butter. Put the futility of resistance into perspective, figures like that.

During the week Mahfouz answered the same questions posed by a number of different people: about the purpose of his visit, about Omar, about his uncle, his father, the money he carried. They asked about the article on American drones they had found carefully folded in a shirt pocket discovered when they searched Ibrahim's house. Then they asked why he had a plastic container of sand in his suitcase. He explained he took it from a beach in Alexandria, as a gift for his friend's daughter. They looked at him dubiously, told him it would be analyzed.

At the beginning they seemed interested in his replies, writing down the exact words he used. Now they just repeated the same questions to check how one response differed from another. When he repeated himself they asked if he had memorized the response. If he said something new they asked if he was trying to change his story. He told them the truth as best he could — scrupulously, repeatedly — but they'd lost interest. They acted as if they'd begun to wait. But for what?

His broken front tooth remained a problem. He tried to protect it with his tongue when he ate or drank. But when he asked to see a dentist they looked through him, as they did when he asked why he was being held. He became angry. He found his imprisonment unnecessary and humiliating. It might be naïve to believe westerners should be treated differently, but surely they realized that a law-abiding Canadian wasn't used to this.

But even when angry he tried to show dignity, to remain calm, to be patient and polite.

Elena had promised to meet the return flight. Probably Sharon had gone with her. Had Josh driven them to the airport? He was a lawyer, he could help. Josh and his father working together would be good. Had they met? Would Elena think to get them together? Yes, she would. She was smart.

Mahfouz had always worked for an hourly wage, ever since he could remember. The focus of any day, every day, was the work to be done and the time it took to do it. It was how he had defined living in the real world. But now, imprisoned, he realized that reality was mediated by the mind, for him as for everyone. When things were going well he had had the privilege of forgetting his thoughts, but how could he avoid the burden of them now? But, if condemned to awareness, why not simply cling to thoughts which are pleasant? It should be easy enough.

Mahfouz wanted to relive the moment when he and Elena first touched; her hand reaching for the light before retreating to his arm, then moving to his chest. But it was impossible to keep the sequence of spontaneous impressions within the frame he had set for it. It took more than remembering to remember, it took composition. So he found himself composing memories within a loosening embrace of the past, somehow always losing what he had thought to hold most firmly.

The first modern Western invasion of a Muslim country was Napoleon's invasion of Egypt. Odd to consider the consequences of that distant event. His parents were born within the receding waters of the French colonial tide, so when looking for a place to emigrate had chosen Montreal, where they thought they would best fit. If no Napoleon, then no Mahfouz in Montreal. But how much could he remember about the defeat of the French in Egypt? Were they defeated or just replaced by the British? Wasn't it something like a changing of the guard? Hadn't the French and the English actually shared sovereignty over Egypt, managing the treasury and ensuring debt payments? When and how had the Americans taken over?

The French were certainly defeated in Algeria. Bloody, so bloody.

He had read a little Fanon. A bit hysterical. No, not so much hysterical as stubborn. Like Omar. Is that true? Maybe Fanon and Omar were neither hysterical nor stubborn, but knew something he didn't. Could Omar actually have known what he was doing and why?

But how could one knowingly engage in such futile resistance? And what, now, would happen to his family: to his wife, to Fadumah and the boys? Had Omar considered that? Did he, Mahfouz, have a responsibility to them? Assuming he would eventually be released from this solitary cell, could he sponsor them to Canada? What would it take to arrange? If he married her would it follow automatically that he could bring her mother and brothers to Montreal?

He was trying to think only of Elena, of that moment in the bedroom when she let her desire be known, but had caught himself wondering about Fadumah, about his responsibility to her and her brothers. How did that happen? For that matter, what did he actually remember of her brothers? What did he even remember of Fadumah, beside her quiet presence and the headscarf pulled low over her forehead?

The British Empire was defeated. Eventually. They say it was defeated by the cumulative effects of the first and second world wars. But not only, it was constantly challenged by liberation movements everywhere around the globe who fought irrational borders imposed by English masters. And who would defeat its progeny, the American Empire with its eight hundred military bases on foreign soil?

It wasn't only America that had to be defeated, but the unified European colonial interests which continued to support it, all clinging to privilege. How many deaths to do it?

How many centuries of struggle from how many places around the globe? With what arms, what tools?

Ten to fifteen bullets a second.

One second.

Two seconds.

Three seconds.

Four.

3

"YOU'RE ONE OF my oldest friends, Josh, but still, you know I'm not in a position to talk about anything too specific."

"I understand that, Dan. I'm not looking for anything too specific, just to get a general sense of what I should do."

"I see this as one of our usual lunches, a bit of time to discuss the world, ask after the family, as we've done so many times before."

"Right, so how is the family?"

"Nothing much new. Busy enjoying summer."

"Isabelle?"

"She's at the family cottage on Lac Memphremagog."

"That's a beautiful place you have down there."

"Yes, it is. She loves it."

"So you're living alone for a bit?"

"I go down on the weekends. Actually, I leave Thursday at noon, come back for Tuesday mornings. The work weeks are short."

"Ahh, lucky you!"

"You?"

"There are so many things on my plate right now."

"Can't get free?"

"Haven't done, anyhow."

"You like it that way. You're a workaholic."

"Not anymore, or at least not a willing one." Josh thought it time to shift subjects. "So, I don't know how clear I was on the phone, but there's a young Montrealer who wasn't on his return flight from Cairo. I'd like to help his family find out what happened to him."

"How did you meet this young man's family?"

"I was introduced to them through his girlfriend, who works at Rachel's store. When he didn't come back she talked to me and then asked, seeing as I'm a lawyer, if I'd meet with his family, which I did."

"She's a good friend of yours?"

"She's more a friend of Rachel's. She's a single mother, bright, hardworking. His parents have called the Canadian embassy in Cairo and the Egyptian consulate in Ottawa, but they didn't get anything other than instructions how to fill out the forms for a missing person."

"You aren't their legal advisor, are you?"

"No, no. Nothing like that."

"I mean, you're an entertainment lawyer."

"I'm just a concerned friend, trying to help if I can."

"Good. Well, obviously, they should get an experienced lawyer on their side."

"If you have a specific person you'd like to recommend, I'd appreciate it."

"I don't really want to recommend anyone, but if you get a name run it by me and I'll let you know what I think. There are a few good ones, and more than a few not so good ones." Daniel picked up the short menu.

"I know this is difficult, Daniel, a difficult question, but are you aware of the case I'm referring to?"

"Even if I were I couldn't talk about it." He considered his choices.

"Let me put it another way, are you aware of any case *like* the one I'm referring to."

Daniel put the menu down. "To state the obvious, Josh, it's not news to tell you that the federal government is very concerned about the financing of international terrorism."

"Is it possible that people from Montreal are involved in that, financing international terrorism?"

"Why not? This is a perfect location. We're close to a very porous American border and we have a large Arab population who are coddled by the laziness of the Canadian legal institutions. Well, that might be a bit harsh, but it's how the Americans see us, and some within our own office as well. The Minister, for one."

"So, our government would be sensitive to any evidence of such activities?"

"Yes, that's right. That's exactly right. Our government would be very sensitive." He picked up the menu again, but his look was elsewhere, scanning the room for colleagues.

"And such sensitivities are usual?" Josh asked.

"Yes."

"I received a call this morning from the mother of this young man telling me that her husband had been picked up on what I think must be a security certificate."

Dan didn't seem surprised. "When things move, they move quickly."

"A certificate is what you use when there's no actual evidence of a crime, is that right?"

"All that it does is to establish a reasonable and limited period to hold somebody, giving authorities an opportunity to investigate their concerns."

"Are these certificates issued on evidence of past wrong doing, or just on current hearsay?"

"You don't have to have any evidence of past wrong doing, but you can't just pick up anyone either. You have to make a case. I guess it's possible that the evidence will be circumstantial and rely on hearsay, but obviously one tries to avoid that."

"Isn't that contrary to the presumption of innocence?"

"Yes, but that's acceptable when we discuss terrorism. There's a need, in such cases, to be pre-emptive."

"What kind of thing would one be looking for?"

"Well, imagine someone couriering cash to a foreign country and then giving it to a person who is a member of an illegal party, that would ring a few bells."

"I suppose it might."

"Then imagine, as a second step, that same money being used to buy into a legitimate business to generate revenue for a group of radical insurgents in a third country."

"That's pretty sophisticated stuff."

"It's the kind of international planning we're up against. It takes time and resources to crack schemes like that. It's a challenge."

"How much cash might someone be couriering, to use that term?"

"I was being hypothetical."

"Would five thousand dollars be about right?"

"Why do you use that number?"

"Just trying to get an idea of the possible scales of operations."

"Five thousand dollars goes a long way in a society where the average annual wage is less than half that."

"You mean in Egypt?"

"Yes, in Egypt."

"And who was the member of the outlawed organization? Mahfouz's uncle?"

"Don't play with me, Josh. I don't like it. How much do you know?"

"I know the uncle belongs to the Muslim Brotherhood. Hardly a terrorist organization, Dan, just a banned political party that fights for the democratic rights we're supposed to defend. And I know the money was for the down payment on a fragrance shop to be run by a Somali refugee family who had fled the violence back home."

"Perhaps the authorities should be asking you questions."

"Look, his father told me. He's anxious to tell people what he knows. He thinks the truth is going to bring his son back. He'd tell anybody. He'd scream it from the rooftops if he thought anybody would listen. You didn't have to jail him on a certificate to get him to speak."

"The father was picked up as an issue of public safety. It's our main responsibility."

"You think the father may be dangerous?"

"There's no reason to take his story at face value."

"Why not? If there's no record of past criminal activity, why not take his story at face value? His wife called me this morning completely at a loss, in tears. Her son has disappeared. Her husband himself called the Canadian authorities insisting they get involved. I don't think it ever occurred to him that the government would turn around and jail him without charge."

"Patience is needed in these complicated cases. He has nothing to fear if he's done nothing wrong."

"What do you mean nothing to fear, Dan? They had to close the restaurant since neither the father nor the son are available to run it, and if it's closed long they'll go bankrupt. That's something to fear, no?"

"Don't jump on me! You have to admit that the financial health of a small restaurant can't be the government's primary concern when faced with organized terrorism."

"The father assumes that his son and brother are being held by Egyptian authorities."

"That might be true."

"Has Mahfouz seen a representative of Canada?"

Daniel paused before choosing his words very carefully, "You know, if I were free to have it, that would make for a very interesting discussion."

"We've known each other for what, almost thirty years."

"Yes. Since constitutional law."

"Well?"

"Can't you imagine a case where our Embassy couldn't get involved? For instance, suppose the Egyptians were asked if they were holding a Canadian and they emphatically denied it?"

"Could that happen?"

"Why not?"

"But the Canadian government would press, wouldn't it, if it suspected it wasn't being told the truth?"

"Well, let's say, for argument's sake, that the Americans suspect there's a sleeper cell of terrorists in Montreal. They would want any known member of it to be immediately questioned in ways that might be too vigorous for Canadian sensibilities. The Egyptians wouldn't have that reluctance."

"That's what happened in the Arar case."

"Except it was Syria, not Egypt. But El Maati was actually sent from Syria to Egypt for vigorous questioning. Do you know about his case? It's on public record."

"No."

"A truck driver from Toronto. He was held for more than two years."

"Should you really call it vigorous questioning? Isn't it torture?"

Daniel ignored the comment and the distinction. "If you analyze those cases from the prosecution side, the mistake is not that they were vigorously questioned, but rather that it was so easy to prove the Canadian government not only knew a citizen was being illegally held, but had supplied information to assist in the questioning. The government was complicit in the treatment administered by others, and that's what both the O'Connor and Iacobucci inquiries concluded."

"Were the Canadians complicit in that torture held responsible? Was anyone fired or demoted?"

"No, but we're not talking about that, Josh. The point is that the government was found complicit. It wouldn't want to make the same mistake again, would it? But in the hypothetical case we're discussing, when the Canadian government asks the Egyptians if they're holding someone they deny it. So, clearly, there's no reason to intervene."

"But there must be a file somewhere. Someone's read it. Someone picked up the father."

"On evidence passed along from the Egyptian government which came from an unnamed Egyptian national."

Josh mulls this over. "So Mahfouz has been erased?"

"Momentarily misplaced might be a better way of putting it. He could be on a jihad fighting our boys in Afghanistan for all the Canadian government knows."

"But you know the Egyptian government is lying."

"Do we?"

Silent pause.

"Is there no shame?"

"I know you interpret your friend's actions with an understandable naïveté, but we're professionals paid not to make that mistake."

"What mistake, the presumption of innocence?"

"It's clear, pretty clear, your guy is part of a bigger unit."

"A bigger unit ... you mean family?"

"The owner of the store in Cairo, the guy who receives the money, he isn't family. The Somali who is supposed to run the store, he sure as hell isn't family."

"You're right, it's bigger than a family. How about a culture, and in that culture, as in ours, people seek ways to organize improvement within their lives by co-operating."

Daniel responded gently: "Wake up, Josh, smell the coffee. You don't really believe any of that nonsense about buying the store to sell fragrances in Canada, do you?"

Josh felt slapped across the face. It took him a moment to gather his wits. "But why your interpretation rather than the father's? The father wasn't lying when he spoke to me. He was pouring out his heart. There were no equivocations, no attempts to conceal. He was begging me to help him on the basis of all the facts he knew. He wasn't, as you are now, playing the angles, assuming unlikely odds."

"You're living in a humanist past, Josh. I know it's more comfortable back there, but you clearly haven't been keeping abreast of the law and how it's executed, not only in Canada, but in all the English speaking countries: the States, England, Australia."

"No more *habeas corpus*?"

"People don't want to be blown up on the subway."

"That's the choice?"

"Ask the people in London, the people of Madrid."

"Are you linking Mahfouz to that?"

"Can we afford to assume he isn't?"

Josh grabbed at the facts he knew. "I know his girlfriend. She's a single mom. Christian! What kind of Muslim terrorist has a Christian girlfriend? What kind of Muslim terrorist takes care of a Christian girlfriend's child?"

"A smart one. And besides, many Palestinian terrorists have been Christian. Think of George Habash. He was Greek Orthodox. For that matter, Yasser Arafat's wife was Christian."

"I'm not okay with an innocent young man being tortured on suspicion."

"The evidence is compelling."

"How can the evidence be compelling if no crime has been committed?"

"You're simply wrong on this, Josh. Conspiracy to fund or organize future crime is a crime. It's on the books. It's legal reality. People want the crime prosecuted. Your friend is involved in precisely that, a conspiracy to provide funds to international terrorists. Look, our ethical responsibility is to eradicate terrorism, not to coddle terrorists."

"But you don't know he's a terrorist!"

"That's right, and someone has to put into place a process to determine if he really is or isn't. So who are you to object to that process? Can you imagine the incredible outcry if we did nothing and innocent people were blown up? Can you imagine the pressure we're under to make sure this community is safe? You don't come at this from the assumption that a danger exists. We do. This isn't the entertainment industry with its fictional plots and clear distinctions between bad and good."

"No?"

"Have you ever met him?" asked Dan.

The question hovered briefly.

"I know his girlfriend. I've met his parents."

"Have you ever met him?"

"No."

"Look at you! Look at what you're doing! You're defending from a position of complete ignorance a guy, a family actually, who represent the very worst in our society, who promote violence and hate. They're indoctrinated by violent and hateful religious leaders who take advantage of our liberties and institutions. These people are not our friends: they're our enemies. Surely you understand that! This is all done to protect people like you. You especially!"

"Why me especially?"

"Never mind."

"No, why me especially? Is there something about me that makes you say that? Because I'm Jewish?"

"It's relevant, isn't it?"

"Look, Daniel, I'll ignore that, for your own sake."

"We're trying to protect you."

"Mahfouz is not my enemy."

"You don't know that."

"The least you can do is get him returned here to be questioned without being tortured."

"I don't have that kind of power, Josh. This is far above me. Maybe this kid is innocent and then, frankly, it's a shame. Okay, I'll say that, a shame. But in the big picture, he's just a tiny blip on a very wide screen. He's interesting for the connections he seems to have and the Egyptians will do a very good job of flushing that out."

"Do you know what you're saying?"

"If he is who they think he is, then he deserves everything they throw at him, and if that's the case and they break him ... well, he deserves to be broken."

"And if he breaks even though innocent, if he confesses even though he's done nothing wrong, what then? Isn't that what usually happens? Isn't that, in fact, what is meant to happen?"

"My conscience is clear."

"Is it?"

"Absolutely. Can you·say the same? Are you one hundred percent certain that he's innocent? A hundred percent?"

Josh hesitated.

"There, you see, you don't know. Then let happen what has to happen. I realize backing off isn't your way, Josh, but it would be wise. This case is not small potatoes. The man who was to run the fragrance store was a known fighter for the Union of Islamic Courts in Somalia. The police are currently sweeping the refugee communities both in Cairo and Montreal looking for any other contacts between the Somali Islamists and your friend."

"I didn't know that."

"The father didn't tell you everything, did he?"

"He told me everything he knew."

"Don't be naïve, Josh."

Josh had nothing more to say.

"I've been open with you," Dan said. "Please don't use it against me."

"I wouldn't do that."

"In my mind I've been discussing hypotheticals."

"I understand."

"You know, we haven't ordered any food yet. Don't you think we should order something before they throw us out?" Daniel nodded at the waiter who hurried over. He ordered the smoked meat plate, lean, with extra coleslaw, and Josh asked for a short espresso and some pickles.

"You're not hungry?"

"Not very."

"Are you paying any attention to the Olympics?"

"No. I just can't get into it."

"You following the war in Georgia?"

"No, not really."

"That's unlike you. You usually follow Eastern Europe pretty closely."

"I try to, but I don't know where to turn to get real information. I feel like I'm always being manipulated."

"I trust the Wall Street Journal."

"Why them?"

"I like their approach. Hard nosed. I like that."

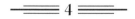

4

THE LIGHT FADED as Josh recounted his meeting with Dan. He said he believed Mahfouz was being held in Cairo for questioning. She asked if that meant being tortured and he replied that he didn't know for sure but that it might. He added that, while Mahfouz might be suffering, he was alive.

When they finished speaking it was dark everywhere save the bright rectangle at the front of the store cast by the streetlamp and shaped by the window. The light framed the headless mannequin on the low table, now wearing an expensive shirt made of taffeta and torn denim, also by the Quebec City designer.

They sat in complete silence, each lost in personal

thoughts. Then Elena initiated the conversation as if to hear everything all over again — as if needing it slowly repeated — all of Josh's questions both asked and implied; each of Dan's answers, cryptic but laden. Then she slowly stood, more as an old woman might, moved to the window and looked out. She spoke to him through waves of nausea. "You have to speak to Ghadir as soon as possible."

"That's his mother?"

"Yes."

"Maybe we could meet after breakfast tomorrow."

"Okay."

When, a few days before, he had arranged to meet with Dan, he thought he'd be picking up a few insights on the process of embassy assistance. But now he was to face a mother to tell her news no parent should hear. He felt heavy. No, not heavy, numb.

"What else should we be doing?" Elena managed to ask.

Josh considered her silhouette, still and flattened. "We start with the obvious. We aim to get him back here and his father released. If there are charges, let them be charged: if not, free them. We need a capable lawyer who can get some kind of due process going."

She turned to face him, still a dark shape. "Will it take long to find one?"

"I don't know."

"You know that Ghadir and I might not be able to afford it."

"I'll help."

"Thanks."

"I want to help. This won't be easy. We need someone who's not afraid of bare knuckle encounters for a client without deep pockets. There aren't many of those around."

"I'm sorry," she mumbled, wiping her eyes with her sleeve.

"Can I drive you home?"

"I'm going to sleep at Ghadir's tonight. Sharon's already there."

"Okay." He reached into his pocket for the car keys and got up to leave. "It's out past Papineau, isn't it?"

"You know . . . ," she said, moving towards him, the vulnerability of her face finally visible, ". . . sometimes I feel that it's only what I don't understand that's real."

He was shocked by her words. Yes, he knew that feeling, had tried to reach for those words himself. He had wanted, but failed, to communicate precisely that to Rachel.

Elena locked the door behind them as they left the store. The leaves tumbling from the hanging plants were faceted orange and silver in the mixed illumination of streetlamp and moon.

"People will claim that no one knows where he is," Josh said, taking her arm. "And they'll say we're making up our story."

"You mean they'll deny what's real."

"Yes, that's exactly what I mean."

5

ELENA CONSIDERED IT intensely for several days, then called her father.

She told him she had too much to say for it all to be on the phone and she needed him to come to Montreal. He had immediately asked if she and Sharon were okay and she said yes, they were fine, but she had a boyfriend who needed help.

What kind of help, he asked after a silence.

She told him she didn't know exactly and he replied she

should just quit fooling around and tell him what was going on. Pushed like that she had finally found the words she wanted, telling him that she didn't trust her own judgment, which was the main reason she wanted him to come. "You're smart," she told him. "I need that."

The next silence was even longer and it was she who broke it. "I need you to come so we can work this out." Somehow she had managed to say that without any of the usual derision.

His attitude changed. He said that while he didn't understand what was going on of course he'd get there. He told her he'd prefer to give the garage some notice, because if he left without warning they'd be short-staffed, it being summer and the guys having all booked holidays long ago. He'd get there tomorrow, if necessary, but was it necessary?

She didn't want to answer because that was the wrong question and she really didn't want him to hear that she was on the verge of crying. Somehow he understood and asked, gently, how much time he needed to book off. She said she didn't know.

He told her that was okay, he'd be there soon and would stay as long as necessary. It wouldn't cost much because he'd be happy to sleep on the couch.

She corrected him, saying she was close to subletting the apartment and she and Sharon were moving in with her boyfriend's parents for an indefinite period. And since Mahfouz's father wasn't home and the mother didn't know him, it would be better if he stayed at a cheap motel. There were several not too far away.

Not understanding a thing other than his daughter needed him, he agreed.

"I've been missing you," he said at the end of the call, as

if to sooth her. "Missing you and the little one. Sometimes it hurts, you not being here."

"Okay. That's good. We miss you, too."

"Is there anything I should bring?"

"Your optimism."

Given her tone, he hadn't laughed.

Chapter Eleven

===== 1 =====

What was left of Omar's family gathered in Ezbet el-Burg, east of Alexandria on the Egyptian north coast. While waiting for their meeting with Wasif, the man handling the arrangements, they looked out at an old fishing boat softly rocking on the waves. The grey and red paint of the hull was blistered and dull, the ropes looped over the sides frayed, but it seemed sturdy enough. With the sun dancing on the vast blue Mediterranean behind, it was possible to imagine this modest vessel as an appropriate portal to a new beginning.

The two brothers knew they would land in Italy with no means of support, but naively assumed that the slender traces of Italian colonization in southern Somalia had prepared them for what would come. The elder had chosen Pietro for his pseudonym, the younger — Vittorio. The mother, although unhappy the names weren't Islamic, understood they would help where they were going. Later, of course, when older and established, they'd proudly retake their true names, but for now such efforts could be made.

The mother had spoken to a friend who had a cousin in Milan savvy to the needs of recent immigrants, a woman who had made a reputation fighting the anti-African belligerence of the Berlusconi government. She has promised to look out for the boys. The mother wrote this blessed woman's name and number on four small pieces of paper, one hidden beneath the inner sole of each of their shoes. She thought that one could never be too careful.

They were to contact that woman as soon as they arrived. Should they ever be separated — although each insisted it would never happen — they were to reconnect through her.

The boys were eager to leave. If they remained it was only a question of time before they'd be caught by the authorities to be imprisoned, beaten and deported. Besides, they detested Cairo now, calling it The City of Sudden Tragedy, and the possibilities of Europe were too close to ignore. Vittorio bragged to his brother that he'd find work in the tourism industry. Knowing himself to be handsome, he hoped a woman from a distant country, perhaps a woman not too unlike his mother, would fall in love, take him home and care for him. Pietro, more practical, intended to go into small engine repair, for which he had a proven aptitude.

About a hundred meters from the shore stood a low building with open windows. A man appeared at the door and waved at them. Fadumah and her mother approached, saying nothing, leaving the boys to walk the pier and gaze at the boat.

The two women stopped at the entrance and peered into the shadows. Wasif had taken his place behind the wooden desk. Two plastic chairs were vacant in front of it. He looked up, wondering why they were waiting and gestured impatiently for them to enter.

"Are you the one who speaks Arabic?" he asked Fadumah.

"If you go slowly."

"You know the price and for two you must double it. How will you pay?"

"My mother wants me to tell you that our father is a martyr. He died fighting for Islam."

"Why does your mother want to tell me that? Is it because you don't have the money?"

Fadumah didn't raise her eyes.

Wasif looked at her frankly, appraisingly, then decided. "Different forms of payment can be negotiated."

Still with eyes lowered, Fadumah replied quietly: "Can I tell my mother that you appreciate that my father is a martyr and are willing to make exceptions?"

It's not the first time Wasif had negotiated for the virtue of a woman. He found it best to be straightforward. He paused only briefly before saying: "My younger brother and I would need a night of your time. Can you arrange that? The night before the boat leaves you must go to his house."

Fadumah knew her father would not have tolerated this suggestion for even half of a heartbeat, but he was neither alive to know nor present to solve their problems.

"What's he saying?" asked her mother.

"He's willing to make an exception for the sons of a martyr. He will accept what we offer."

"It's not much," said the mother excitedly. "Tell him we don't have much."

"What we have is enough," replied Fadumah tersely.

The mother continued: "Tell him we thank him for his understanding. God is great and will certainly reward him."

Fadumah didn't translate.

"Well?" asked Wasif, wondering if she was going to make herself available or not.

"Has the boat ever made the journey before?" Fadumah strained to remember the questions she had prepared to ask.

"The boat has crossed successfully twice before and, of course, it will be three times lucky."

"When will it leave and do my brothers need to bring their own containers of fresh water?"

"The boat will leave five nights from now, just as the high tide is turning. They should bring water and whatever food they need for three days, which will be more than enough. They need to dress for warmth during the night and to cover themselves from the sun during the day."

"Will you be on the boat?"

"No, I have to stay here."

"Who will guide the boat?"

"There's an experienced captain. He will follow the shore until Darnah, then . . ."

"Where's that?" Fadumah said, interrupting.

"Almost to Benghazi, then he will head northwest to Sicily. That's the only difficult part, should the weather be bad. When the weather is fine the distance is short."

"Where will the boat land?"

"It's a long coast, wherever it lands will be the right place."

Fadumah turned to her mother and shared the information. The mother explained her deepest anxiety and Fadumah turned to Wasif. "Will there will be enough gas on the boat to get there? My mother has heard that some boats ran out of gas and then drifted for weeks. People died."

At which point Wasif threw up his hands and proclaimed that no one was forcing anyone to do anything. They didn't have to go to Italy if they didn't want. They were free to find another boat if that's what they preferred. They could even lease their own small seaplane and fly over in comfort. He'd be happy to give them that phone number. Did she understand? Whatever they did was of their own free will. Everything was their choice.

"How many will be on the boat?" asked Fadumah, her voice trembling. "That's my final question."

"Less than the vessel can carry. Do you think I want to lose my boat? It's old, yes, but it's still worth a lot of money. Besides, why would any captain be stupid enough to risk his own life by carrying too many?"

"The lives of my brothers," she said, "are precious beyond riches."

"Where did you learn your Arabic?" he asked. "You don't speak well, but you speak with Alexandrine habits."

"I assisted an Egyptian doctor for two years in the refugee camp in Kenya. He was from the University of Alexandria. He insisted I learn Arabic."

"And he helped you into Egypt?"

Fadumah didn't answer. Wasif rubbed his hands over his face. It's a strange world, surely. He almost wanted her not to accept his offer. Why hadn't they just stayed in the refugee camp? "Where's that doctor now, perhaps he could lend you the money?"

"He's in Kenya."

"Tell him that we're happy to meet a man of God," the mother urged her daughter, worried that she was not following the correct form of things. "You didn't tell him that."

"My mother is happy her sons will be safe," Fadumah said.

"You're very pretty," Wasif said. "And now that I've answered your questions, why don't you answer mine?"

"I will do what's necessary for the safety of my brothers."

"This is the address." He wrote it down on a piece of paper the size of a business card. "Be there at sundown four nights from now. Be prepared. I don't want crying. The boat will leave the next night."

Fadumah took the piece of paper and stood, her head bowed. Her mother followed her out. The two women walked beside the tear-filled Mediterranean towards the pier where the boys still sat, gazing as if mesmerized at the continuous rocking of the boat.

"God is merciful," said the mother.

Fadumah inhaled deeply. "He wants me to spend the night with him and his brother. I'm the payment."

Her mother stopped walking. Her face twitched. She looked out over the water, looked back at the building.

They continued walking, the silence strained, and then, as if answering an unspoken question, Fadumah added angrily: "Father would kill him if he were here." It was only then the mother crumpled onto the rocks of the beach, but Fadumah grabbed her arm impatiently and insisted that she stand. "Don't be weak," she cried out. "I can't stand weakness." The mother stood, hearing Omar's thoughts in her daughter's voice. They continued walking.

"What about your future?"

"It won't change anything."

"No man will want you afterwards."

"No man need know. I was cut and sewn as a girl and you can arrange to have me sewn again."

The mother knew this was not a practical thought.

Fadumah wondered if her father had ever discussed with Mahfouz the possibility of their marriage. He had certainly mentioned it to her, but had he ever discussed it with him? She didn't know. When Mahfouz emerged from prison—for he, too, was either in prison or dead—would he expect her to be waiting? Was he, wherever he might be, counting on her steadfastness? Did he think of her to keep himself strong? Fadumah considered her situation from this angle. Perhaps, as soon as he was free, they would race to Canada to marry and have children. They would name their first son Omar, and he and the other children who followed would be raised with the help of the grandmother. They would send messages to her brothers in Italy, offering the choice to live with them. The family would reunite, prosper and grow. And then, one day, she would mention to her brothers the price of their escape to Europe. They would say nothing, but return to the shores of Ezbet el-Burg to ensure that the snake and his pig brother met their maker sooner rather than later.

But Mahfouz need never know. For him, it would never have happened.

Her brothers turned to look at her as she approached. Fadumah stared back, then stopped. Her eyes tried to take in the bigger picture: her shamed mother, her ignorant brothers, the old boat, the sparkling water, the unbroken horizon and, not least, the infinite sky which arched all the way from where she stood to the invisible opposite shore.

All of a sudden Fadumah imagined Mahfouz. He was strolling towards her smiling and youthful, relaxed and confident. She took this as an omen. "Everything will turn out well," she said suddenly to her mother. "One day, not that far away, we will all be together in Canada."

Her mother attempted to grasp the sequence of events that could possibly lead to such an exotic outcome. Finally, as if having joined distant dots, she tilted her head and smiled at her daughter. Fadumah couldn't help but smile back.

The gentle waves rolled in, one after another, each foaming slightly before softly subsiding into the sand between the rocks.

$$=== 2 ===$$

SHARON WAS UNDER the care of Mahfouz's mother for the day. She sat on the top of the outside steps waiting for her friend Leila, just as Mahfouz used to sit waiting for his friends.

She looked up and down a street carved by the sun, noticing that most of the opposite sidewalk was in light and much of her side remained in shadow. She stared at the place where sun and shadow met. Why is it that the colour in the sun, when in the shade, wasn't the same only darker, but a different colour? She could see that by looking at the sidewalk. On the grass, too. Odd. How could that be?

She stood and stepped into the sun. She looked down at her pale yellow dress and lifted her arms in front of her. The created shadows weren't a darker yellow, but a kind of light mauve. Was that really possible?

She closed her eyes and turned to face the searing sun; saw blood-orange swirling on the inside of her lids. She squinted, compressing the skin tightly and the colours turned a cooler black-green and then, as she relaxed, returned to simmering reds and smouldering oranges.

She spun her face away from the blistering orb and her body followed. She began to twirl with her eyes shut; a small sun-drenched dervish, perplexed by the nature of light, spinning on a quiet street.

Sharon lifted into the air, floated higher and higher until she was viewing the houses from above. She continued to rise as, far below her, the organizational grid of the city's wires, lamps and avenues became ever more apparent. Higher yet she rose, remarkably high, and below her all the trees were little and childlike and each roof was but a small coloured square.

She lifted her head and looked about to all horizons.

Everywhere colours met. There was no place where one hue didn't meet another. Woven tightly like that, with no space in between, it was the integrity of colour that protected her from falling.

Or was it the sheer happiness of being alive in the light that lifted her on that gorgeous day?

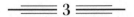

3

"NICE," JOSH SAID, entering the hallway of the apartment where Rachel now lived on a side street off Jean Talon, west of Park Avenue. "I like it."

"Honest?"

"Yes."

"Why?"

"Why what?"

"Why do you like it? I thought it was everything we didn't like. It's in the wrong part of town, it's small, it has a terrible view. What do you like about it?"

"You're in it."

"Oh for God's sake! Don't do this! Don't pretend you love me now."

"It's nice because it's unpretentious, very welcoming in a homey kind of way. It's obviously freshly painted and the colours reflect your sensibility. Is that better?"

"A bit. Would you like a coffee?"

"If you're making some." Rachel retreated to the aisle kitchen and Josh remained standing by himself in the small living room, quietly waiting.

"You wanted to speak to me?" he asked, as she entered with two demitasse of espresso.

"Don't you think we should talk?"

"We do talk. We talk more often than I thought we would. I think we're communicating better than when we lived together."

"You think that a good thing?"

"I do."

"So maybe living separately is good for us. Maybe I did well by leaving."

They sat on opposite sides of the room in comfortable chairs. Both considered what Rachel had just said to be true, but neither knew where it might lead. She broke the growing silence, voicing a long-held question. "Why do we talk more easily on the phone than when we're in the same room?"

He'd wondered the same thing and had concluded it had to do with the conversation of bodies in space: how you position your body makes words redundant. Maybe he should shift his position.

"I don't think you should have given notice to Elena," he said instead. "It was kicking her when she was down."

"She's been distracted at work, not the same salesperson. Besides, her high school French is atrocious. Other girls have applied, and some of them have the right kind of experience."

"You're rationalizing."

"You think I can run a store in Westmount waiting for the inevitable article in the *Gazette* about the girlfriend of a terrorist and where she works? You want the fruit of my hard work to disappear overnight? Maybe you don't understand, but Elena does. She doesn't hold it against me."

"Which reason did you tell her? The first or the second?"

"It's none of your business."

"You shouldn't have done it. It's giving in to fear and hysteria."

"Some judge thought it appropriate to lock the father up. I'm not in a position to question his decision."

"That judge was acting on unsubstantiated information. He hasn't a clue what's going on any more than we do."

"Okay, that's your opinion. It won't change the fact that her last day is in two weeks."

Josh sighed, but didn't stand to leave. "You asked me here. You wanted to talk to me."

"Are you sure you want to pay for their lawyer? Isn't that going to come back and bite you?"

"It's the least I can do. Besides, I'm not paying the full amount."

"Let them get a court appointed lawyer."

"He won't be as good."

"He, or she, will be good enough. Do the owners of the production company know what you're doing? I don't think so, and I doubt if you want them to find out."

"I don't care if they do. I have a private life. I have no obligation to tell them."

"Are you sure about that? With this kind of thing they might think differently."

He knew she was right. "I suppose I should tell them. But it won't change what I do."

"They might want to knock some sense into you."

Josh finished his espresso. "Have you said everything you want to say? Should I leave now?"

"You drank that fast. Would you like another?"

Josh nodded. Rachel rose to make it and this time he

followed her into the kitchen. "You remember the slate of films I was trying to finance with the help of investment from the government of Quebec?"

"I thought it was a done deal."

"It is."

"What about it?" She ground and compressed the beans, fit the filter into the threaded receptacle, pushed hard against its polished handle, then hit the button and looked up.

"An American major wants to broadcast the first of them in a prime Thursday night slot. For us that's a breakthrough."

"Congratulations. I know you worked hard on it."

"I did. I worked very hard. In terms of financing, I broke new ground."

The pressure forced the water through and rich black coffee dripped out. Rachel kept the shot short and reached for the saucer. Josh began to explain the film.

"There's an explosion at the beginning and a female executive and her child are separated. Then the woman, American, regains consciousness in the hospital. She immediately asks for her daughter but of course she's not there. So she rallies and begins to search for her within the political intrigues of two foreign countries, one vaguely in Eastern Europe and the other somewhere in the Mideast. There are scenes where the mother has to question the bad guys to get the information she needs. Finally, near the end, she gets the last, critical piece of the puzzle from the youngest bad guy, to whom she had been secretly attracted, and that enables her to save her daughter. The end is happy."

"Thank God for that," said Rachel, making fun of Josh's obvious lack of enthusiasm. "Let's go back to the living room."

"The U.S. network loves the story. They're over the moon. They think the lead actress perfect for the part, which she is. She's pretty in that girl-next-door kind of way. It's impossible not to like her. Extremely intelligent, very talented. The director says the script has great visual action, well spread out, and that it builds nicely. Everyone loves the final sequence where she's wearing a hijab and gets chased through an Arab city."

Josh, still agitated, fell silent, and moved to the edge of his chair.

Rachel settled in hers. "You helped finance the film. You don't have to believe it's a great work of art."

"In the pictures of prisoner abuse from Abu Ghraib, there's an image of a woman soldier who has this Iraqi guy on a leash, like he's a dog. He's actually lying naked on the floor with his hands tied behind him and there's a collar around his neck attached to a leash. When you look at the photo you just see this blatant . . . what, a pornography of some kind, a sexual sadism. And now I discover that I'm working on a film that does exactly the same thing but for a mass audience."

"She walks one of them on a leash?"

"During the interrogations. The leash is only a small part of it."

"It doesn't have a critical sensibility?"

"It pretends to, but no it doesn't. When it's acted well, and it will be, the audience will want her to inflict pain and will cheer it like a victory when she does. I guess it goes without saying she becomes very inventive."

"Why are you telling me this?"

"In the end she's an almost naked white woman in stockings and underwear facing a gang of men, all brown skinned, which isn't exactly coincidental, is it? She kills them with the machine gun hidden beneath her robes before it got pulled off. She blows them away—all except the one she likes. She could polish him off, too, but she doesn't. He lies there bleeding and she walks away."

"She shows a moment of compassion."

"Right, after torturing and killing how many she has this moment of so-called compassion. I'd like to tell you this is satire, but it isn't."

"It's just a film, Josh. It's destined for television. It's used to sell advertising."

"At one point I thought it was going to be a serious work. At one point it seemed to have content. Her sympathy for her lost child was supposed to open her eyes to the losses of the people around her. At one point she wasn't just a victim, she had a consciousness. But then the broadcaster got involved and, you know, they suggested a chase sequence be put here, a dialogue scene be cut there, stick in a few guns to 'raise the stakes'—you have no idea how I've grown to hate that expression. They insisted on silly scenes in a forensic lab which weren't in the first draft, while cutting any dialogue which could be mistaken for intelligent conversation among mature adults. A tweak here, a chop there, all designed to emphasize clichés so familiar only an audience of five-year-olds could find it confusing . . ."

"You doubt the writer's integrity?"

"What integrity?"

"The story isn't your responsibility."

"No. I'm not responsible. That's a small mercy."

"So?"

"But how am I supposed to feel having helped finance a film that glorifies the sadistic interrogations that take place in god knows how many hellholes? And why does no one else see the problem? Why is everyone happy? Why do

Canadians consider getting this shit on network American television the epitome of our cultural achievement?"

"You know the answer to that better than I."

"I can't do it."

"What's to do, if it's already financed? What are you trying to say?"

"I think of Mahfouz and the others like him and I don't want to go through with it. We call it entertainment but it's propaganda. There's no other word for it. It's designed to weaken our natural horror at what we know is happening."

Rachel looked at him silently.

"Do you remember," he asked, "why I got into this industry? I mean, at the very beginning? You knew me then. We used to watch films together in the Hall building: Resnais, Wertmuller, Goddard, Bergman. We were fascinated by the intelligence, the moral viewpoints. But now, here I am . . ."

"You're a successful lawyer for a successful production company and this is just one film among many. Don't dwell on it, move on."

"Is it so simple, move on?"

"Besides, you're helping to save jobs in a sector vulnerable to a high Canadian dollar. The investment did what it was supposed to do."

"Public money used to further public ignorance."

"Why are you talking as if a film is meant to be history? It isn't."

"No? Why, then, do we present it that way? We spend huge amounts to get every aspect as real as possible. We insist on all the details: the hair, the make-up, the clothing, the accents, the props, the sound effects, the locations . . . fucking everything! Everything, that is, except the essential, who is suffering and why."

"Terrorism happens."

"Terrorism might happen, Rachel, but it's sexual sadism that's on the screen."

"Your heart opposes."

"Doesn't yours?"

"Is this really how you feel? So bitter?"

Josh drained his second cup. He seemed exhausted and angry. Rachel finished her first. Silence.

She stated her position bluntly. "There are times I think you've never understood the business you're in. Film is a popular media. You go with the flow. You find the wave in a market and you ride it. The directors you mentioned, they were all part of waves, too. It's just the way it is. You simply don't understand today's wave: what's happening now and how people feel about it. You're out of touch. The broadcast executives aren't."

"Alright. I used to disagree when you said things like that, but not now, not anymore. It would be nice to use my skills differently."

"You want to change jobs?"

"Did I tell you about my most recent conversation with Dan?"

"No."

"I told him that I was in the razor wire business."

Rachel looked at him blankly.

"He looked at me just like you are now. I said that society needs a good razor wire to keep people herded together. The wire shouldn't be visible, because everyone wants to believe in their freedom, but it should be sharp, so that no one wanders in any direction they're not meant to go. And that's what I do. I write the contracts that create the thinnest, sharpest, razor wire possible. And the general population is so incredibly naïve that they enjoy paying to have it installed in their own heads."

"What did Dan say?"

"He said that he could hardly recognize me, I had become so cynical."

"He's right."

"No he's not. The problem is that I'm not cynical enough. If I were more cynical then I'd be okay with it. I told him that he and I are in the same business, only with different tools. The media industry uses thin razor wire placed in the mind and the justice department uses cops and prisons."

"You shouldn't disrespect your own hard work and good fortune."

"Why call it good fortune if it gets me upset like this?"

"It didn't use to."

"But it does. Once you start to see these things it's like living in a madhouse."

"The film has a statement, Josh, it's just not the one you want to hear. It says that terrorism is real, which it is, and that terrorists do things so low that they can and should be treated like dogs, which they do. And it says, at the end of the day, that even though we have to fight our enemies with no holds barred, we shouldn't reduce ourselves to the same level as them."

"That's what it says?"

"Doesn't it? Perhaps films like that help us achieve the social cohesion necessary for a long and difficult fight."

"Anti-Arab bigotry is a good thing because it helps us all think alike?"

Silence between them. And the silence endured.

Rachel thought she'd scream. He was so obstinate, so thick, so self-satisfied with his moral superiority. Had he always been that way? She should scream. That might wake him up.

Josh, dismayed by the impasse, reached into his pocket, pulled out his cell phone and punched in numbers. The phone in the kitchen rang.

"Why are you calling me, Josh?"

"I thought maybe we could get the conversation moving again." He was trying to amuse her.

Rachel smiled thinly but, willing to oblige, entered the kitchen to answer. "Hello."

"Rachel?"

"Yes."

"I'm glad I caught you in."

"I have a guest over, Josh. It's not a good time for you to call."

"A guest? Is it a male guest?"

"I don't think that's any of your business."

"Is it a he or a she?"

"A he, since you're so insistent. And he's young and handsome."

"Really?"

"Maybe not as young and as handsome as he used to be, but not a bad catch, in the great scheme of things."

"The great scheme of things? What's that?"

"Everything considered."

"I'm glad to hear that you've considered everything. Can't be easy, to consider everything. Especially when you have a young male guest in your new apartment."

"But he makes me so mad I want to scream."

"To scream?"

"I want to scream and scream and scream. He's arrogant and blind. He thinks the world is supposed to be perfect."

"Why don't you scream at him, then?"

"Maybe I should. So tell me, before I go back to my guest and hurl abuse at him, what did you want to talk about?"

"Maimonides."

She laughed. "But of course, your friend Maimonides."

"You know him ... philosopher extraordinaire, medical doctor, wrote in Arabic and Hebrew, exiled from Spain, settled in Cairo."

"I've heard a little about him, yes."

"Wrote a Guide for The Perplexed."

"With a title like that it should be a best seller."

"It is. Or at least, it was."

"When was he, anyhow?"

"Eleven hundreds."

"Listen Josh, I'm going to hang up on you now. I'm going to rejoin my guest."

"Okay."

Rachel hung up and re-entered the living room.

"Why Maimonides?"

"He said that we limit reality by our own ignorance, so rather than pretending we know what God is we should understand what God is not. They call it the negative way, the *via negativa*. Maimonides wasn't the first to use it, but he was clear about it, and tried to be consistent."

"And why are we interested in the consistency of a twelfth century Rabbi?"

"I was actually thinking about it in terms of righteousness. I can't really tell you what righteousness is, but I can tell you what it's not. The film, it's not."

Rachel didn't know what to say.

Josh continued: "I've spent so much time trying to define myself by who I am, I've forgotten to define myself by who I'm not. Do you understand?"

That made sense to Rachel. "Maybe it really is time to leave, if that's how you feel."

"I often think the negative way is misunderstood."

"I don't think anybody is evaluating it, frankly."

"Strauss did. He interpreted Maimonides' statement that God has no positive attributes as another way of saying God didn't exist, but that we should have faith in him for reasons of social cohesion, the same defence you gave the film. You see, he believes Maimonides, too, was only a razor wire salesman."

"And what do you think?"

"I think Strauss couldn't imagine there was an age of deep belief before this age of hypocrisy. It made no sense to him because he couldn't reach it inside of himself, so he presented Maimonides in the only light he could: a consummate liar with good intentions."

"Strauss couldn't imagine you, either, could he, Josh?" she added thoughtfully. "A smart man in the twenty-first century who still believes."

"I take that as a compliment, Rachel."

"I know you do."

"It's kind of you not to laugh at me."

"I've never done that. I don't agree with you. I don't think righteousness is a way to God. I deny the destination. I think we do what we have to do to take care of our own as best we can. To me, that's pretty straightforward, and it's enough."

"Do you think I'm a coward to believe?"

"That never occurred to me. No. I would never call you that. If you do leave your job, what will you do?"

"I don't know but I'm thinking about it. I have skills."

Rachel surprised herself by a leap into the dark. "If you do it, Josh, I'll understand."

"For the soul I don't have?"

"Yes, something like that."

"I want to sell the house."

"We should have done that long ago." She felt liberated to say it.

"The market is dreadful right now. It couldn't be worse."

Rachel laughed. "Don't worry about that. The views will seduce someone, same as they seduced us."

"I'll be looking for a place to live. You wouldn't want a roommate would you?"

"You are a very impertinent guest, Josh."

He smiled. "I love you, Rachel."

"I'll consider your offer."

"Can I offer you a bite to eat? There's a Punjabi restaurant around the corner."

"Alright, I'd like that."

Rachel felt lighter. If Josh was actually willing to change jobs and sell the house, then he must be envisioning a very different future. Maybe he was willing to work on the relationship, really work on it.

4

THE MONTREAL LAWYER who represented both Samih and Mahfouz spoke softly.

"I reached a representative of the Muslim Brotherhood in Cairo. He is aware that one of their members, Ibrahim, is being held. They've not been able to contact him, but have spoken to others who shared a cell with him. When I asked after the owner of the fragrance shop, he said he was not a known member, although he may have sympathized with the movement. Many sympathizers, he said, are too frightened to join. He had heard of a third man who had been gunned down by Egyptian security forces, but they knew nothing about him. I don't know if that is true or not. When I asked about Mahfouz, he said my call was the first he had ever heard of him."

The lawyer tried to gauge the reaction of the individuals he faced: the disappeared young man's mother, stolid and aware; his girlfriend, quick and attentive; the girlfriend's father, apparently just arrived in the city, out of context and distracted; and Josh, voluble, intense, frustrated.

"When I asked where the government might be holding Mahfouz, if they are, he replied that he could be in various facilities around Cairo. He could be in the Lazoghli, which is the SSI headquarters — they're essentially a police force tasked to ensure the maintenance of the Mubarak regime — or at the Gaber Ibn Hayan, their facility in Giza, or at a third centre in Nasr City." He peered over his reading glasses. "While none of those are officially places of detention, people are held and interrogated there. He could also be in ..." — and he lowered his head to refer to his notes — "the Abu Zaabal Liman, the Wadi Natroun Liman, or the Istikbal Turrah Liman."

He leaned back and faced them.

"The three limans have maximum security capabilities," he said in his faultless if slightly accented English. "All of them hold people incarcerated under the National Emergency Laws, and all of them are dreadful institutions. When I asked if the Brotherhood could help us locate Mahfouz, he said that although they would like to their hands are full trying to help their own members. He mentioned that more than a thousand Brothers are currently imprisoned. He repeated that our best bet is to maintain pressure on the Canadian government to publicly acknowledge that Mahfouz is being held by Egyptian security. When I told him that our Foreign Affairs Ministry insisted it couldn't be true if it was denied by the Egyptian government, he said such a statement was obviously absurd."

The lawyer knew that nothing he had to say at this meeting could be considered as comforting. No choice, then, but to plough ahead. "Frankly, we all know this won't be the first time the Canadian government has claimed ignorance while standing aside during the torture of one its citizens." He tapped his finger on the desk to underline his personal disapproval. "I spoke to a range of people in Cairo, all of whom said that Mahfouz is almost certainly in the hands of security. One of the groups I spoke to was a non-governmental human rights organization. They have literally hundreds of torture cases on file, many of them of prisoners identified by American intelligence. They gave me a rather sobering statistic. Roughly forty percent of the known torture cases in Egypt end in the death of the prisoner. As bad as that is, that's only up to 2004, and most believe the situation has deteriorated. A CIA agent was recently quoted as saying, quite openly, that Egypt is the place to send a prisoner if you want him to disappear."

He turned to Ghadir who looked back at him steadily. He noticed that Elena was holding her breath, her face extremely pale. The girl's father continued to stare out the window, strangely calm. Josh leaned forward in his seat, struggling to remain silent. The lawyer forced himself into the lengthening pause. "God only knows what percentage die among those who never have a file opened."

Ghadir bowed her head and closed her eyes, wincing as if to ward off a blow. The small gesture filled the room.

"I'd like you to put a lawyer on retainer in Egypt," Josh said. "I want that person to pursue all leads to find Mahfouz, wherever they go and whomever they implicate. We're not going to back off and I want it understood by all who are watching that we won't back off. I want our efforts to be seen, to be public. That's important to me. Can you do that?"

"Yes, and I think it's a good idea to put an Egyptian lawyer on retainer, someone with experience in these security cases. I already have a short list of those with the right experience. I understand you want to be aggressive, Josh, and to be seen as aggressive for strategic reasons, but I have to tell you that the most prominent defence lawyer in the field, one Abd al-Harith al-Madani, was picked up by the security forces one day and found tortured to death the next. No charges in his case were ever laid. That was years ago, but let's be reasonable with our expectations about what any lawyer will be willing to do on our behalf."

"I remember when the emergency laws were announced," Ghadir said, fighting to regain composure. "I was still in Egypt at the time. It was in 1981, after Sadat was assassinated."

The lawyer nodded. "They've just been renewed for another two years. Mubarak has ruled non-stop for a quarter century under their umbrella." Yes, the mother understood what they were up against, but did the others? "If you say in public that Mubarak is getting old you can be thrown into prison for insulting the state. If you're a young man with a religious looking beard you can get swept up and detained. You can get fifteen years in prison for being at a demonstration."

He was being drawn forward by his desire for the others to grasp the steepness of the hill yet to be climbed. "There's a veneer of freedom and civility in Egypt associated with projects like the new Library in Alexandria, holiday excursions on the Red Sea, the Museum in Cairo — what the tourists see — but for the majority life is not like that. This past year the government spent most of its time fighting bread riots and a series of wildcat strikes in the factories. When the police arrested hundreds, thousands more appeared. The most effective strikes were led by women. It's one thing to beat up male militants — no one thinks it unusual — but to publicly attack working mothers is something else."

"The tide is going out for a government if it's the women they fear," Victor suggested, turning back to the group, his unexpected words hanging in the air.

Ghadir didn't believe the Egyptian government was about to change anytime soon, no matter how many women were opposed. Didn't he know that Mubarak's son Gamal waited groomed in the wings? However, it would be impolite to disagree, so she looked away and said nothing.

The lawyer, however, appreciated Vic's comment and betrayed his own analysis: "What all the conservative governments in the Middle East fear is unity between a popular cause and Islam, and that's an alliance the striking women successfully forged, if only briefly."

Elena heard this and wanted to know more. What was this alliance the women forged 'if only briefly' that frightened those in power? She wanted to discuss it. She opened her mouth to ask a question but the lawyer had already gone on to say that he had nothing else to report, that he expected to meet with them again in about two weeks and, by then, would have a better understanding of how to contest the certificate under which Samih was being held. He'd communicate sooner if anything important came up.

He stood and so they all stood, preparing to leave.

At his office doorway the lawyer engaged in a discussion of some length with Ghadir in French, to whom he showed genuine concern. Josh listened attentively, but the words washed over Victor and Elena. Ghadir, at the end of it, managed a smile.

The lawyer shook Elena's hand in a perfunctory manner, smiled gently at Victor while shaking his, and told Josh to give him a call later.

Ghadir, standing in the hallway by the elevator, wanted to cling a bit longer to the cohesion of the group and invited everyone back for coffee. She didn't want to be alone with her confusion and grief. She wanted that initial period of shock, impotence and anger to have passed. She wanted, more than anything, to discuss plans, to co-ordinate actions.

Josh drifted a few yards distant, flipped open his cell and called Rachel. She didn't answer so he left a message: "I wanted you here, Rachel, I really did. If we're trying to get back together then you have to try to understand this through my eyes. You have to give me that chance." He paused briefly. "Ghadir has invited us to her place for coffee. I'm hoping you can make it. I'll take you out after. You have the address."

But he knew she wouldn't come.

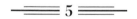

5

THE CAR GATHERED speed travelling east along René Lévesque Boulevard on what had become a cold, overcast day. It rained in small, sporadic gusts and the wipers, on a delay, hesitated before reluctantly clearing the glass.

Everything Victor had learned since his arrival surprised him. His granddaughter, whom he noticed speaking a smattering of French and Arabic, treated Ghadir with more familiarity than she had with him. When he spoke German to her, as he used to, she struggled to remember. And for reasons no one explained, Josh, the husband of the person who fired Elena, was paying the lion's share for the lawyer in whose office they had just attended a meeting. And that was just the beginning: Elena's boyfriend, seemingly a normal kid liked by everyone, was being tortured in Cairo while the Canadian government knowingly denied it; and the boy's father was imprisoned under a law where neither the accused nor his lawyer knew the evidence against him.

He looked over at Elena, remembering when she first had her baby — a child having a child — but now she was easily old enough to be a mother. She had, in fact, a certain competent air about her. Had she that quality when she left home? Yes, though definitely not so defined. But if so capable, why hadn't she finished her first year of university? Why had she been fired from her job? And how had she chosen a boyfriend who would find himself in such an awful predicament? God knows life is full of surprises and rarely does anyone travel a straight line, but still ...

It could only make sense in a world he didn't recognize. So how did she, his daughter, leaning forward with her hand resting on Ghadir's shoulder, make sense of it?

To lose Elena and Sharon at this stage of his life would be to lose more than he could bear. Could he convince them to come home? Why were they staying in Montreal if Elena was no longer going to school? She could apply to Brandon University, as he had always hoped. It wasn't exactly world famous, but that might prove a virtue as it wouldn't be riding on past laurels. She could study social work. She'd be good at that.

But Mahfouz ... Mahfouz ... how could he forget the young man who had changed his own life in such unexpected ways? She wasn't about to desert him. No, face it. She and Sharon were in Montreal for the long haul. If they wouldn't move, should he? There were more brakes and mufflers here than there and with his experience he'd land a job. But he didn't speak the language and the few friends he had were back there, as was the grave of his wife.

"I think you should go to Egypt."

"What? I'm sorry. I was lost ..." He waved his hand about, trying to tell his daughter that she had interrupted his thoughts.

"One of us should go to Cairo. We can't just abandon him. Sharon's in a new school and she needs me. Ghadir has to stay for Samih and besides, if she leaves the country there's a chance they won't let her return. You're not taking care of anyone, you should go."

"How would it be useful, me going?"

She looked at him with frank, wide-opened eyes. "We can't just pretend everything will work out, dad. We can't do that. We have to find evidence that he's there so we can pressure the government to bring him back. That's what the lawyer said we needed to do."

"Isn't that why the second lawyer will be hired?"

"We can't leave it up to the lawyers. They'll do what they can but only through the channels they know. One of us has to go."

"I don't speak Arabic."

"Yeah, but so what? You're smart, you'll figure it out."

It pained him that she was counting on abilities he doubted. It occurred to him, though, in some deeper place, that she was right — you don't abandon loved ones — you walk down all paths and proceed to the very end, no matter how unlikely or difficult. He was out of the picture in Brandon, a redundancy in Montreal, but could perhaps be useful in Cairo. And even the slightest of possibilities should be embraced in an urgent situation.

He remembered what his own father had told him: "Judge your life by the character of your grandchildren." His father, now deceased, would have been proud of Elena.

"Okay," Victor answered, without any idea of the nature of the challenge he was accepting, "I'll go."

"Thanks," a relieved Elena said. "My dad will go," she proclaimed to Josh and Ghadir in the front, as if a new player had just joined their team. "He just said he'd go."

Had they been discussing this, Victor wondered, while he was lost in his thoughts? When he looked again at his daughter he couldn't help but see traces of her mother. It wasn't just the physical features, although, of course, it was that: the forehead, around the eyes, the shape of the ears, perhaps even the shape of the lips; but more, it was the impression she gave of . . . of what?

Gathering and weighing.

Yes, she gathered thoughts and then weighed them, just as Arden had. He remembered his wife's intelligence, how he had never known from which direction the spoken synthesis of her silences would come.

Why had she been taken by cancer in the prime of her life? Why had she died so young? Who knew how her thoughts might have evolved, the repercussions they might have had? Certainly her daughter's life would have been entirely different, and his, too. They had needed her.

It slowly dawned on Victor that his relations to his daughter and granddaughter, for reasons he could never have predicted, would now be judged on his willingness and ability to help Mahfouz. He really had to commit. In Cairo he'd have to find someone with a conscience. It wouldn't have to be someone who knew everything, just someone with a conscience and therefore willing to help him find someone who knew a little more than either of them, and so it would grow, living link to living link, a chain of concern and trust until the problem was correctly identified and the right action taken.

Not so easy, though, getting that chain started. That would be the hard part. Everyone thought they had a conscience but most had only the shadow of one. It was much easier to live with the shadow than the conscience itself. To maintain a conscience meant to seek out the relevant knowledge: starve the knowledge, wither the conscience. It was implicit in the word: *con science*.

Sometimes the feeling of the infinite gripped him. It did. A moment opening and again opening and yet again opening, and yet again, all infused with a strange inner light. It had been there for a moment in the lawyer's office when he had looked out the window. He had felt the glow of the infinite within the spark of that instant. What had Arden called it: "Seeing the lotus in the clouds"?

The car turned on Avenue de Lorimier, then right on Rue Masson, before turning left again. Victor peered out the window to the grey, overcast sky, listened to the stuttering wipers, then lowered his gaze to the rows of walk-up apartments which filled street after street. It sure wasn't Brandon.

The eternal — was it a concept or an emotion?

Maybe it was an emotion: that sense of a connection between all events rippling through time. All religions tried to deliver that emotion packaged with their distinct symbols, trying to brand the eternal as their own. Yes, religious history as written, nothing but an endless arrogance. So hard to free oneself. So hard.

But why want freedom? Why not accept the emotional comfort and clear definition of self which comes with a group's regulation of what to remember and why?

But he hadn't wanted that. Nor had his daughter.

Stubborn stuff from prairie soil.

Chapter Twelve

══ 1 ══

Something had changed and it wasn't for the better.

They knew things about him they could only have learned from people who knew him well. They mentioned his work schedule back home, the names of regulars at the restaurant and the times they were likely to show up. They knew who was at the party the night before he left for Cairo. They also knew aspects of his past better than he remembered them himself: courses taken in University, marks received, friends from high school.

No, he hadn't realized that particular person travelled regularly to the United States. No, he hadn't a clue where he stayed when there. Yes, it was true he took a chemistry course in college. Yes, it was true he did well in it.

They had access to bank records for the restaurant and questioned him on the pattern of cash deposits and withdrawals, looking for discrepancies between amounts received and amounts deposited. Mahfouz was not frightened by these questions: he knew the fastidious financial habits of both himself and his father.

They again closely questioned him about his father. He answered them easily and with confidence. He depended on his honesty.

Then they introduced a new series of questions that made no sense. Knowing his life in Montreal, they superimposed over it a possible world of which he knew nothing. They asked about Somalis in Minnesota, Palestinians in Florida, Egyptians in western Pakistan. It was a world he didn't recognize. He told them that.

They broadened their field of enquiry: his access to plastic explosives, his familiarity with cell phone technology. They asked his opinions about Iraq, Afghanistan, Israel and Iran.

Mahfouz became angry. What did all that have to do with anything? Why had no Canadian official spoken to him? Why had no one from the Embassy been to see him? The delays could no longer have been caused by their ignorance of his plight nor the slowness of large wheels turning. And why was he not allowed to reach out, to call? What had he ever done to deserve this? What did it matter what his political opinions were: he had done nothing wrong.

They were interested in this outburst, and then repeated the same questions more slowly, as if to give him another chance.

Mahfouz, with a sickening awareness, finally understood that the future would not be the correction of misrepresentations for which he had been patiently waiting, but rather the misrepresentations themselves would be the basis on which his future would unfold. He drew inward. He stopped answering. He stopped speaking. Better to be silent than to collaborate in this strange farce.

A crust of despair thickened around him.

But to the jailors, Mahfouz's sudden and emphatic words followed by a resolute silence were entirely provocative, his political naïveté incredible. They wanted their questions answered. What did he know of the Somali group Al-Shabab and its links with Gama'a al-Islamiyya in Egypt? What had been the effect of the recent death of Aden Hashi Ayro on the coordination of the Somali insurrection? What did he know of leaders within the Habr Gadir, Omar's clan? How did Omar get into Egypt and where was his family? How much money was coming from the Egyptian community in Montreal to support the Brotherhood in Cairo? Was any of it getting to Al-Shabab? How was it being transported? And most insistently, who were the other members of his cell in Montreal, and what connections did they have within the United States?

Mahfouz said nothing.

And so positions of stress were introduced. He was left for hours with his hands shackled to his feet while bent backwards over the seat of a chair. Later, he was hung from the ceiling by his bound wrists, his toes just touching the floor. When still he would not speak, his hands were retied behind his back and then he was again hung from the wrists, the feet not touching at all. After a period of strain his shoulders dislocated and he passed out. When Mahfouz revived in excruciating pain, lowered to the floor, the man in front of him asked why he wouldn't speak. Why did he ignore even the easy questions designed to get the tongue wagging? But the previously earnest and accommodating young man had gone adamantly mute.

The man in front of him stepped on the four fingers of his outstretched right hand and ground them with his heel. The thick heel, made of hard rubber, met bone, cartilage and tendon, and ground relentlessly.

How could it be, wondered Mahfouz, whose dislocated arms wouldn't move properly to protect him, that this man, a Muslim, was willing to do such things? Mahfouz felt, in spite of the pain, that he was waking up.

The path of resistance had always been there, but he had never taken it. He now considered that everything he ever thought, said, or did since being imprisoned— all of his presumed dignity and considered manners —has been a shameful form of self-delusion; an absurd grovelling which had fooled himself and no one else. He had tried to present himself as an aspiring member of an international business elite, when he was only an inconsequential pawn trying to help a family even poorer than his own in a constant fight against economic annihilation.

Why had he, his uncle and Mr. Ahmed-Naeem taken their supine positions, acquiescing so easily? Why had they assumed benevolence from their enemies? Omar had known his opponents. He had known they were neither benevolent nor just. Only when one began to resist did one see the world as it was. None of what he had thought previously was relevant. He had understood nothing. Nothing! Nothing!

How Omar must have felt contempt for them lying with their faces to the floor, while he fought a dozen by himself.

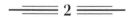

=== 2 ===

GHADIR RECEIVED A call at nine in the morning asking if she would meet two representatives of the Canadian Security Intelligence Services. They wanted to have an informal meeting at her place. She agreed and then immediately called the lawyer.

"He said they'd be over about eleven."

"I'll be there."

"I didn't tell him I was going to call you."

"That's alright. You have no legal obligation to tell them I'm coming. Will Elena be there?"

"No, I'm alone. Sharon's in school and Elena's out with her father. If you're here, will that change what they say?"

"Probably, but it shouldn't. You've never spoken to either of them before?"

"I don't think so. I didn't recognize their names. Why do you think they want to see me on such short notice?"

"We'll know soon enough. Let's just listen to what they have to say."

Ghadir put the phone down. She figured an hour would give her more than enough time to tidy, put together a plate with olives and crackers, change into more presentable clothes and prepare tea.

The lawyer arrived first. A freshened Ghadir led him into the living room and guided him into one of the two sturdy chairs, upholstered in green damask, which matched the small couch. The woven oriental carpet was worn and warm. The walls, like the ceiling, were a pale yellow. Ghadir returned to the kitchen for the plate of food while the lawyer gazed over a small flotilla of treasured images in standing frames on each side table. Many were older photographs of people he couldn't identify. Among them, however, was an old black and white snapshot, maybe three inches by five, of two young men he presumed were Samih and Ibrahim, each with an arm over the other. There was also a coloured photo of a young, dark-eyed, very pregnant Ghadir holding Samih's arm, and another of her in a different dress, now cautiously holding a swaddled baby.

The lawyer moved those two pictures to better see the one behind. It was a coloured five by seven in landscape format of Mahfouz and his father, both about the same height, the father clearly thicker than the son, standing in front of a small box truck with the family name written on the side of it. What was it, the lawyer wondered, that had unified them so completely in that distant moment of genuine laughter?

He gazed up at the larger images harboured on the walls. There was a marriage portrait in sepia tones, Ghadir sitting gracefully with Samih standing behind, his gaze artificially stern and penetrating; and a very recent shot of Mahfouz in university graduation robes, standing alone, smiling shyly. There was another of Mahfouz, obviously taken the same day, in which he was bracketed by his smiling, proud parents. On the opposite wall hung two etchings of views of Old Cairo. European in inspiration, dating from the end of the 19th century, the passage of time had, perhaps, added a lustre of importance not inherent in their artistry.

All in all, the lawyer concluded, gazing about, the living room exhibited a narrative of familial continuity, recent pride and modest success.

The CSIS agents arrived a few minutes later.

"I'm sorry," said the elder agent as he entered the room and turned to the lawyer, his grey hair and professorial beard neatly trimmed, "but we've never met before. You are?"

"I'm her legal counsel," he answered, standing politely and shaking the proffered hand. "She called me after you called her."

"Ah."

"You don't mind my being here, do you?"

"No, no, you have every right to be here."

"And you?"

"With CSIS, trying to help a bit with community relations. He's my assistant ..." — and the younger agent also shook the lawyer's hand.

"Please, eat something," offered Ghadir. "Can I make you some tea?"

"No, no, we just had coffee," replied the elder agent, and the younger nodded in agreement.

"I'd like a tea, Ghadir, if you don't mind." The lawyer didn't want so much to drink tea as to open up a bit of space to observe the two men.

Ghadir anxiously re-entered the kitchen, filled the teapot with the water she had already set to boil, and returned with a tray set with four cups, in case the agents changed their minds, which they didn't.

She herself sat on the sofa beside the younger agent, who gave her a lopsided smile. She poured cups for herself and the lawyer, then settled back with hers cradled in her lap. She looked to the elder agent. "What would you like to ask me?"

"Very simple things," he responded, happy to be received in such a friendly fashion.

"Alright. I can probably manage that."

"About people you may know. I would like your help to ensure we aren't getting the wrong impression about anyone in your community."

"I'd like to help the people of my community."

"Of course, and I want to make that possible."

The lawyer didn't like the sound of where this was going, "Are you suggesting that she inform on her friends and neighbours?"

"That's not a word I would use," replied the agent easily.

"You want her to give you information about people she knows, is that right? I've always thought that the verb for giving information is to inform. But you're a native English speaker and I'm not, so perhaps I have that wrong."

"I think it would be useful to all of us if more information were shared."

"Shared? You would like us to recognize some kind of reciprocal relationship between us?"

"I would hope we could share information, yes."

"Alright, I think that's a wonderful idea. So if Ghadir does answer your questions, will you share with us the specific evidence you have to substantiate the charges against her husband? Will you, at the very least, identify specific charges beyond telling us that he's a threat to national security?"

The younger agent looked at the elder and he, in turn, more reluctantly answered: "I don't think I've given you grounds to interpret my words as looking for some sort of *quid pro quo*. What I said, and I think I was clear, was that we're hoping to learn more about the Muslim community here in Montreal from people who actually know. I can't help but imagine that everyone would find that a good thing."

"I'm just wondering how you intend to reciprocate the generosity you expect."

The elder agent wouldn't be drawn. "As we learn more about the community, it's less likely we'll make mistakes, hold people for the wrong reasons, or hold the wrong people." He turned back to Ghadir. "I'm asking you to help save other people in your community from the kind of suffering you've had to endure."

Ghadir turned to her lawyer. "Why shouldn't I answer his questions? I don't know any terrorists, there's nothing I could say that would hurt anyone, and perhaps something I say might help."

"They're not looking for terrorists, they're looking for people who fit the profile of terrorists, which is an entirely different thing. They're trying to identify the guilty through values, not actions. There's a great deal you might say that would hurt people."

"I know," the elder agent said drily, "that I can't stop you from interpreting this however you want, but I have to say that's an extremely negative twist on why we're here."

The lawyer spoke earnestly and directly to Ghadir. "People in the community feel sympathetic to you and tell you things either in hope or bitterness they wouldn't tell anyone else. These gentlemen want to turn that fact to their advantage. What you might think a passing moment of justifiable anger they'll interpret as a predisposition to violence. What you hear as a reasonable response to prejudiced government policy they'll hear as a desire to destroy the state. Don't think I'm exaggerating. Everything you say will be noted and seen through a lens that assumes the worst. Before you answer his questions, ask yourself why they didn't have a friendly conversation like this before they dragged Samih away. Ask yourself about the other Arab-Canadians they're currently holding without proper legal recourse. And ask yourself why they won't tell you the truth about your son."

The agent had better sense than to try to respond point by point, but sighed in a way as if personally hurt. "Look. Why don't we forego the polemics? I'm just here trying to do my sincere best to improve relations between CSIS and the community."

The lawyer bit his tongue, but wondered how it had

come about that here, in Canada, when he asked for clarity on charges against a defendant he was accused of engaging in polemics.

"If I answer your questions," asked Ghadir, still trying to get a clear grasp of the dynamics at play, "will the treatment of my husband change?"

"I don't think you should take that approach," replied the agent. "I'm not qualified to offer any kind of deal." But he said it in such a way that one could reasonably conclude that he was cautiously surveying the lay of the land, rather than denying the possibility.

Ghadir, uncertain if she should reveal so clearly what was on her mind, knew what she wanted. "If you bring my son back to Canada, then I'll answer any questions you want to ask."

The lawyer inwardly winced: he hadn't expected that, yet understood why she had offered it, and admired her directness.

"I sympathize with your anxiety about your son." The elder agent clearly felt the conversation was back on track. "I do. I wish I knew where he was. We all do. But we don't, so can say nothing about him. I do, however, know where your husband is, and the charges facing him, and I guess, if you really are willing to help us, that I could bring up issues about his treatment to the people who do have the proper authority."

"You guess?" asked the lawyer, not amused, entering a slow burn.

"I want my son," said Ghadir firmly, understanding that masks were off and very serious negotiations had begun.

"I can't help your son. I can help your husband. Please, consider your husband."

"I am. He would rather die a thousand deaths than have anything hurt Mahfouz. Help us get our son back to Montreal, even if he remains in prison here, and I will do whatever you want. I will inform for a year, two years, whatever you want."

"Are you sure you want to say that?" the lawyer asked.

"Yes," she replied, "the longer he stays in Egypt the less chance he has of ever coming home. I know that. You know that. They know that."

None of the three men rushed to disagree. The younger agent seemed to have found something absolutely fascinating on the floor, for he looked down at it with undivided attention.

"Why don't you agree?" cried Ghadir, looking at both agents. "I've agreed to answer your questions, any question, and I'll tell you the truth, but only after my son has been returned to Montreal."

"Are you wired?" the lawyer suddenly asked the younger agent, realizing that of course he was. "Not that it makes any difference, but ..."

"Don't dignify that question with a response," the elder agent said.

"So I can assume he is," retorted the lawyer.

"Where is my son?" pleaded Ghadir.

"We don't know, and that's the truth," replied the elder agent.

"When will he be released?"

"How can I tell you that if I don't know where he is?"

"Why are you holding him?"

"We aren't."

"Why aren't you pressuring the Egyptian government to let him go? Please!"

"We don't know if that's where he is. You tell us he's there, but they repeatedly deny it."

"How can you lie to her so brazenly?" snapped the lawyer, who had had enough.

The elder agent abruptly stood, looked briefly about him as if he wished to remember his surroundings, and the younger stood awkwardly in response. "Look," the elder one said, again finding his initial relaxed tone as he directly addressed Ghadir, "I'm sorry, but this meeting has been a mistake. For reasons I understand you thought it necessary to invite your lawyer, but he has twisted this occasion into something it was never meant to be. I think you and I could have had a useful conversation, but it wasn't to be. At least not this morning. Maybe we can try again some other time. It would be wrong, however, for you to think that I've asked you to inform on anybody." He turned to the lawyer. "There is no deal to be negotiated, either actual or implied. None. Zero. Rien. Nada. Is there any part of that you don't understand?"

Ghadir escorted the agents to the door without the lawyer having answered or risen, or in any other way acknowledging their departure. He was quite comfortable in his expression of contempt.

Ghadir returned and took her place on the small sofa. She sat on the very edge of it, her hands anxious in her lap. She suddenly tilted forward to reach for her cold cup of tea, which she held tightly, as if for comfort. "I'm not sure what just happened."

"Then I'll tell you. They aren't getting useful information out of your husband so they're willing to change his situation, but they want to pretend that any change is their decision to make, and to trade it for you becoming an informer. To your credit, you didn't go along."

"I did go along, I agreed to give them whatever they wanted."

"For your son, but not for your husband. They thought you would agree for the sake of your husband."

"Will they call again?"

"Oh yes. You'd be quite a prize for them, and they know you're half-way there. They anticipate, after several more weeks of anxiety, that you'll do whatever they want. They'll come with specific questions about people you know."

"I would agree to meet with them again."

"Would you?"

"Yes, and I'll have exactly the same answer, not until they return my son."

"Are you going to invite me to the next meeting? They're expecting that you won't."

"I don't know," she muttered honestly. "I don't know."

"If we can't maintain completely open communication between us, Ghadir, then I can't be your lawyer."

She was surprised by this hard line but, considering, realized it was for the best. "What does it mean that they're willing to change Samih's situation?"

"I think they'll offer to put him under house arrest. He'll have to wear an electronic bracelet so they can track where he is twenty-four hours a day. Your guests will be monitored, your phone line tapped, but that's happening already, so wouldn't be a change."

"But he'd be released?"

"He would live here, not in prison."

"How long would that last?"

"Who knows? At the same time they'll be trying to deport him and will comb through all of his dealing with the government, especially his initial application process for citizenship. If there's any detail amiss they'll win their case. If he were still a permanent resident they'd simply call him a security risk and fly him out. All of these procedures occupy a legal grey zone where hearsay can be taken as fact and where an incredible amount of discretionary power is given to the government. The deportation hearings will be brutal, believe me. That's another reason I don't want you speaking to them. Whatever you say will eventually get quoted back to you completely out of context, proving the opposite of what you meant. I don't want that happening in court."

"I trust you."

"Thank you."

"What do I do if they succeed in deporting him?"

"There won't be much you can do. You'll have the choice of living with him elsewhere or living alone in Canada. But we're not there yet. We have to play this out step by step. You have to stay strong and fight them, day by day for many years, and you have to realize that your life will never return to what it was."

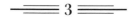

3

WHEN THEY ARRIVED at the same place where she had last embraced Mahfouz, Elena asked her father: "Are you sure you'll be okay?"

"Yes, of course."

"How do you know?"

"I know," he replied, without any shadow of doubt. He then leaned down and, very gently, took the earbuds out of Sharon's ears. She let him, knowing it was time to say goodbye. "You like this new gizmo?" he asked.

Sharon smiled radiantly. She was thrilled with her grandfather's choice of an iPod as a belated birthday gift. They hugged.

"If I let you, you'd spoil her," Elena said.

"When I come back," Victor said, again bending down to the child, "I want to hear the music you've chosen."

"Okay," she said. "Will you be away long?"

"I'll be back as soon as I can." He straightened up and added to his daughter: "She's one incredible child."

"Got everything?" Elena asked, one last time.

He patted the breast pocket of his short leather jacket. "The passport, the confirmation for the hotel, my list of things to do and the initial contacts to make it all happen." He paused. "You know, I've never been off the continent before. That's odd, isn't it, given my age?"

"Are you worried?"

"No. I regret the circumstances, that's all."

"You'll get a phone in the first few days?"

"Yes and I'll call you with the number."

"Buy those long distance cards, they're not expensive."

"I know."

"So stay in touch."

"I will." Victor again leaned down to hug his granddaughter. "I love you so very much."

She whispered in his ear that she loved him, too.

Then Elena and her father embraced with the renewed deep feelings that their recent weeks together had confirmed.

Looking like the distracted mechanic he was — grey cotton pants and heavy shoes, dark brown jacket, red baseball cap — Victor moved towards the security screening area. It occurred to Elena, not for the first time, that although her father appeared confident in his abilities and undeterred by any qualms, perhaps his going wasn't such a brilliant idea. Who'd be able to find him in a foreign country of eighty million souls?

As though hearing her doubts he turned to say: "If he's there, I'll find him."

She rewarded him with a quick smile, which was all he needed. Sharon waved, he waved back, and then he, too, walked out of sight.

Mother and child started to wind their way back to the bus stop, picking through an anxious flow of morning flyers pushing towards the gates.

4

RACHEL, ON HER way to visit her son studying economics at the University of Chicago, landed at O'Hare Airport at the end of a week of heavy rains. Not wanting to be stuck in a taxi in the usual congestion, she walked the long underground corridor to the blue-line subway station, her tote bag rolling smoothly behind her. She passed the travelling sidewalks, none of which were working. The smell of mould noticeably increased as she walked under a pool of stagnant water gathered in a plastic sheet positioned beneath a still dripping ceiling.

She heard singing. She noticed the young woman at the far end of the corridor and appreciated her full, mature voice. The familiar lyrics bounced off the walls and echoed behind her.

Michael row your boat ashore, Hallelujah

Michael row your boat ashore, Hallelujah
The Jordan river is chilly and cold, Hallelujah,
Chills the body, but not the soul, Hallelujah

As Rachel approached she noticed the upturned hat on the ground and not much in the way of coins or bills to cover its lining. As she reached for change she was momentarily distracted by a poem cut into the wall, *The Negro Speaks of Rivers* by Langston Hughes.

"A song about a river performed in front of a poem about rivers," she remarked as she put an American bill into the hat, "and all the while the roof keeps leaking."

"Water is life," smiled the singer.

"You have a beautiful voice."

"Thanks."

And the exchange was over. Or almost. Rachel noticed the button with 'Yes We Can' on the singer's shirt. She hesitated, then asked the obvious: "Are you for Obama?"

"Yeah. This is Illinois. You?"

"I'm Canadian, I don't get to vote."

"But you like him, right?"

"I don't know. Too soon to say."

"You wait. He's the next President. He's the one. Change is a comin'."

Rachel smiled and said nothing. It irritated her when Josh and others went on endlessly about how America could change, should change, must be better. They were silly, hoping for a future of more perfect people running about on the same but cleaner streets. That wasn't the future. The future was different people running about with different ideas of better. People couldn't really imagine the future at all, she concluded, which is the best reason not to rush towards it. Better to accept the world as it is, rather than pretend it can become what you want.

Was Elena's boyfriend a terrorist? Elena was convinced he wasn't, but how would she know? She was naïve to a fault. She never bore down hard enough to maintain a straight line of thought. Josh didn't think so either, but he'd never even met Mahfouz and, to be honest, was infatuated with Elena. He had never yet been able to resist the crying eyes of a pretty girl.

The police weren't stupid. They didn't operate in a vacuum. They must have had a good reason to imprison Mahfouz's father or they wouldn't have done it. Maybe the father had used the son, sent him unwittingly as a courier to Egypt, which is why Mahfouz's innocence appeared so genuine. It appeared genuine because it was. How tragic! But it wasn't the first time, was it, that a Muslim man would use his innocent child as a front, a shield? They insisted on bringing tragedy upon themselves.

She breathed a sigh of relief that the scheme to sell fragrances had ended before it began. She herself would have been guilty of supporting terrorism. They had almost, but not quite, taken advantage of her kindness. It was amazing: evil that close.

Josh ... Josh ... so confident of his own virtue that he was a soft touch for the idealism of others. Without being aware of it, he was a mark. It was written on his forehead. It wasn't enough that he personally paid out of pocket for Mahfouz's lawyer, he tried to invite friends to a fundraising evening for the legal costs of both father and son. She had tried to talk to him out of it, to save him from himself. Nor had she attended, wanting to avoid the experience of the inevitable disaster. Very few of his friends had attended, and those that had had done so to argue. In the eyes of the community he had disgraced himself and humiliated her. Although, of course, that was not how he talked about it. He had called it a good beginning.

He needed her, that much was clear, and perhaps he loved her, but she hadn't the patience necessary. Not anymore. He had transgressed reasonable limits.

Her phone rang. She looked at the call display. "They're probably bugging your phone," she said to him.

"Do you care if CSIS is listening? I don't. Maybe they'll learn something."

"Just so you know. If you're going to help terrorists you have to face the consequences and a loss of privacy is one of them."

"Fuck 'em."

"Why have you called, Josh?"

"Rachel, we have children together. You carry memories I share with no one else, you have been the love of my life, how can I not want you back?"

"Did you practice saying that before you called?"

"No, I don't rehearse my conversations."

"I don't understand you, Josh. Sometimes I think I do, and then it disappears."

"You understand me well enough. Besides, is it important if you understand me completely or not? Can't you just trust me?"

Rachel considered the questions. Was there, in fact, some missing element which she needed to grasp for all the pieces to fit, or would it be more honest to admit that she had grown tired of what she knew the whole of him to be? And given what she knew, could she trust him?

"Where are you?" she answered.

"In my car, almost home. I calculated that you must have just landed." He paused, then again reached out to her. "I'm struggling, Rachel. We're both struggling, but we can help each other. I want us to listen to the future together. I want us to hear it talk."

This, she noted, was a novel twist. "The future talks to you?"

"To all of us willing to listen. To each of us in different ways. But yes, the future speaks."

"You think so?"

"Sometimes I hear it."

"Really?"

"Yes."

"Josh, if this is who you are then I can't do it. I can't start again with a make believe prophet who pretends he hears the future while helping people who support terrorism. I can't do it."

There was anger in Josh's quick reply. "Is that how you see me?"

"Don't get angry at me."

"Can't you at least question your assumptions?"

"Why should I believe your delusions? Because you ask me to?"

"Yes."

"Well, since the future is talking to you, you must already know the answer, which is that I can't do it. I won't. I'm not going mad like you."

"I didn't expect you to say that."

"So maybe it's not the future you're hearing in your head." She hung up.

Josh, miserably alone, sat in his car now idling in the driveway in front of his house. He turned off the engine and gazed out the windshield at the desolate October sky. He wished he could somehow stop the cold sun in its tracks, get Rachel back on the phone and pour eloquent words into her inattentive ear. If the sun could be stopped so that a slaughter of Amorites might continue without profaning the Sabbath, why couldn't it at least pause when words of reconciliation needed to be spoken? Shouldn't that be possible, at least during the Days of Awe?

He re-dialed, she answered.

"Why don't you ask Ghadir," he started, "if her husband is a terrorist? Why don't you ask her directly? This isn't a situation where you're being forced to guess something about people far away. Talk to Ghadir. And if you don't have the courage to ask her in person, then you have no right to judge her."

"Do you really think she's aware of what her male partner has done?"

"Why wouldn't she be?"

"I don't think so. She and her son have been duped."

"Then tell her that. Come with me to meet her and tell her that her husband is a terrorist but she just doesn't know it. She'll respond. She'll share her thoughts. She's not ignorant."

"I didn't say she was ignorant."

"That's what I heard."

"Her husband is being held because he invented a scheme to get money to dangerous people who advocate violence. He got caught. Does she think she can just spread a white tablecloth over the ruins and invite everyone over for tea? Is that what she thinks?"

"Is that what's she doing?"

"And you're the idiot who's helping her do it."

"She's trying to protect her family from unproven charges. You'd do the same."

"How she must be laughing at you!"

"She's not laughing at me."

"Do you think she respects you?"

"I'm sure of it."

"It's an illusion, a conceit. Why do you need her respect, anyway?"

"Even if your worst fears are right, Rachel, and they're both terrorists, which I don't believe for a second, does Mahfouz deserve to be tortured in Egypt? Does Samih deserve to be held without knowing what the evidence is against him? Why shouldn't they have experienced lawyers to defend them?"

"It's a war, Josh, and you're helping the wrong side."

"It's not a war. We're talking about the nature of our civil society, the kind of justice any Canadian citizen should expect. That's the issue. This is not about Israel, Rachel, it's about legal procedures for all Canadians. I expect support from my friends for the position I'm taking, not to be attacked and shunned."

"That's just naïve. There's a war going on and you want to pretend that Canada is so isolated we can sit it out."

"I can't believe what you just said."

"I don't understand why you can't see it."

"Rachel, if you keep pushing yourself further into this extremism, how long before . . ."

She cut him off. "Now you're accusing me of being an extremist? That's too rich. I won't tolerate it. I can't stand it." Rachel snapped her phone shut, pushed it deep into her bag.

Josh, stunned, got out of his car, cell phone in hand, and leaned with his back against the car. The heavy October sky continued to lower.

Rachel took her seat on the commuter train and looked about her. Two elderly women chatting together and a middle-aged man lost in thought shared the car. She tried to look out the window, but the darkness ensured there was nothing to see except her own reflection. She leaned back and tried to exhale her immense irritation. No, not irritation, her immense anger. No, not anger. Rage. How to rid oneself of it? But who could possibly remain balanced after a call like that?

She had been thinking something interesting before he called. It had absorbed her. About the singer? About Obama? What had she been thinking? It was gone now, whatever it was. It's hard to hold onto thoughts when you're seething.

Why did he insist on inverting the world?

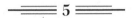

5

JOSH FOUND THE will to take out his key and walk towards the house, but a strange thing happened as he stepped through the doorway. The tumbling October sky moved from above his head to below his feet and he was held suspended in the air unable to land. It occurred to him, hanging there mid-step, that there were other words he should have spoken to Rachel, and if he hadn't known them and hadn't spoken them he couldn't blame her for not understanding. Yet it also occurred to him that there were other words she could have spoken and she, too, had not found them. Neither had reached for what needed to be said, or didn't know how to do so.

Buffeted by gathering winds and a deluge of unfinished thoughts, Josh eventually noticed that the sun was not moving. It hung in the air, still and covered by cloud as he hung in the air, still and blanketed by sorrow. The wind brought freezing rain, followed by snow. The snow blew through open windows and doors, filling every room in his house with mounting drifts. How did it get so high? Why was it so cold? Why was he shivering?

Then followed a brief spring. In all the rooms the drifts melted and the water streamed into the hallways, gathering force as it fell down the stairs from one floor to the next, and then passed beneath him in the doorway. Carried in the flow he saw fading invoices and stapled receipts, jotted notes and torn envelopes, early drafts and signed contracts. He watched as the paper preoccupations of his daily life were swept away. In among the documents he recognized a copy he had made of the letter written to President Wilson, published in 1919, in March, an analysis of how Zionism would lead the community astray. And all that had happened after that date, he wondered, had it rendered that analysis irresponsible, as some claimed, or prescient? And what was the relation of that letter to the failure of his marriage? Were the universalisms of normative Judaism a thing of the past? But that's what he had held sacred, not the powers of a Jewish state. Had he misunderstood the primary beliefs and hopes?

Then he noticed that his books, sodden, were also being swept away beneath him. For some reason the loss of these, his most precious possessions, caused him no pain. Summer followed, long and hot. The air filled with the contrasting rhythms of air conditioners, lawnmowers, water sprinklers and crickets, some close and some distant, all punctuated by the barking of guard dogs. A cat entered the house beneath him only to race out with a red cardinal flapping in its mouth. The irrationality of it made him laugh. The heat was such that he wanted to strip off his clothing and run through a sprinkler, like he had as a boy, but his churning feet still hovered above the firm ground.

Then, of a sudden, the bracing coolness of the first autumnal winds again appeared. The seasons had completed an annual cycle and the sun had moved not an iota. Just as suddenly as he had been held aloft by an inverted sky, he found himself gently lowered to complete his stride. He entered the house and softly closed the door behind.

No one he spoke to the next day appeared to have noticed anything unusual about the day before. They seemed completely unaware of the year of reflection he had gained while suspended in his own doorway.

If I am not for myself, who will be? But if I am for myself alone, then what am I? And if not now, when?

It's not that nothing was sacred, but rather that what was sacred must be renewed for it to remain so.

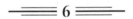

6

AFTER THE ELECTROCUTIONS, the stress positions, the incessant interruptions of sleep, the hoodings and beatings, Mahfouz had lost any sense of how long he'd been imprisoned. It was a lifetime ago when he smelled Omar die. It was a lifetime ago when he last held Elena. It was a lifetime ago when he last spoke to his father and mother.

Life was a lifetime ago.

He still wanted to believe that through acts of concentration he could resist physical pain, reach such levels of mental discipline that his body would vault to new thresholds well beyond normal limits. But physical anguish daily triumphed.

Are those his cries? It must be so.

Is that his pain? Listen . . .

As for the authorities, preparing for the annual fast of Ramadan due to start soon, they were happy to discover Mahfouz was not as he had presented himself, that he was more important than he initially appeared. We almost missed it, they concurred, he almost fooled us. But that's why we are paid to do what we do: we are the select who can see below an innocent surface to the deeper, malignant layers.

Drawn forward by their image of surface and depth they worked to delaminate him, to rend his life so painful and full of agony that he would call out for relief, exposing to the man with the wedge the existence of the next seam. They intended to separate him layer by layer until he was completely exposed. Like torturers throughout history, they believed that when the layers of a self are separate, the wholeness of the enemy lies visible before them.

Chapter Thirteen

Fadumah's mother refused to eat, not even to break fast after dark, preferring to grasp at any stray rumour rather than the meal in front of her. Her lips had retreated into thin lines between hollowed cheeks, her large eyes were sad and emptying. She had heard that the boat to Sicily drifted and all in it died; that it drifted and some died, the rest being imprisoned and awaiting deportation; and, most recently, and what she prayed to be true, that the vessel never left Egyptian waters, having been boarded by security forces who were holding everyone on it.

Stung by the impotence of past illusions, Fadumah bore in silence the growing conviction that her act of sacrifice, meant to be selfless and noble, had paid for a final voyage in which her brothers had died. How was that possible? How could she have been so misguided and wrong? How could her brothers, so young and full of hope, be drowned?

She didn't dare imagine their journey and its end, yet images arose before her of swelling waves and horizons swallowed. She heard their voices calling out for her, as they had for so many years — as clear as before — yet now unanswerable. Nor did Fadumah dare imagine her mother's unspoken imaginings.

She tried to deny her night with Wasif and his brother, but it was difficult. The humiliations of that night deepened and festered. She felt wholly desecrated and defiled, in body and spirit, as if a serpent had bitten into her soul with poisoned fangs. She knew the cure would not be found in greater humility, further prayer, nor dreams of foreigners. Her illusions of future bliss with Mahfouz had dried without a trace. It was, she had concluded, a future that had never been hers to consider.

God is compassionate, attempted the mother.

God can go fuck himself, said Fadumah.

An unregistered immigrant working under the table, Fadumah was a member of no union, but found herself wishing she were. Riding the same crowded busses, finding refuge in the same subway cars, waiting in the same hour-long lines at the bread store, she befriended a few older women working in the established factories. They told her scarcely believable fables about successful actions, led by women, in the cotton mills of Malhala. By refusing to collapse in the face of mounting intimidation, by persevering in a growing solidarity of thousands, they'd achieved a double victory, the first over the deceits of their state-run union, and the second over the organized repression of the Mubarak regime. Their example led to a series of successful actions throughout the delta.

Fadumah learned that the Muslim Brotherhood, so central to her father, had a long history of breaking strikes and opposing effective unions, having a deep prejudice against worker's organizations which they considered communist and anti-religious. "That seems to be shifting," an older woman told her, "but we don't trust the Brotherhood." The woman explained that the wages of Egyptian textile workers were only sixty percent of those in India. "We're poorer than the poor, and the least well paid are always the women." But when the woman asked Fadumah how much she made, she was astonished to hear that Fadumah earned precisely half her wage. When asked to explain how she could possibly afford to live and support her mother as well, Fadumah spoke of the necessary charities received from others almost as needy as she. The woman, understanding, didn't press. "Listen," she stated, "your present doesn't have to be your future."

Fadumah wanted to believe her. She didn't want to continue working for less than the cost of living and she was frightened that her future, forced by financial necessity, would become as an object of sexual attention and barter. She wanted to work honestly and hard beside others working honestly and hard, and to be appreciated for what she contributed. She also wanted, should it be at all possible, that her life experiences, and those of her siblings and parents, be acknowledged.

Her allegiances shifted from the certainties of her deceased father and emaciated mother to the possibilities of the women with whom she daily mingled. She volunteered to distribute information to non-unionized workers within the factories and warehouses nearby, including her own place of employment. It was not a machine gun she carried beneath her outer garment, it was printed material giving up-dated information on union actions, mixed with articles on the fate of workers hauled in front of repressive courts.

At meetings Fadumah asked questions and found herself surprised that others took the time to answer. The women discussed many things, including the siege at Gaza. They were shown pictures of Israeli settlers bulldozing Palestinian olive groves and orchards, and discussed reports of women dying in childbirth while detained at checkpoints. They were presented with statistics of children suffering stunted physical growth due to malnourishment, and were enraged by official Israeli statements that there was no humanitarian problem. They discussed the strange but uncontested fact that one and a half million people were suffering blockade and that no government in the world was lifting a hand to end it. They discussed the tunnels dug deep beneath the Egyptian border, and marvelled at the resilience of a people being collectively punished and intentionally crushed.

Fadumah was not surprised that the hypocritical west called the repression of Palestinians a peace process, just as it had called the foreign invasion of her country a liberation, but she wondered how the Egyptian people could accept such idiocy. Of course there was no shame in the west, but was there really no shame here either? Why was the crossing at Rafah shut? How could that be tolerated? The shame of Gaza, it was agreed among them, was another reason why the Egyptian government must be overthrown. The siege had to be lifted.

Intelligent, bitter, yet naturally hopeful, Fadumah was constructing a new family while in mourning for the dissolution of her own. She turned eighteen having chosen sides in Egypt's on-going, unannounced, civil war. She began to dress to merge more easily into the pedestrian traffic on the crowded streets.

ELENA AND GHADIR helped each other through punishing times. Their friendship buffered the harder edges of a city whose news media, politicians and public spokespersons looked to win favour by endorsing the prejudices of the day. Together they discussed the letter from the finance company summarily withdrawing the insurance policy for the restaurant. Together they researched and took the necessary steps to declare the business bankrupt, voiding the leases to the space and the equipment. Together they discussed and tried to tackle the fears of those who believed helping Ghadir would expose themselves and their families to surveillance, as well as charges of aiding terrorism.

Ghadir found a moment to laugh at Elena's uncannily accurate impersonation of the sputtering, indignant, CSIS agent after his second and third visits, wherein Ghadir again refused to inform on her community in return for promises of better conditions for her husband. Ghadir's laughter may have been bitter and short-lived, but it was spontaneous.

In spite of their unexpected friendship and mutual support, Elena found living in Mahfouz's childhood house more difficult than she had anticipated. In his bedroom, now shared by her and Sharon, she had taken his few posters off the walls and replaced them with Sharon's drawings. She had folded his clothes and tucked them neatly in a garbage bag at the back of the closet, as if hiding the evidence of his existence. But what was she to do, there being only one set of drawers?

In her mind the room remained his, on temporary loan. The house certainly remained, overwhelmingly so, the house of his parents. Living there might be appropriate during this crisis, but not longer. When Mahfouz returned, as surely he must, the three of them would find another place. She knew in which neighbourhood they would look. She imagined them having breakfast together at Byblos Café, on Laurier Avenue near Papineau, and living not too far away.

Without being aware of any transitional moment she considered her future permanently united with his. There had been one dreadful moment in the lawyer's office when she had doubted his return, but she had succeeded in defeating that short-lived despair. She had used common sense to dull the sharp fatalism that had sucked the air right out of her, making it impossible to breathe.

She missed Mahfouz. His infatuation with her had been straightforward and unapologetic. He had been smart enough to let her lead and kind in his hopes. He had sincerely cared for Sharon, and her affection had grown unobstructed towards the man within him.

She believed, if she could talk to him, that he would understand the dreams now haunting her. She had tried to explain them to her father but the memory of the rapidly changing images grew more vague as she spoke. The sequences she had thought bursting with deeper meaning had seemed ridiculous when exposed to the light of day. Her father had tried to sympathize, had asked a few questions, but her inability to answer only added to her confusion and uncertainty.

Realistically, Elena concluded, no matter what she did or said, or the maturity of the pressing insights forming within her, she would never be for her father much different than Mahfouz was for his mother, a beloved child. It wasn't their fault.

Mahfouz, however, would understand. Yes, because they would touch and then talk, or talk and then touch, or touch and talk together. The strange images would inevitably make sense, all of them, even the most ephemeral and unusual, because their meanings would be slowly nurtured in that fertile space between her body and his, capturing a significance beyond the spoken.

There it was again, she thought, the on-going issue of reality—what it is and how best to approach it. She found herself struggling, again, with the unavoidable limitations of language. Words could only ever point to a truth, while they could define a falsehood accurately. Or to put the same thing another way: falsehoods themselves are verbal creations, while the truth is not.

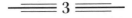

3

SLEEPING IN MAHFOUZ'S bed, the warm body of her daughter beside her, Elena dreamt that Sharon was painting a triptych. But it wasn't Sharon eight years old, but Sharon as a young woman in her early thirties. Disconcerting, but a touch wonderful, too, to see one's child grown up. Her hair was cropped shorter than Elena ever remembered seeing it. She wasn't sure if she liked that, but did admire the firmness of her daughter's strong stance, the muscular arms.

The scene was lit by innumerable small fires fuelled with scraps of broken office furniture on a concrete floor in a cavernous basement. Elena's father was there, too, as were Josh and Samih; three mature men sitting on lawn chairs in the flickering light, as if to witness.

Sharon began to dip her brushes into a bewildering mix of jars on a cluttered side table. Using vigorous strokes, each loaded with pigment, she created life-like images on the wall in front of her. She started by painting a young man with what seemed to be a falcon's head, one eye piercing and fierce, the other lost in shadow. Falcon-Man held something. It was a scale, a balance, suspended from a string above the centre point. On one side of the balance he placed a feather—a tiny feather!—and the balance shifted ever so lightly, as if the weighted side was only slightly more than nothing.

Then Sharon painted a man with a dog's head; a small, sly figure, a trickster of some sort, leading someone. Dog-Man was leading Mahfouz! But she painted Mahfouz exactly as she had years ago in the kitchen of his restaurant: flattened, schematic, a stick figure; not fully rounded and commanding like Falcon-Man and Dog-Man.

Dog-Man reached with both hands into Mahfouz's flat chest and withdrew a heart that immediately throbbed in three dimensions. Dog-Man gave the heart to Falcon-Man who placed it on the scale to be weighed against the small, single feather.

The chorus of three old men shifted and stirred in their chairs as the balance tilted and tilted again and then righted itself. It balanced! The chorus stood and cheered, all three of them, as they saw with their own eyes that Mahfouz's heart weighed no more than the feather of righteousness. Josh, Samih and Victor threw their arms over each other's shoulders and cried out in vindication.

In the soon forgotten dream, even the dreamer was happy, so happy.

DOES GOD, AT every moment, recreate the universe, preventing its annihilation? If God's compassion were withdrawn, would the world disappear forever? Was it possible, in the early years of the twenty-first century of the common era, for such strange questions to make sense to a young man of twenty-three? Could they be asked in good faith?

And yet, to Mahfouz, that is where his resistance had led: a search for the meaning of suffering in the face of indifference. Who cares when no one cares? The obvious answer is no one, and yet if he, himself, cared, was there not again a caring mind? And if his caring mind was an integral part of the universe and its history, wasn't God as close as his own jugular?

Mahfouz nurtured these questions within him. He considered them Islamic, reflecting the nature of an inexplicable yet compassionate universe. Why hadn't he thought about this before?

And in yourselves - what do you not see?

His struggle was alone and outside the public's attention. His victory was neither in hundredths of a second nor fractions of a metre. If he were to succeed he would not climb a pedestal to be adorned by precious metals, nor would his national anthem be played. His was a struggle everywhere ignored, and if considered, denigrated.

He no longer saw the imprint of the divine only in the distant and chosen, but also in the close and inflicted; no longer heard the music of the spheres only in the harmonious and measured, but also in the discordant and random. Among the ninety-nine sacred names, consider:

the Slayer,
the Harmer,
the Depriver,
the Severity,
the Justice,
the Wrath.

The voice of God spoke through all of creation, and creation — beautiful, remarkable, wondrous, infinite — was also burning, diseased, finite and cruel.

Which, of the favours of your Lord, do you deny?

But his interrogators were irritated and frustrated. Why didn't this frail, broken, delirious youth with the trembling limbs wipe clean their crimes through a confession? Why didn't he speak of a desire for revenge, a plan to reciprocate pain for pain and affirm the existence of the secret organization they had sworn to destroy?

They didn't want to hear him say once again that God was present in the shit of the world. They thought it madness, and didn't understand it as the origin of the strength they were tasked to break. They pursued their list of questions but neglected to ask any of each other. They didn't encounter their enemy because they didn't encounter themselves.

Behind closed doors it had rapidly gained profile, this sleeper cell in Montreal. Its discovery was considered a major breakthrough. Reputations were consolidated and careers advanced. Considered to link extremist elements of Somalia, Egypt and the United States all within the too safe haven of Canada, its inner workings needed to be revealed and smashed. A series of green lights were quickly given for resolute action.

Of a sudden then, surprisingly, the interrogators relented.

The CIA, they'd been told, were to send a team. The Muslims of Egypt had had their chance and failed. It was the turn of the Christians of America to show them how it was done.

Mahfouz's treatment changed in the interim: he was allowed continuous, unbroken sleep; his body was neither contorted nor beaten; nor his testicles electrocuted; no headphones were taped over his ears; nor were his hands bound behind him; nor his feet shackled; nor was he suspended from the ceiling. A cotton mat replaced the folded cardboard on the concrete floor. On that thin mattress a new blanket lay folded.

He was, for the first time since Omar's death, allowed to walk outside. During that rather astonishing half hour in a courtyard, body bent, hobbling forward as best he could, he looked up at a blue sky which, in its richness and depth, reminded him of something, of some other place. Yes, and for the briefest moment, in the dry dust of Cairo, he remembered the colourful autumnal leaves of his hometown, and wondered if he'd ever return.

He tried to remember life as it was, to put together the fragmented pieces. He exclaimed, once, the name of Elena, and believed he felt a living volume beneath his palms. He wondered how he might get the promised sand to Sharon. He wondered how he could still wonder such precious thoughts.

At first dimly, but then with increasing precision, he began to regain the rhythms within a common day. Grasping a sequence of such days, he began to count. Counting, hopes of release surged within him.

5

THE LATE AUTUMNAL sky of Montreal was an opaque and cobalt surface poised to remain forever, not yet the retreating, cerulean sky of winter. Beneath it, Elena, Sharon and Ghadir climbed the south side of the long extinguished volcano around which the city had been built. They lost count of the endless stairs and were breathing heavily when they reached the top. Sharon ran to the stone wall. Elena and Ghadir soon followed, and together they looked over the suddenly endless vista. From this height the city's sirens and squeals were heard as soft punctuations within a distant moaning. A breeze wafted in from the north-northwest, replacing the sweat of the working city with the evergreen scents of the low hills and narrow lakes of the nearby Laurentians.

They stared into the distance at two other ancient volcanoes, each rising from an otherwise flat plain on the other side of the broad St. Lawrence. The river itself — seemingly frozen in time, but flowing without cease towards an ocean still a thousand miles east — reflected exactly the colour of the indelible sky. They all noticed, each in her own way, how the artifact of city jumped the river and spilled onto the far bank before quickly fading.

They left the lookout to walk along a path of colourful leaves beneath almost naked branches. They discussed simple ways to make their living together easier.

Chapter Fourteen

Victor hadn't expected the Nile delta to remind him of home. Although the fields were smaller and the crops different, he recognized the land stretching flat towards an ever-retreating horizon, the intense cultivation beneath a reigning sun.

The glare of the horizon turned the palms into silhouettes. Those close to the train flitted by as a series of dark animations, while those at a greater distance appeared and disappeared more slowly, though still as cut-outs against a white background. He wondered if he had ever before seen a sky so blanched. Perhaps he had, on one of those dog days in Manitoba when a sharply angled sun gripped the earth's edge with a light so white it blinded you.

He was intrigued by the patterns of the palms. He imagined they had been set hundreds, if not thousands, of years ago: planted so the roots would hold firm the precious soil along the banks of the irrigation ditches; so that the broad leaves would shade the precious water and lessen evaporation. He enjoyed that, the informed and effective choices of long ago still visible.

In the deep shade of the train he opened his notebook and began to jot down the type and number of cars visible on the highway running beside the tracks. They were mostly smaller European cars and their Asian counterparts, almost all with four cylinder engines. There were far fewer American cars than he had expected. Nor had he anticipated that all of the higher-end vehicles would be German: BMW, Mercedes Benz, Audi. Those sped along a good deal faster than the train from which he watched, weaving confidently through the slower traffic. He recognized most of the car manufacturers, but not all. Would that unfamiliar car be a Khodro or a Saipa? He had never worked on an Iranian built car, and would have liked to put one on a hoist and examine it from underneath.

Every now and then he saw a motorcycle in the field scurrying from one location to the next, raising dirt along the paths beside the ditches. Most often there were two riders, but on several occasions there were three, one holding the handle bars and the other two sitting behind, hugging the person in front with one arm and gripping tools in the other. A small pick-up would have been used on the prairies. But there were far fewer ditches needing attention in the fields at home, irrigation being increasingly delivered through the large circular sprinklers that, from the air, created haunting patterns of verdant circles.

Then, surprisingly, he saw a donkey standing placidly in the shade of a palm at the side of a field. He wondered what purpose it could possibly serve. Yet he knew — it just being the way it was in farming communities — that if it didn't serve some purpose it wouldn't have been there. For a brief moment it made the whole scene look timeless and biblical, which irritated him.

He wondered if he still remembered the Aramaic he had taught himself. Could he write, as he used to: "Your kingdom come, your will be done on earth as it is in heaven" in the evocative alphabet of ancient Palestine? He turned to a fresh page in his notebook. Yes, he remembered. There it was, a small display of esoteric knowledge. He questioned, however, if that was the fruit of it, whether he'd achieved anything beyond a petty conceit, a party trick. Frankly, why would any non-specialist study Aramaic, given that all the important documents were available in English at a level of interpretation difficult to match, impossible to better?

On the other hand, to read only in English was to ignore the differences history struggled to reveal. As a child the German language had been the key to his community's past, but he had felt it necessary to push even further back. Thinking about it, perhaps that had been the problem, preferring to look back rather than around. He should have learned Arabic, not Aramaic. He should have woken up to the world as it is, not to the world as it might have been. Then he could have asked questions to the people living in the small villages through which he was passing. Was it true that the Nile gathered no water in Egypt, actually losing more to evaporation than it gained through rainfall? Was it true that the flow depended entirely on the sweet waters gathered in the highlands of east Africa, sourced through the Blue Nile and the White?

At home on the prairies, in the cities and out, one never stopped asking questions about water: who owned it and what they wanted to do with it; about water tables and run-off; about floods and droughts; how to interpret the clouds and how to interpret the trade agreements. It was understood that one could evaluate a civilization by how it used its water.

There had been a moment when Arden was ill — well, many moments, if truth be told, she was sick about two and a half years — when he had wanted to again believe in miracles. He had told her that they'd meet in heaven. He had actually said that to her. She hadn't welcomed his opinion. She had replied from her bed: "Don't say stuff like that. I don't need it. I want to die with dignity, not delusions." Later, as if to forgive him, she had added in a lighter tone: "Honestly, Victor, it's not about my feelings for you, it's just that I think nothingness a sufficient reward."

At the time he had thought he understood. But more recently he wondered what she had meant by nothingness, for it was a concept difficult for him to grasp.

He saw again in his mind's eye the downpour during the last week of Arden's illness. Massive thunderclouds, dark grey like wet stone, had rolled across the prairie heavens and drenched the earth with torrents of cool, clear water. The rains caused the Assiniboine to spring to life, turbulent and fierce. Since then he had remembered the two events as one, her dying and the river flooding.

He thought again about Mahfouz. Was it possible that one day he would feel for Elena the same way he felt for Arden?

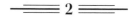

2

"YOU HEARD FROM your dad and that's why you're calling."

"How did you know, Josh? We just got off the phone."

"I've been anxious to hear from you and figured you must be waiting until he called."

"He said things had started slowly but were going better now. He met with someone at the American University in Cairo and that person arranged for him to meet a woman who defends the rights of foreigners in Egyptian prisons. She runs an NGO in Alexandria, which is where he is now."

"That's positive."

"He thought so."

"I guess that's fast."

"He also thinks he's about to get a meeting with someone at the Canadian Embassy. He's unsure if it will be with the right person but, like he says, you have to start somewhere. He told me to tell you that he keeps detailed notes of his conversations and will share them soon."

"Good."

"It helped to lift Ghadir's spirits."

"How is she?"

"Strong. I don't know what other word to use."

"She's a fighter, isn't she?"

"She hasn't much of a choice. Think about it, both husband and child have been taken from her." She switched topics. "Dad told me he was going to visit the Ben Ezra for you."

"Do you know what that is?"

"A synagogue."

"Not just any synagogue, Maimonides' synagogue in Cairo. I asked him to do that for me."

"How are you, Josh?"

"I'm fine. Sort of, anyway. I feel a bit . . . I guess the word is isolated. I'm not exactly making friends right now."

"New friends don't count?"

"They count. But there are old friends I've known since high school who are less than happy with me. They tell me I'm doing one thing, I tell them I'm doing another. We're talking past each other."

"Do you regret knowing me?"

"Honestly?" And then he laughed. "Let's just call it a testing time."

"Have you heard from Rachel?"

"Not recently."

"Are you going to manage?"

"I'll manage. What have you been doing?"

"Taking care of Sharon, looking for a job."

"Anything out there?"

"If I want to take off my clothes and serve alcohol." In the pause that followed she, too, began to laugh.

"You're toughening, aren't you?"

"Or coarsening. Which do you think it is?"

"You sure as hell have never struck me as coarse."

"Do you like shadow puppets, Josh?"

"Shadow puppets are performing somewhere?" he asked, intrigued. "Is an Indonesian troupe passing through, or has culture in our city evolved that far?"

"Leila and Sharon have a sheet hung up in the living room. They spend hours inventing stories told with shadows. It's fascinating the shapes they can make with kitchen utensils. They're tired of Ghadir and I being the audience."

"I could come at the end of the week, Saturday or Sunday."

"Okay, come for dinner Saturday."

"I'll bring dessert."

"That's good."

"I like to hear you sounding so up."

"It's good to be up."

ON THE FIRST night of Mahfouz's renewed interrogations, Elena again dreamt her daughter was painting. Falcon-Man reappeared, again weighing Mahfouz's heart. But Sharon wasn't finished and painted beside the scale a low squat animal with small eyes. It was a fat short alligator, or maybe a deformed miniature dragon. The creature turned to Falcon-Man with an open mouth. Visible within its thick maw were more than a dozen partially chewed human organs. Falcon-Man glanced down scornfully before placing Mahfouz's still throbbing heart in a vase-like container, away from the consuming jaws.

The beast closed its mouth, chewed and swallowed, then opened it again and turned to look directly at the dreaming Elena. She suffered a moment of panic gazing into the empty eyes, the abysmal mouth. This, she thought, was the origin of hell, the ever-present hunger of the indifferent beast. Hell did not begin with the naked perversions and physical atrocities of the Middle Ages. Those were later developments on a theme. Falcon-Man began to speak but in an ancient language the dreamer couldn't grasp. Sharon drew a bubble from the beak in which she wrote: "Who accuses, and of what crime?" Her feet were quick and her movements confident as she stepped back, repositioned, and moved forward to begin again. Her brush moved ever faster.

Osiris, the god of the underworld who died annually and resurrected with the floods, emerged on the far left of the panel, his skin green as spring grass. He held in one hand the royal flail and in the other a short-handed hook. Now the royal flail was painted over and it was Jesus holding the long-handled shepherd's hook. He held out his free hand, as if welcoming children towards him.

This was quickly replaced by an almost naked man on a cross, arms outstretched, palms and feet nailed, wearing a crown of thorns. A Roman soldier thrust a long spear into his side. Then the soldier, now an American member of a Special Operations Force, attached electric wires to the outstretched arms as the cross itself was painted over. The sacrifice, wearing an orange jumpsuit with a black bag over his head, stood on a small wooden crate, trembling.

The soldier laughed loudly and, speaking English, played rocks-scissors-paper with his young female colleague to determine who would throw the switch to electrify the anonymous man.

Mahfouz's father had risen from the broken lawn chair and, in the shadows, pounded his fists against the wall trying to smash through, for he believed it was his son whose head was beneath the bag. Josh placed his head into his hands, covering his eyes, not wanting to see, and Elena's own father had such a silly expression of ineptitude and foolishness on his face that she would laugh, were it not so sad.

The small fires on the floor now raged, and the wall on which Sharon painted burst into flame. The three old men gathered in a distant corner, inept and fearful, trying to flee the heat.

The electrified man re-emerged as a female Buddhist monk calmly engulfed in rising flames, her hands pressed together in front of her heart, her shorn head bowed. It was Elena's mother, as thin as Sharon the grandchild had once drawn her, sitting in a wheelchair. The grandmother's head lifted and the emphatic wheels on either side of her emaciated body spun and spun. The sound of that spinning was as the chant of thousands of voices raised together, then of millions.

Sharon briefly stopped. Her eyes closed, she concentrated as if to better hear the massing voices. She repositioned her feet and opened her eyes. Still gripping the brush she stretched her arm towards the wall of fire. Elena, asleep, cried out in fear for her daughter. Sharon didn't retreat. Her arm erupted in flame as she continued painting.

4

SHARON AWOKE BESIDE a sweating mother who had tossed and turned all night, sometimes calling out in pain.

"Mommy?" prodded the child carefully, trying to get her attention.

"What?"

"Should we get up?"

"I'm tired. I can't sleep. I haven't slept."

"Why?"

"I don't know what to do," Elena whispered. "I try and I try and I can't figure out what to do."

"What do you mean?"

"They're hurting him. They're hurting Mahfouz."

"Who is?"

"I don't know, people."

"What do you mean, they're hurting him? What are they doing?"

"They want him to say things and they hurt him until he does."

"That's stupid."

"Yes, it is. Very stupid. I'm hurting him, too."

This was a new and frightening thought for Sharon. "No, you're not hurting him. How are you hurting him?"

"I don't think of him enough. I forget him. I sometimes wonder if I ever knew him. I think about him and he changes. I'm forgetting who he is."

Sharon began to panic. "Why are you saying that?"

"It's true. I think about him and then it isn't him anymore."

"Mommy!" Sharon cried out loud. Then she began to cry.

"It's alright," Elena said soothingly. She turned on her side to hold her daughter closely. "It's alright," she repeated, smoothing her child's hair. "Everything will be okay. Sometimes I remember his scent, and then all of him comes back. I like that."

"You scared me," Sharon said, calming. "You shouldn't scare me. Why don't you remember him? I remember him."

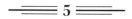

5

ON THE FIFTH day of renewed interrogations Mahfouz was oblivious to the fact that they were asking him questions in English, not Arabic. The lead inquisitor, a well-proportioned man in his early forties from North Carolina, a stylish multi-coloured tattoo running as a band above his left elbow, asked a series of prepared questions. None of them made any sense to Mahfouz. He might as well have been asked if he had gills, if he were a fish. Then, at least, questions and questioning would correspond.

The inquisitor was extremely patient in front of Mahfouz's stubborn silence and gestured again for the Egyptian assistants to submerge him beneath running water.

Once again Mahfouz was baptized, and once again he remained silent.

Another time, yet again, they lowered the plank and continuously poured water over his exposed nostrils, his gagged mouth, until he again attempted to breathe by inhaling water. His proximity to death was calibrated by the duress of his convulsions, which were extreme, as well as the oxygen level in his blood, monitored by a simple device taped to the tip of one finger.

They stopped the water, raised the board, removed the gag.

Mahfouz, entering shock, tried to wretch and inhale at the same time. He managed to mouth: "I am a fish. I breathe through gills. I am. Yes. Yes. Whatever you say. I am a fish. I confess."

And they, the new team, enchanted by the efficacy of their actions, nodded to each other. The inquisitor, naturally cautious, turned to the videographer: "He was pretty faint, are you sure you have it on tape?"

"I got it. I'm sure I got it."

They had what they came for and the tension in the room began to wane. They were doing their jobs and it was, finally, going well.

"Wait a minute, I want to change memory cards," said the videographer, anxious that nothing important be said while the memory was full.

They paused while he quickly slotted a new card into the digital camera. Somewhat uncomfortable recording this sort of thing, he took pride in his attention to what he considered the professional aspects. His images were well lit and in focus and the sound quality always excellent. He insisted on using two microphones where most operators only used one, and he never relied on the camera microphone alone.

Mahfouz had confessed. To what, he did not know, but small matter.

The medical officer took another sip from her can of Coke. She noticed with interest just how disoriented Mahfouz appeared: the unceasing trembling of his limbs, the marked paleness of lips and hands, the unfocused, dilated gaze. Yes, certainly he was in physical distress but his pulse, which she measured through a stethoscope to the inside of his strapped down arm, though both racing and sluggish in turn, was within norms for a healthy young man his age.

What concerned her was the possibility of a spasmodic larynx, the involuntary clenching of the hollow muscle that surrounds the air passage to the lungs. When waterboarding interrogations were repeated the larynx could spasm so tightly as to lock in an airtight position. If necessary, she would perform a tracheotomy to bypass the locked muscle before the subject suffered brain damage or death. She had a small kit with her precisely for that purpose.

Straps were tightened, the mouth gagged, the board lowered, and water again flowed over mouth and nostrils. Again the convulsions and oxygen levels were monitored as they sought new evidence for the plans Mahfouz had confessed.

But the racing heart faltered, then stopped.

The camera also stopped, the operator confused. He'd never seen this happen before. Should he continue to record?

Amidst a flurry of curses the man from North Carolina began to loosen the straps, getting in the way of his Egyptian assistants who were trying to raise the board. The can of

Coke inadvertently spilled as the medical officer reached for the vial with which to inject adrenalin. She, too, cursed, as she slipped slightly plunging the needle directly into his chest.

The camera restarted, the videographer having decided he should capture the heroic efficiency of the team as they worked to save a life.

Later, over lunch, they debriefed on the events of the morning. The medical officer shook her head: "I've never seen that happen before. I didn't expect it. I was caught by surprise."

"I wonder if you should have intervened," the lead inquisitor said. "I mean, he had confessed."

"I had to follow protocol."

"We have what we came for, that's all that counts." He hated Cairo and was eager to leave. He considered how to work in a visit to the modern splendours of Dubai — with the medical officer if she'd be willing — but had better sense than to invite her in front of the videographer.

Given the new circumstances, the videographer requested and received fresh instructions from CIA headquarters. He was to return to Virginia and edit there. Traces of the American team were to be removed: any parts of their bodies captured on screen were to be edited out and all traces of their voices were to be stripped from the sound track. All that was to be kept were Mahfouz's responses to the questions and the confession that emerged, nothing else. The master memory cards were to be handed in to be physically destroyed, not simply erased.

The written report, composed to parallel the audiovisual evidence, confirmed the existence of a secret cell confessed during the interrogation of a twenty-three-year-old native Egyptian male.

About The Author

Michael Springate's writing for live performance includes: *Historical Bliss* (Studio Altaire); *Dog and Crow* (The Necessary Angel Theatre Company, published by Guernica Editions); *The Consolation of Philosophy* (composed by Helen Hall, The Toronto Music Gallery); *The Geese Sonnets* (New Music Festival of the Winnipeg Symphony Orchestra); *Kareena* (Ukrainian translation pub. Вітуизна); *Freeport Texas* (Sodium Glow Theatre); *Küt: Shock and Awe* (Craning Neck Theatre); and the short libretto *I should bring them water* (composed by Alfredo Santa Ana). He has lectured in the dance and theatre departments of Concordia University, in the School for the Contemporary Arts at Simon Fraser University and, most recently, at the Institute of May 18 at Chonnam National University in Kwangju, South Korea.

Born in Montreal, he currently resides in Vancouver where he is Artistic Associate with Full Circle: First Nations Performance; a member of the Board of Directors of the Vancouver Latin American Cultural Centre; and a founder of Commercial Drive Productions.

The Beautiful West & The Beloved of God is his first novel.

Printed in June 2014
by Gauvin Press,
Gatineau, Québec